THE DEVIL'S
DIARY

BLOOMSBURY READER

Discover books by Patrick McGinley published by
Bloomsbury Reader at
www.bloomsbury.com/PatrickMcGinley

Foggage
Goosefoot
The Devil's Diary
The Lost Soldier's Song
The Red Men
The Trick of the Ga Bolga

THE DEVIL'S DIARY

PATRICK McGINLEY

BLOOMSBURY READER

LONDON · NEW DELHI · NEW YORK · SYDNEY

This edition published in 2013 by Bloomsbury Reader

Bloomsbury Reader is a division of Bloomsbury Publishing Plc,

50 Bedford Square, London WC1B 3DP

First published in Great Britain 1988 by Jonathan Cape Ltd

ISBN: 978 1 4482 0952 1
eISBN: 978 1 4482 0953 8

Visit www.bloomsburyreader.com to find out more about our authors and their books
You will find extracts, author interviews, author events and you can sign up for
newsletters to be the first to hear about our latest releases and special offers

To Bernadette

Contents

Part I

Brennan

Chapter 1

Below on the Glebe a fire burnt dimly within a circle of low tents. A woman came forward with an armful of brushwood, and sparks flew up into the extinguishing haze above. Figures moved round the fire in a slow dumbshow that had no overt purpose, no discernible beginning or end.

He drew the curtains and went downstairs to the kitchen where two glasses of milk stood on a tray beside a plate with two biscuits. He carried the tray into the study and put more peat on the fire in the grate. The room was spacious, high-ceilinged and sparsely furnished. It was a good room for reading, a room in which to be alone. He placed a beer mat over each glass, took a black mackintosh from the coat-hook under the stairs, and went out. Through the window he could see the welcoming fire in the grate and the chairs on either side, one with arms and one without. In front of the armchair was a pair of black slippers with red insoles. He walked slowly down the avenue and picked his steps across the cattle grid in the gateway. All round him the starless April night held its peace.

To the east the village street lights gleamed naked between houses that rose steeply in steps on the hill. He crossed the road to the footpath leading north towards the fire and the ring of tents on the Glebe. The grass was slippery with dew, and, as he walked, he could hear a murmur that was too monotonous and regular to be mistaken for the murmur of the sea. The land dipped before him. He left the path and leant against a rock above the clearing of light where seven men and nine women sat round the fire holding hands. High-pitched voices chanted. Fire-light danced on upturned faces and closed eyelids. He strained to catch the words as they rose and fell:

Peace … peace … days of peace
Peace … peace … dreams of peace
Peace … peace … endless peace

He lingered for half an hour while the flames of the fire died down. The chanting stopped. Men and women reached out their joined hands to the fire and kissed each other with ritualistic indifference. He turned and walked briskly up the slope to the parochial house, aware of nothing but the heavy exhalations of the sea. From the driveway he glanced through the study window. One of the glasses was empty and his slippers now lay in front of the chair without arms. On the hallway floor was a battered knapsack and a rolled anorak.

'Who's there?' he called. 'Who's there?'

When he got no reply, he entered the study and drank the remaining glass of milk. He felt excited and at the same time disappointed that the unknown visitor had left the biscuits untouched. Returning to the hallway, he rummaged through the knapsack and found among the shirts and trousers a policeman's truncheon and three clothbound books – *Totem and Taboo, Cannibalism and Catholicism* and one battered volume of *The Golden*

Bough. As he put the books back in the knapsack, a knock at the door echoed in the rooms upstairs. The door opened to reveal a bearded stranger, broad-faced and burly, with a corncob pipe in his mouth.

'Jerry?' The stranger smiled as he came forward.

'Yes, I'm Father Jerry,' he replied.

'Don't say you don't recognise me.'

'Hugo! It was the beard that threw me. Your voice hasn't changed, I'm pleased to say.'

They shook hands. He felt short and slight beside his brother whose handshake had communicated a strength of will and limb that he had quite forgotten.

'The first time I called there was no reply, so I dumped my things and went to the village for a drink. I was pleased to find that you still don't need to lock your door here.'

'I like to think that my neighbours are at least as honest as myself. So far they've given me no cause to think otherwise.'

'Good old Jerry, still the same.'

'I'm Father Jerry now, that's change enough. But where have you been all these years?' He led the way into the study.

'Travelling up and down and to and fro, mainly in the southern hemisphere. I drank some of your milk. I hope it wasn't meant for someone else.'

'I lay out milk for two every evening. Once in a while a parishioner calls, or maybe a tramp. If no one calls, I drink the extra glass myself.'

'And the extra biscuit?'

'I put it back in the barrel for next time.'

Hugo laughed as he dropped into the armchair. He stretched his legs before the fire and locked his hands over his wide midriff. Though he had put on weight, he looked solid rather than flabby.

5

His forehead was suntanned, his hair thick and black with no trace of grey except at the temples. His beard was broad and curly and his strong teeth gleamed as he smiled. He was forty-one, three years younger than Father Jerry, and he had the frame and features of a man who has led an active, healthy life under the glare of a warm sun.

'What have you been doing in the southern hemisphere?'

'Fighting a losing battle against women, if you must know.'

'Are you married?'

'Not yet. I live in hope.' He laughed again and banged the arms of the chair with both hands.

'I once knew a general who used to say that some battles are best lost.'

'You have a housekeeper to see to your needs, I suppose.'

'I believe in the untrammelled exercise of free will. No priest with a housekeeper can seriously claim to be a free agent.'

'So you live here in this large, commanding house on your own?'

'Yes, I do. There are ghosts of course.'

'And now I've arrived to add to their number.'

They both looked into the grate where a darting flame singed the threadbare pelt of white roots that hung from one of the peats. Red embers fell into the pit beneath. Neither moved. Each waited for the other to speak.

'In which countries have you been losing battles?' Father Jerry asked at length.

'The Ivory Coast, mainly skirmishes. Solomon Islands, a long siege that ended in no surrender. The Amazonian jungle, guerrilla warfare under cover of dense foliage. I'll say nothing about New Guinea, where I've just come back from.'

'You're an old soldier. You must be weary of war.'

'When did Mother die?' Hugo enquired with a casualness that failed to conceal unease.

'Ten years ago. In her last illness she kept asking for you. I was never her favourite son.'

'What did she die of?'

'A cerebral haemorrhage. She'd had a stroke the year before.'

'I often thought of her while I was away.'

'You never wrote.'

'She had you, didn't she?'

'I was in London. There was little I could do for her except during the holidays. I came to see her every summer. She was lonely and depressed. At the end I put her into a nursing home. I had to sell the house to pay the cost.'

'You shouldn't have sold the house. It was the family home.'

'I tried to get in touch with you but I didn't know where to start looking.'

'You expected me to come back one day. I like to think that the extra glass of milk was for me.'

'Why *did* you go away?' Father Jerry asked.

'I didn't know why at the time. Now I realise that I went away in order to come back. I wanted to see this place as Mungo Park saw the interior of Africa.'

'I can tell you here and now that you won't.'

'My immediate reason for returning was perhaps a loss of certainty and the drive that goes with it. In my youth I had a gambler's faith in luck. I was passionate and single-minded, dedicated in everything I put my hand to. One morning about a year ago I looked down on my shadow running thinly before me. It was the shadow of a just steward, a man whose only distinction in life was that he tended another man's garden to the other man's satisfaction. The garden was spacious and well ordered but it was not my own. I envisaged a simple vegetable patch with carrots, cabbages, onions and runner beans, and I knew that I must head for home. If I stay here long enough, I suppose I shall start dreaming of coconuts, yams, and papayas under a hot sun.'

'If you stay here long enough, maybe you'll find out why you've really come back. I hadn't realised that you were a gardener.'

'Not a gardener! I ran a plantation as big as this parish.'

'I opened your knapsack and got the impression that you'd served in the police.'

'I can explain all that.' Hugo laughed. 'The truncheon I acquired from the widow of a policeman who'd died keeping order during an intertribal row. The books were given me by the widow of an anthropologist who'd died of Legionnaire's Disease. As you may imagine, widows were a great source of comfort to me on my travels.'

Father Jerry looked non-committally at his brother whose eyes gleamed with self-delighting merriment.

'You must be tired after your journey. Would you like a drink? A cup of tea perhaps?'

'I'll have Scotch if you've got any. I haven't changed as much as you seem to think.'

Father Jerry went to the sideboard and poured a measure of Balvenie that looked embarrassingly small in the tumbler. Hugo held the glass up to the light and with exaggerated gusto drank his brother's health.

'I approve your taste,' he said.

'I don't touch it myself, I buy it for the parish priest who calls once a week. He's a devotee of Highland malt, and ever since he made his preference known to me I try to please him. The bishop calls once a year. Now, he enjoys a glass of brandy.'

'You know how to please your superiors. You can't go wrong.'

He regretted having mentioned the parish priest and the bishop. He stared at the twisted bars of the grate and crumbled a piece of biscuit between his fingers.

'I had a drink in the village on the way here. The pub was full of youngsters speaking French and German. I was a stranger among strangers. Not even the locals saw through my beard.'

'If you've come back to find the past, you won't find it here. And if you've come back to escape from all things alien and unpossessable, you must look for another haven.'

'What I hope to do is buy a house and farm and keep myself occupied providing life's necessaries. I've saved a bit over the years. With hard graft and good husbandry I should get by.'

'You couldn't have come at a more opportune time. Burke's is up for sale. You could do worse.'

Father Jerry rummaged beneath the coffee table and found the local paper.

'Here's the advert.'

For sale by auction on May 15th (unless previously sold by private treaty), farmhouse, barn, outbuildings and forge with 18 acres of arable land and 30 acres of mountain pasture, as a whole or in two lots.

He handed Hugo the paper, who studied it while he finished his whisky.

'Do you think you could put me up for the night?' he asked.

'Of course. There are two spare bedrooms. There's linen in the airing cupboard and enough blankets for a platoon.'

He showed his brother to the south-facing room across the landing from his own.

'I'll be getting up early tomorrow,' Hugo said. 'I've got

9

business in town. When I get back, I'll tell you about my plans.'

After he had said good night, Father Jerry came downstairs again and put more peat on the fire. He was not in the habit of going to bed early. He liked to read into the small hours, because he could get by on five hours' sleep or less. This evening he did not go to the bookcase. He sat in the armchair that Hugo had vacated, with his stockinged feet on the fender. He was a man of impulsive and irreversible decisions, was his brother, and by all appearances he had not changed. In his early twenties he had been 'an underpaid and less than zealous schoolteacher', to use his own phrase. One evening he packed his bags and left without giving the headmaster as much as an hour's notice.

He did not move until the fire had shrunk to ash. On his way to bed he paused outside Hugo's room and listened to the deep, untroubled breathing coming through the door, an animal sound that reminded him of his boyhood when Hugo's snoring used to keep him awake in the bed they both shared. He crossed the landing to his own room and stood by the north-facing window. The haze had lifted. The moon was shining on the sea. The fire on the Glebe had gone out and nothing moved in the shadowy circle between the tents.

He lay on his back in bed, aware of little except the presence of his brother in the house. The hiss of the toilet cistern woke him at four and he listened for Hugo's footfall on the landing. In his dream he had seen four boys and a girl sitting in the open round a flat, grey rock, chanting rhymes and holding hands. The girl's hand was hot; her palm burnt into his. He wanted to break the circle. He was about to shout when the sound of trickling water washed all pain away. He heard Hugo's door click closed and he fell asleep immediately with the warmth of a lost past flowing through his trunk and limbs.

Chapter 2

He woke at eight and knew that Hugo had already gone. His bedroom door lay open, the bedclothes formed a twisted pyramid on the bed. He washed and shaved with edgy deliberation, and as his fingers sought the collar stud at the back of his neck, he counted eleven gulls on the roof-ridge of the fishmeal factory, eleven gluttons with beaks on breasts facing wind and sea, eleven women sunk in satiety and intermammary introspection. On the Glebe below, the flaps of the tents were closed against the light of morning, and in the centre a dark mound of ash and embers waited to be stirred into life to warm leftover scraps for breakfast.

He walked to the village and said Mass before a congregation of eight. Throughout, the thought of Hugo hitching a lift to town occupied the hinterland of his mind. Afterwards, as he disrobed in the sacristy, he kept thinking of something prickly and rough, a solitary furze bush in winter on a hard, black hill-side after a late autumn burning. He returned to the parochial house, ate a light breakfast, and read Hugo's book on cannibalism in his brother's bedroom till noon. Over lunch he decided to spend the afternoon in his vegetable garden. He was planting onion sets

11

when Hugo drew up in a Land Rover with a boat on tow.

'Back already?' he called.

'When I move, I move fast. It's been a perfect day. I was in town by ten, and by twelve I was the proud owner of a Land Rover and boat. A man drew up in the square with a "For Sale" notice on the boat. I said I'd buy her if he sold me the Land Rover as well. He named his price and I didn't haggle. Are you impressed?'

'I hope you don't live to think yourself impulsive.'

'The Land Rover's as sturdy as a tank and the boat's a beauty. Don't say another word. All further praise is superfluous.'

Father Jerry walked round the boat, waiting for Hugo to ask him to bless her. He didn't.

'Come into the garden and let me show you my handiwork.'

'Are you doing it for therapy or the pot?'

'To work is to pray. Laborare est orare.'

They both looked at their watches as a bell began tolling in the village. Father Jerry said the Angelus while Hugo stood in front of him with his eyes on the ground.

'It's my first Angelus in twenty years and it's fifteen minutes late. You should have a word with your sexton, Father.'

'My sexton is Mandamus McDaid. He hasn't changed, he's still Arty Brennan's dogsbody.'

Father Jerry showed Hugo round his vegetable garden with the pride of a landowner for whom every square yard is an estate of latifundian proportions. He pointed out the carrots, parsnips, swedes and cabbages, and he counted the potato drills and bet a pound that he would be the first to eat new potatoes in the glen come summer.

'It's the garden of a vegetarian who loves his gut. I'll bet you keep thinking of the goodness of the cellulose and the blessing of regular bowel movements as you hoe. I'm not poking fun. When I see a bullock, I imagine a plate with a fourteen-ounce T-bone steak.'

'I grow vegetables because I like to watch them grow.'

They both looked up as McDaid returned from his bell-ringing. Tall, spare and weathered, he was a year younger than Father Jerry, yet he looked at least ten years older.

'You're back,' he called to Hugo.

'So everyone keeps telling me.'

'Now all the men are back, you and Arty Brennan and Father Jerry. I'm the only one who never left. Pity we haven't got Mary Rose. How can we ever play the Game again without her?'

McDaid looked from Hugo to Father Jerry who was pretending to examine the crosspiece of his spade.

'The Game?' Hugo said. 'Those of us who have been away have had other games to think of.'

'There's only one Game and it must be played again.' McDaid went off laughing. Father Jerry dropped his spade and hurried after him.

'The Angelus is always late, Mandamus. Why is that?'

'It could just as easily be early.' McDaid turned and faced him.

'I want it rung at twelve and six on the hour.'

'At twelve and six. Message received, Your Reverence.'

He watched McDaid's narrow back which seemed at least as long as his spindly bow-legs, as he retreated.

'It was the Game that was on his mind, not bell-ringing,' Hugo smiled. 'Nothing ever changes here.'

'You're wrong. We're no longer children, we must think and live like men.'

'Surely, if we're mature men, we must acknowledge the past in all its diversity. Childhood isn't something you try not to tread in.

13

It must be accepted and allowed to work its way through the conscious and unconscious designs of our waking and dreaming lives.'

Hugo drove up the avenue and parked the Land Rover and boat outside the door. In the boat he had stowed a cargo of provisions: meat, vegetables, fruit, six bottles of malt Scotch and a bottle of brandy.

'The brandy is for the bishop,' he said, as Father Jerry helped him unload. 'The Scotch is for myself, not the parish priest, you understand.'

'It looks as if you intend holing up here for quite a while.'

'It's just that I'm fond of my food.'

Father Jerry made tea and Hugo prepared what he called a mixed grill – lamb cutlets, bacon rashers, sausages, tomatoes and black pudding. He must have been peckish. While Father Jerry talked, Hugo bent over the mountainous meal and ate without once raising his head.

'I've been to see the auctioneer,' he said, when he had finally cleared his plate of everything except a single rib. 'I made a pre-emptive bid for Burke's but he wouldn't budge. Someone else had bid before me. I'm not the only man who's keen.'

Father Jerry told him that his rival must be their old school chum Arty Brennan. Arty had spent ten years in America and had come back seventeen years ago a prosperous man.

'Now he owns everything worth owning here: the fish-meal factory, the vegetable factory, the motel, the supermarket and the folk museum. He built them all. At present he's planning to build a holiday village, and for that he needs Burke's. If you want it, you'll pay through the nose for it. Arty Brennan is one of those men who don't take kindly to being blown off course.'

'Ah, the local boy made good. That makes two of us. The plot,

Father Jerry, is about to thicken.'

'Brennan is an egomaniac. I'm convinced he came back here because they wouldn't put his name up in neon lights in New York. Here his name is everywhere: on the supermarket, the motel, and on the vans and lorries in and out of his fishmeal and vegetable factories. He's in love with his own idea of himself. He's had his portrait painted and hung in the motel restaurant, a big, gilt-framed oil painting, as wide and as high as Michelangelo's "Last Judgment".'

'Surely there's no money in any of these things. The motel can be busy only in the summer, and a folk museum is just a civilised way of collecting coppers. He sounds to me like a man of straw.'

'He's a tireless milker of government departments. He spends his time up and down to Dublin lobbying politicians to give him grants. He lobbies God as well. He's first to the altar for Communion on Sundays.'

'A goody-goody. You must love him.'

'Only in so far as I love my neighbour. I don't love him specially or specifically. He is not a lovable man.'

The following fortnight was mild and calm. Hugo took him out in the boat once or twice. They caught pollack and cod which Hugo cooked in a thick sauce flavoured with celery. As Father Jerry didn't eat meat, he was delighted to have fresh fish, if only because it made a change from the flavourless fish fingers he normally bought in Brennan's supermarket.

Hugo was a rough and ready cook who spent as little time as possible in the kitchen. First, as a notional aperitif, he would announce that dinner would be ready in two hours. He would then vanish into the kitchen for twenty minutes, put something in the oven, and place two or three pots to simmer on the hot plate. Lastly, he would go for a walk or a drink in the village and saunter back to find everything 'done to a turn'. Surprisingly, he always managed a happy confluence in his cooking. Everything was ready at the same time, yet it seemed that everything had been left to chance. His shortcomings as a cook were that dinner could be at any time between six and nine, and once he had eaten he lost all interest in washing up.

'Every good chef needs a scullion, just as every good priest needs a deacon,' he said.

Father Jerry, who was pleased to be spared the bother of cooking, gladly assumed the role of scullion, washing up every evening with an old shirt tied over his cassock as an apron.

Hugo gradually established a routine. He would spend the morning walking on the hill, the afternoon fishing, and the evening drinking in the lounge bar of Arty Brennan's motel. He came back around midnight and went straight upstairs to bed. The only signs of heavy drinking he ever evinced were his frequent visits to the toilet during the night.

Soon Father Jerry grew accustomed to sharing the house with him. At first he was afraid that Hugo might intrude on his privacy, but before long he came to realise that Hugo himself was a private man. He spent hours alone in his room, and when Father Jerry once asked him if he had been reading, he replied, 'Not reading but thinking. Reading is only a way of letting other men do your thinking for you.'

On the morning of the auction Hugo was up early. He had cooked and eaten a hearty breakfast of poached eggs and haddock before Father Jerry left for Mass at nine.

'You'll come to hear the bidding?' Hugo enquired. 'I shall need moral support; and, who knows, a bidding prayer at Mass may do no harm.'

They spent an hour looking over Burke's farm before the auctioneer arrived at half-past eleven, both of them in raincoats and wellingtons, as the morning was wet. Local farmers smoked their pipes in the shelter of the haysheds and discussed the likely price, though it was obvious that most of them had come to watch rather than participate. Brennan was nowhere to be seen. Just as Hugo revealed to Father Jerry that the opposition had got cold feet, McDaid arrived on a bicycle with a spade tied to the crossbar so ostentatiously that Hugo immediately saw it as a weapon of offence.

'Arty Brennan has bigger fish to fry. More than likely, he's frying them in Dublin,' Father Jerry said. 'If you want Burke's, you'll have to bid against his scullion.'

The auctioneer took them round the farmhouse and outbuildings. He was a neat middle-aged man who was short of breath and gave persistent questioners the impression that he could also be short of patience. The sky darkened. As they crowded into the bare kitchen, it began to rain. The auctioneer stood on a chair and faced the grey light that seemed to leak accidentally through the dusty windows. When he had finished his preliminary remarks, a young man who had got married the previous month opened the bidding. A shopkeeper from the village bid fifteen thousand pounds. The auctioneer waited. One or two farmers looked at McDaid who looked out at the falling rain. The auctioneer told them that the reserve price had not been reached. McDaid bid seventeen thousand. The newly married man hung his head. As Hugo bid twenty thousand, everyone in the kitchen turned to look at him, except Father Jerry who was gazing steadfastly at the ferrule of his umbrella.

The rain lashed the window panes with louder insistence as

Hugo and McDaid battled it out. Hugo's face had set, or rather his beard had set. He looked alien and demonic in his single-minded concentration; he had lost all awareness of everyone except McDaid.

Each time McDaid raised the bidding by five hundred pounds, Hugo would raise it by a thousand. The murmur of conversation fell away, and the beating of the rain on the concrete of the farmyard died to a whisper. The tension of single combat showed in every face except the auctioneer's. When McDaid raised the bidding by a thousand pounds, Hugo's immediate response was to raise it by two thousand. Silence followed the auctioneer's request for another bid. McDaid stalked out of the kitchen. The auctioneer announced that the property had gone as one lot to Hugo McSharry for the sum of thirty-seven thousand pounds.

On the way home Hugo was jubilant. He talked and talked, unable to contain his excitement. When Father Jerry reminded him that he would have to spend at least another ten thousand on general repairs to the house and outbuildings, he said, 'Ten thousand! I'd give twenty thousand to see Brennan's face when he hears the news.'

'If you'd waited, you'd have got a better farm for less,' Father Jerry said.

'I fell in love with the forge. Maybe I fell in love with all those afternoons I spent watching Old Burke working the sooty bellows.'

'It's a lot to pay for a memory.'

'I wasn't out for a bargain,' Hugo replied. 'I was out to make a point.'

Chapter 3

A fitful morning breeze was coming in from the west. They could feel it on their faces but only now and then.

'I'm afraid I still can't get it,' Hugo said.

'You will when the weather gets warmer, believe me. The stink of rotten fish guts hangs over the shore townlands like a haze you can't see. You'll taste it on your tongue when you wake up in the middle of the night, and you'll get it again first thing in the morning.'

'Hasn't anyone complained?'

'The fishmeal factory provides employment. Employment brings money. If money stinks, it's just too bad.'

'I think I got it that time,' Hugo sniffed.

'It ensures that you're always aware of Brennan here. His works simply cannot be ignored.'

'Not all his works are bad. Think of the tourists he's attracted. The village pubs are crowded with comely French and German lasses every night.'

'He's brought the riff-raff of Europe and America here: artists, writers and hippies who have never turned an honest penny. They're corrupting the morals of the young.'

'I wish they'd corrupt mine.'

'It's no joke. They spend the days swilling plonk, the evenings smoking pot, and the nights in sexual orgies. You can get the smell of pot on the wind whenever the fishmeal factory isn't working.'

Hugo plucked his beard and laughed irreverently.

'I'm going to spend the day at Burke's,' he said. 'I'll take in the Glebe on the way. If I manage to get a prurient peep into the tents of ungodliness, I'll describe for you whatever perversions I see over dinner this evening.'

After Hugo had gone, Father Jerry lingered by the parochial house gate, looking west to the fishmeal factory, a long shedlike structure with a low, grey roof. Six or seven gulls came in over the sea and perched on the roof-ridge, squawking and screaming with irritable aggression. Gradually, they settled down in a broken row. They had become a somnolent parliament of evil old women, sitting on privies, pressing and pressing with small heads sunk below their shoulders.

He sauntered up the avenue and climbed the stairs to his brother's bedroom. The bed had been made, and from beneath it peeped two shoes with a sock stuffed into each of them. The local paper stood furled in the waste-paper basket and the book on cannibalism lay next to *Totem and Taboo* on the night table. Last night his brother had stayed out late, and instead of going straight to bed he looked into the study where Father Jerry was reading by the fire. Without waiting to be asked he sat down in his donkey jacket and lit one of his short, sharp whiffs.

'I realised this evening how lovely it is to be home,' he said. 'Here we are protected by hills. We live in a womb, a big, soft, warm womb with nearly all mod cons provided. As I walked back from the motel, I could swear I heard the word "womb" on the wind.'

'What you heard was the hippies on the Glebe chanting mantras.'

'Forget the hippies, they're harmless. They seem alien to you because you've always lived a sheltered life.'

'I've lived in cities and ministered to the down and out.'

'You've always lived among Christians or at least among people who could relate to your cassock. You've never been outside the realm of your Christian god; you've never slept in the jungle surrounded by the shrieks of hell on earth, and you've never been invited to a feast at which human flesh was to be consumed. If you had accepted such an invitation in all innocence, would you have had the courage to make your excuses and leave before the soup?'

Hugo showed his well-preserved teeth in silent laughter. His broad shoulders shook, his eyes gleamed with self-approving merriment.

'You've had an exciting day. You've been celebrating. Now it's time you went to bed.'

Hugo closed his eyes and continued smoking. His bushy beard was curly, almost unkempt, and the fine hair on his forehead shone with perspiration.

'On my first evening here you asked me why I'd come back. Would you like to hear the real reason?'

'It's as good as any you're likely to give me, I suppose.'

'In New Guinea I got to know a woman who kept pestering me to run her plantation. She invited me to dinner and sent her chauffeur to collect me. In the glove compartment of her car was a copy of *The Donegal Democrat* which the chauffeur said belonged to his wife. I picked it up, and there on the front page was your picture and a caption saying that you'd been transferred from London to Glenkeel. You'd lost your boyish looks. You were thinner and more serious. I realised that you were the only kin I had left. I knew immediately that I had to see you and talk about certain things that were on my mind.'

'It's late now. We'll talk about them another time.'

Hugo flung his half-smoked whiff into the fire.

'We may not talk about them at all,' he said.

Over dinner Hugo made no reference to the tents of ungodliness. Instead he said that Brennan had been to see him at Burke's.

'He's hopping mad with McDaid for letting the property slip through his fingers. He made me an offer of forty-five thousand. "You'll make a profit of eight thousand," he kept repeating, as if repeating it could change my mind.'

'What did you say?'

'No dice.'

'That must have pleased him.'

'He left in a huff. "You're standing in the way of progress," he shouted. "You got Burke's just because I happened to be in Dublin on the day and McDaid misinterpreted my instructions. You got it by accident, and accidents have no place in my planning." He was so incensed that he threatened me.'

'How?'

'By the way he stood. He was standing in *my* farmyard, and he deliberately made me shift my ground.

'Don't exaggerate, Hugo.'

'You weren't there. When two civilised men stop to talk, there's a holy ground between them, a no man's land that must not be trodden. Brennan, I tell you, invaded the holy ground.'

'He always liked to have his way.'

'I'm going to his motel tonight. If he's there, he may find

22

himself taking a backward step or two.'

'Don't court dissension. Best to ignore him. You made the auction into a contest which you won. Now it's time to be generous. Just let him see that all enmity comes from him.'

That night he dreamt of a glen where lean and weathered faces had grown flabby and soft, and hippies with backpacks defecated shamelessly on the roadsides. The rangy walk of mountain men had gone the way of their native language; it had no place on the factory floor or on the dance-floor of the motel ballroom. He woke with the feeling that he had not slept, and as he went to the bathroom saw that Hugo's bedroom door was ajar. His bed had not been slept in. From the window he looked down into the garden where a shapeless bundle dangled from one of the sycamores, an ungainly wasps' nest that moved before his eyes. Slowly it dawned on him that he was looking at an old fishing net with Hugo curled up inside it. He ran down the stairs and into the back garden. Hugo was making a moaning sound as he struggled, his big bushy head trapped between his knees.

'Don't move in case the branch snaps,' he shouted.

Father Jerry got a rope and ladder from the garage and within ten minutes had lowered Hugo to the ground. He opened the net and cut the gag that covered his mouth and chin. Hugo staggered as he scrambled to his feet. He tried to say something, then suddenly bent forward and retched over his boots.

'Wait till I get my hands on Brennan,' he spat between gasps.

'Surely Brennan wouldn't do such a thing.'

'Not Brennan himself, he just gives the orders. While he's got McDaid he needn't lift a finger.'

'Did you see either of them?'

'It was too dark to see. I was walking home from the motel when someone jumped me from behind. The first thing I knew I was bound and gagged and hanging upside-down from a tree. I managed to free my hands but the knot on the gag was too tight to undo. I thought I was about to pass out. It was lucky you got up so early.'

He sought the support of the wall and hobbled stiffly towards the house. Father Jerry put him sitting at the kitchen table and gave him black tea laced with Scotch.

'Will you go the police?'

'Would *you* spread the news that you'd been left hanging upside-down from a tree?'

'I think the police should know.'

'They wouldn't believe me. Brennan is a pillar of what passes for society here. Besides, where's the evidence? This is something that requires a more subtle riposte than a summons. Or do you suggest that I turn the other cheek?'

'Don't do anything rash is all I say.'

'The objectivity of your advice is commendable, Father, but then you don't have a splitting headache and you don't have cramp in your left leg. All I can say is that I appreciate your concern.'

He drank three mugs of tea but declined to eat. He looked pale and shaken, and when Father Jerry suggested that he should go to bed, Hugo took his advice with uncharacteristic docility.

'One thing I'd like to know,' he said as he climbed the stairs. 'Was the net the first thing that came to hand, or is he trying to tell me something special?'

Though he felt sorry for his brother, Father Jerry could not help feeling that he had brought about his own humiliation. Throughout breakfast the thought of the bearded stranger upstairs steeped him in disquiet. With a gesture of impatience he took his father's old shotgun from the cupboard under the stairs

24

and climbed the hill, as his father used to do whenever his mother launched into one of her homilies on etiquette, public morality, or the weather.

His father was a doctor who had been brought up in the glen and returned in middle age with a wife who did not share his passion for country living. She came from the city. She had social aspirations, while his father liked nothing better than the solitude he found on river banks and on long walks to unfrequented loughs in the mountains. On his strolls he carried a gun solely for companionship; he never pointed it at anything more sensitive than a clay pigeon.

He often accompanied his father on these walks, because his father saw Hugo as a mummy's boy. Consequently, Father Jerry used to feel that he himself had been chosen to share a secret world of fantasy, eccentricity and subversive humour which his mother saw as a challenge to her femininity, her family back-ground, and her longing for the social round of a doctor's wife in a prosperous Dublin suburb.

Thoughts of his childhood brought him closer to his father's life in which courtesy, culture and philosophical speculation were paramount. As he zigzagged against the face of the hill to avoid the steepest banks, he knew that he found his ideal of manhood not in the lives of the saints or the popes but in the uncelebrated life of an obscure country doctor. At times he felt that it was only his belief in the kind of life his father had led that kept him from lapsing into the impassivity of despair.

He reached the top. Swags of thin mist whirling in from the west touched his face like fine rain. The glen lay veiled beneath him: the fishmeal factory, the vegetable factory, the folk museum, the flat-roofed supermarket, the encampment of hippies on the Glebe. Though there were other things to see – white cottages, meandering roads, the wide, grey bay and the curving shore – it was to the works of Arty Brennan that his eye obsessively returned.

He crossed a plateau of moorland towards a basin in which lay a grey lough with a black, peaty shore. Looking down on the dull water, he became aware of a gangling figure approaching on the right.

'You're out early, Father. Out for a shot?'

Mandamus McDaid drew level. Father Jerry did not move, though he could not help feeling that the other man was standing too close to his shoulder. He was carrying a triangular board with a kind of fin sticking up and a row of fishing lines and lures attached to it.

'You know I don't shoot. The gun is unloaded, I carry it for company like my father before me.'

'A gundog would make better company than a gun.'

'You've brought your own company.' Father Jerry eyed the wooden contraption under McDaid's arm.

'Ah, the old otter. I haven't used it in years.'

'Ottering is illegal. As a sexton who calls people to prayer, you should try to give a better example.'

'If ottering is all I do wrong, we're certain to share a seat in heaven.'

McDaid gazed down at him from under the peak of his cap which formed an awning over the bright blue of his eyes. He stood straight as a pillar-stone, weathered and seemingly immobile. The lines on his hard, lean face turned into an ogham inscription, and the grey stubble of his chin into prickly lichen. There was a hint of mockery that was not self-mockery in his eyes. They seemed to say that the burin of life had passed over Father Jerry's clean-shaven cheeks without marking them.

'Ah, here comes Arty, the man himself.' McDaid raised a hand

26

to salute Brennan who had appeared from behind a turfstack with a fishing-rod on his shoulder.

'Good morning, Father Jerry,' he smiled. 'You've come to ensure fair play, I'll bet. Mandamus and I are having a little fishing match. He's got the otter and I've got the rod. Are you going to put your money on me?'

'The otter should have the advantage,' Father Jerry said.

'It depends on the water and the day,' Brennan replied. 'The choice of day was mine. Need I say that I chose one to suit myself?'

He was standing on the slope above Father Jerry, burly and bear-like in a thick pullover. His large, round face gave off a rosy hue that spoke of health-giving pursuits on exposed mountains by the sea. Above each ear two or three wisps of fine, red hair swept back in oily wings, and above the wings rose a bald crown not unlike a hogbacked island in a lake of rusty water. A thin, red wisp uncoiled in the breeze and blew across his freckled but unlined forehead. He looked well-fed and self-satisfied, the kind of man who is in no danger of getting a peptic ulcer from nights of worry about problems of philosophy that have no bearing on his annual income.

'You've come up for a mouthful of bog air?' Brennan smiled at Father Jerry. 'Now, if I were you, I'd have taken out Hugo's boat for a wheeze of sea air in the bay.'

'I considered that. This way I'm getting the bog air and the sea air all together.'

'What's so special about bog air?' McDaid turned to Brennan as if he were not just his master but his mentor.

'Strictly speaking, there's no such thing as "bog air",' Brennan explained. 'The air on a bog is a mixture of many smells that are never mixed in the same proportions. One day the smell of heather will predominate, and on others the smell of moss, turf, sedge, rotting fibres or even stagnant water. That's why no two visits to a bog are alike, but if you go to a bog every day for a year, you'll have a fair idea what bog air can smell of.'

Father Jerry studied the surface of the lough without responding.

'Do you remember the English professor who was staying at the motel last summer?' McDaid said. 'Now, he was mad about bogs, and he was an educated man.'

'He was a sexual pervert,' Brennan replied. 'He once told me that bog air is essentially cloacal – I'll tell you what that means later. Staying at my motel was only a cheap way of satisfying his lust.'

'Ah, go 'way!' McDaid's lean face crinkled in laughter.

Father Jerry turned and glanced warily from one to the other.

'I must be off,' he said. 'I'm sorry to have to leave you, you're such ingenious conversationalists.'

'There's something I'd meant to ask you.' Brennan moved closer. 'Hugo is being difficult. As you know, I'm going to build a Holiday Village. I've bought land on both sides of Burke's and I need Burke's to complete the site. Without it I'm stymied. I may never get the right site again.'

'There's nothing I can do about that.'

'If you had a word with Hugo, he'd listen. You could tell him that by selling Burke's to me he'd make a handsome profit himself and do everyone else here a good turn.'

'He's fond of Burke's, that's why he bought it. Surely, if you'd considered it so important, you'd have come to the auction.'

McDaid sniffed twice. His lower jaw was that of a dog gazing dolefully at his master. Father Jerry expected him to allow his tongue to loll. Instead he took his pipe from his pocket and blew through the stem to clear it.

'The best-laid schemes of you-know-who get all screwed up,' Brennan said. 'I'm a man of many ventures. We'll take it no further now, but you might come to dinner for a chat one evening. It's too important to let slide.'

'Which lough are you going to fish?' Father Jerry asked non-committally.

'We'll try the Lough of Silver,' Brennan replied.

'In that case I'll walk in the direction of the Lough of Gold.'

'See how many brown trout you can shoot in an hour. Who knows, you may shoot more than we'll hook.'

McDaid laughed as Father Jerry walked away.

'You're a true clergyman,' Brennan called after him. 'Every true clergyman has a gun that never goes off.'

When he had put a hill between himself and Brennan, he sat down under the lee of a turfstack on the heathery slope above the Lough of Gold. A grey trail of mist rose from the cold, glassy water. For half an hour he sat staring at what seemed to be a mysterious and unnatural phenomenon. Brennan had tried to give an impression of confident authority but Father Jerry had seen not the man but the boy: a carroty urchin with large hands, hacked feet, and patched trousers that had never been less than an inch too short. It was the feet he remembered most clearly. Broad, flat and splashed brown with bog-water, they could have belonged to an aquatic animal that plunged rather than ran.

Above him the sun broke through the mist, a small, yellow sun no bigger than a moon, which had about it the remote and cheerless look of a sun in December. Two seagulls planed in over the hill, touchingly innocent in their silence. They had returned from the years of his childhood when he and his father used to watch their unfathomable comings and goings and wonder why

29

they lit on one field rather than another. His father was fond of seagulls. On their mountain walks they would both stand and observe them rising and falling on the wind, and his father would say, 'They are a lonely and desolate bird. Even by the shore they never stop crying for the sea.'

Brennan's gulls were different, a thin, white line on a roof-ridge, beaks tipped with the red of gluttony, an obscene metonymy. They no longer fed in fields or on the shore. They sated themselves on the orts and offal of Brennan's materialism. They had the look of birds that had been debased and defiled. He had defecated and urinated on their soft, round heads.

One of the seagulls rose off the water through a finely drifting veil of grey. He cocked the safety catch, took aim, and pulled both triggers. Click! Click! No cartridge fell on the heather.

He got up and made for home, unaware of the brightening light on the greens and browns of the rough-edged landscape. He found Hugo doing press-ups in the kitchen while the kettle boiled madly on the cooker.

'Where have you been?'

'Up the hill. I met Brennan and McDaid by the loughs.'

Hugo got to his feet and rubbed the small of his back with both hands.

'I'll bet Brennan looked thuggish.'

'He looked like a country gentleman. Moisture from the mist had made little bright pearls in the wool of his pullover.'

Hugo laughed.

'Did he threaten you?'

'Of course not.'

'You notice all the wrong things. You're a very lucky man.'

Hugo resumed his press-ups with fanatical concentration. He saw no world and knew no life but his own.

Chapter 4

After lunch he looked out at the quietly falling rain, a billion threads from a billion bobbins unrolling endlessly, binding the day in mindless torpor. From below the road came the thin unassertive lisp of the tide, though what he was most aware of were the movements of his brother mending a puncture in the kitchen. However spacious the house, Hugo contrived to be present in every room.

Towards evening the rain stopped. He pulled on an old pair of trousers and low Wellingtons. The air outside was pure, the newly drenched landscape fresh-smelling and bright under the opening sky. He walked down the garden path between rows of carrots and parsnips with tops that looked greener than yesterday. The clay was soft and swollen round the stems. He stooped over his cabbages to watch gleaming droplets turn into darting blobs of quicksilver on the thick leaves. He felt comfortingly enclosed, sheltered by ash trees from the north and by sycamores from the west. His vegetable garden was a world in miniature, a private domain within the public world of pastoral duties. More important, perhaps, it was an hour of contemplation and prayer in a day of humdrum tasks, and it was a place where Hugo never came.

He worked steadily and meticulously, weeding and digging and earthing up. As he grilled a brown trout for tea, he kept thinking about his father, a calm, unworldly man who took pills for angina and had to pause for breath on hills before he was fifty. Their walks together were both an education and a delight, an incessant flow of observations and anecdotes that made him prefer his father's company to that of other boys. He read his office in bed and fell asleep before Hugo returned from the motel. He was awake again before dawn, waiting patiently for daylight and listening to the swish of the sea.

The sea was a continuous presence in the glen, just as the whine of traffic had been a continuous presence in London. Here, as he slept, it made haunting chamber music in the next room, and again as he woke in the morning, spinning a thread of continuity between day and day. If it should cease to sigh in his sleep, he felt certain that he would wake up in alarm because his dreams would no longer have a great, amorphous, wandering world in which to occur.

He must have dropped off again, it seemed to him that the room had suddenly filled with light. He got up and went to the window, delighting in the fresh June morning and the rosy bank of translucent cloud that coloured the hilltops in the east. He blinked as a movement in the vegetable garden caught his eye. An animal's head appeared between the trees, then another and another. He counted four young bullocks as he staggered into his trousers.

'What's the matter with you?' Hugo moaned when he roused him. Grudgingly, he got up and accompanied Father Jerry to the garden. The gate was closed and there was no sign that the cattle had broken through the fence.

'An enemy hath done this,' said Hugo, untying the twine that served as a hasp on the gate.

Nine black bullocks lifted their heads and sniffed the smell of unshaven men on the morning air. They had made mush of the drills. They had broken the potato tops and trodden the carrots and onions into the ground.

'You'll have to start from scratch again, and you won't be the first to eat new potatoes this summer,' said Hugo, as he drove the last of the bullocks from the garden.

'Whose are they?' Father Jerry wondered.

'They're neither Brennan's nor McDaid's. Now, that would have been too obvious. They probably belong to your most devout parishioner.'

'It's obvious that they didn't break in by themselves.'

'They were druv,' said Hugo.

'Who could have done such a thing?'

'Father Jerry, among your parishioners is a man who does not love you. Dwell on that, and also think of this. If an enemy comes and sows tares among your wheat, the Good Book tells you to let both grow until the harvest. What does it advise when you discover nine black bullocks making shit of your vegetables?'

'I can guess what you'd advise.'

'Don't be druv. After all, you're not a bullock. The salmon net and now this prank are what indulgent headmasters put down to "boyish high spirits". Something more serious is bound to follow. When it does, I'll shout, "Action!" Not till then.'

'I think I'll have a word with the police.'

'Don't make a fool of yourself for Brennan's sake. I'd like more time to think. I'm leaving for Dublin after breakfast. I forgot to tell you that my trunks have just arrived. I'll be back tomorrow evening with a well-planned plan of campaign.'

As soon as his brother had gone, he opened every window so that the morning breeze might blow away the stale stagnation that hung in every corner. He couldn't face the mess in his vegetable garden, so he drove up into the mountains in the east and spent the day visiting old people who were no longer able to come to church on Sunday. The houses were scattered far apart over a wide and barren territory. They stood at the end of laneways among two or three green fields that had been reclaimed over centuries from the surrounding sedge and heather. They gave him a reassuring sense of the essential. He rejoiced in the knowledge that the life they represented was austere and true.

'I must remain aloof,' he told himself. 'I'll live like these mountain farmers oblivious to second-hand imitations of twentieth-century glitter. Brennan, McDaid and Hugo are mere distractions. Let them distract one another; I'll pursue the life of work, study and prayer alone.'

When he got home, he found a young woman peering through the window into his study. She was tall and lightly built, in trousers that she must have pulled on with difficulty.

'I was wondering if anyone was home.' She spoke precisely, as if words were hard-won and deserved to be pronounced distinctly.

'I'm Father McSharry, most people here call me Father Jerry.'

'I'm Olga Petersen, your new neighbour. I arrived this morning, I just wanted to say hello.'

He led the way into his study. She sat in the low armchair and stretched two long, trousered legs half-way across the hearth rug. She was no more than thirty, and her fine, blonde hair, parted precisely on top, fell down in thick tresses in front of each shoulder. It was so straight that each tress looked taut as a violin bow, and so fine that no individual hair could be distinguished from the rest.

'You're here on holiday?' he enquired.

'I'm here to earn a living. I'm a wood carver, I need peace to practise my art.'

'You plan to stay?'

'For a while. I have rented a cottage from Mr Brennan for six months. After that I may be able to see a further six months ahead.'

'You know Arty Brennan?'

'I answered his advertisement and met him yesterday for the first time. He was kind enough to give me a lift all the way from Dublin.'

'What made you choose Glenkeel? Arty Brennan's persuasive publicity?'

'I didn't really "choose" it. I looked it up on a map and liked it because there could be no through traffic.'

She fished a packet of cigarettes from inside her pullover and offered him one. The packet was crumpled and the cigarettes were short and thick with dark, strong-smelling tobacco. He took one and tamped the end on his thumbnail.

'Have you got a light?' she asked.

As the match flared before her face, he noted a light-blue eye that moved and a dark-blue eye that didn't.

'So you wanted a place with no through traffic?' He bent down and put a match to the turf fire in the grate.

'I wanted solitude and stillness. Here there is no going forward.'

'You mean it's a dead end?' He smiled at the flame from the firelighter curling between the peats.

35

'I meant that if you don't like it here, you have to go back the way you came. There's only sea for a thousand miles to the west.'

He inhaled and coughed against the back of his hand.

'Those are foreign cigarettes.'

'They're French,' she said.

'You're not, are you?'

'I was born in Munich and came to Dublin before I was twenty. I'm self-supporting. I'm my own meal-ticket. Is that how you say it?'

'It's a phrase we don't use here.'

He got up and offered her a glass of milk and a biscuit.

'Ah, you were expecting someone.'

'Most evenings someone does call – a parishioner with a problem, a fisherman with a lobster for my dinner, a hungry tramp.'

'You're lucky to be living here. You'll never have a visit from an overdressed businessman with a briefcase and umbrella.'

'Believe it or not, we have at least one businessman here.'

She sipped the milk and stared at the digestive biscuit. In profile her face did not look in the least Germanic. It had some of the subtle refinement of a face by Botticelli, expressing an elusive spirituality that seemed to shine from the dark right eye, the eye that had not moved since they met. As she raised her head to exhale a puff of cigarette smoke, her face took on a hint of heaviness that belied the fine, straight hair and slender neck.

'You know Mr Brennan?' she enquired.

'He's our businessman.'

'I got to know him a little on the way from Dublin. He's full of good ideas.'

'You mean profitable ones. The best ideas have no monetary value.'

'If he's a businessman, what does he do in a place like this?'

'He owns things: a motel, a supermarket, factories, cottages. He adds a new string to his bow every time he goes to Dublin.'

'String to his bow. I understand.'

'He's a businessman who never ceases to do business. When he asks you the time of day, rest assured that it isn't an idle question.'

'He's an unusual businessman. He's a conceptual thinker and he can see with other men's eyes. For most men only what they have experienced themselves is real. Mr Brennan isn't afraid of what he doesn't know. He had never thought about wood carving before I met him but he saw immediately how I could relate it to the life here. That's exciting.'

'As you say, he's a conceptual thinker.'

'I can tell from how you say it – *you* find your meaning in things.'

'I don't see concepts as foxhounds to be set on the heels of things. I like to leave things as they are.'

'When I get the cottage in order, I'll show you my carvings. They are things that have swallowed up concepts. The best of them are just things.'

He followed her to the door. Though her hair fell forward on each side of her face, there was still a profusion of blonde tresses left to fall down her back almost to the waist.

'I'm pleased to have found such a good neighbour,' she said.

'The glen is full of good neighbours. Here you can have as many good neighbours as you like.'

He closed the door softly behind her, holding back the catch to keep it from clicking.

'Brennan has found himself an admirer,' he said aloud. 'Or has he added just one more string to his bow?'

He sat by the fire till after midnight reading a book on patristic theology that the bishop had lent his parish priest Canon Hackler. The parish priest, who was not a scholar, had asked Father Jerry to summarise the argument in two short paragraphs so that he could show some acquaintance with the text in his next letter to the bishop. He wrote three long paragraphs, about nine hundred words in all, and put them in an envelope which he stood behind the clock on the mantelpiece. He felt tired and at the same time excited. The luxury of reading and making notes in a large, empty house late at night was not the kind of pleasure that the Fathers of the Church considered dangerous. Yet it had left his mind so restless that it was well after two when he finally got to sleep.

Chapter 5

Hugo returned from Dublin the following afternoon, bulky and overbearing with a tang of stale Scotch on his breath.

'What a cock-up,' he snorted. 'Only one of my trunks has arrived. The other is the one I've been waiting for.'

'Don't worry, it's bound to turn up.'

'You'd better say a prayer to St Antony or whoever looks after lost property these days. It contained all my diaries, nine fat volumes, every one of them as big as a ledger. It's twenty years of my life, a record of every day and every night.'

'I hadn't realised you kept a diary.'

'It's more than a diary, it's a historical document. I wrote over five hundred words a day, nearly four million words in all, every one of them meant for publication.'

'Well, at least they haven't been pinched by Brennan.'

'You don't know what this means. My diaries are irreplaceable. I'm not the same man without them.'

He drove off to Burke's with six bags of cement that he had bought in town. Father Jerry decided to spend the rest of the afternoon clearing up the mess in the vegetable garden. Towards evening Brennan came through the gate looking as burly and overbearing as Hugo. He was wearing green tweeds and a green beret whose leather rim shone with oil from what remained of his sandy-red hair. He stood among the broken tops, tall, broad and planklike, without a hint of either humour or flexibility.

'This place looks like a battlefield,' he said with an air of accusation.

'I had an invasion of bullocks the other night. They trod everything back into the ground.'

'You must look on the bright side. They left you their manure. You'll get the benefit of that next year.'

'I'm a simple country priest. I prefer blessings that are not quite so heavily disguised.'

'Let me offer you a blessing you will recognise, then. I've come to invite you and Hugo to supper at the motel next Saturday.'

'There are two kinds of suppers: those you sing for and those you don't. Which is this?'

'You won't have to sing, I do assure you. I have a pop group from Dublin on Saturday nights to provide the music. We'll talk of course. All three of us have travelled, we won't be short of anecdotes. And for your added enjoyment, I shall have a little proposition for you and Hugo to think about.'

'I must warn you I don't eat meat.'

'Do you eat fish?'

'I'm fond of fish, except in fishmeal, fishcakes and fish fingers.'

'You needn't worry, there's lobster, crab, salmon and wild trout on the menu. For special guests I sometimes buy in crayfish.'

'I'll tell Hugo. I'm sure he'll be delighted.'

Hugo was suspicious. He said that he would go only on condition that Father Jerry agreed to act as his taster. Father Jerry said no more, and Hugo spent the next three days at Burke's bemoaning the loss of his diaries and clearing out the house in readiness for reroofing. On and off Father Jerry thought about Brennan. It was difficult to know what to make of him. He probably meant well, yet he never created anything without leaving a swathe of destruction behind him. The things he built were monstrosities that leapt aggressively to the eye; the things he destroyed were invisible because they had resided in the hearts and minds of men. People praised him for his monstrosities, and he believed them. He saw himself as a builder rather than a demolition man. The German girl had said that he could see with other men's eyes; the truth was that he was blind to all ideas except his own.

As a boy Brennan had known poverty. His mother, a poor widow, was barely able to clothe his fast-growing frame, let alone provide the hearty meals his physique demanded. At the age of sixteen he was still running about barefoot and in short trousers, which made him a butt for cruel humour among the other village boys. Yet he had been spared the extremity of destitution because he had in McDaid a disciple who worshipped the ground his bare feet trod. That must have been a rare solace to Brennan in those straitened days, and when he returned from America, a man of conspicuous means, he appointed McDaid his factor, land-steward and major-domo extraordinary. McDaid was grateful. He repaid his patron with an unquestioning loyalty that took time off only for sleep.

Brennan's first move was to buy the local hotel which at the time attracted starchy middle-aged couples on tight budgets, who spent as little as possible and complained volubly and frequently about rising prices and poor service. Round the old hotel Brennan built what he called 'a leisure complex' which included a ballroom, three lounge bars, an indoor swimming

pool, a snooker room and a fast-food restaurant. He put up a
large sign in red lettering which said ARTY BRENNAN'S MOTEL.
He introduced rock music, which drove the careful middle-aged
couples several hundred miles down the coast and attracted the
spendthrift young from all over the county. The fame of the
'motel' spread. In next to no time the glen people had declared
it a rip-roaring success and its proprietor a man of genius who
instinctively knew what people wanted before they themselves
did.

Like many self-made men, Brennan had a blind faith in material progress. Looking round the glen, he saw the remnants of an
ancient society that had changed little in two hundred years. He
saw men who wore homespun tweeds and lived almost entirely
off the produce of their meagre farms. These men, who made
neither profit nor loss but still found time to lean on their scythes
and converse over a ditch in idioms of infinite subtlety, affronted
him in their culture which was a culture of noncompetition and
an implicit negation of the strenuous years he had spent in
America. He saw a place that had been forgotten by the twentieth century. At last he had found his mission in life: 'to put Glenkeel on the map, where it belongs'.

The poverty of his upbringing had given him a genuine desire
to better the lot of his fellow-man. As he walked the lonely
beaches of the glen, he had visions of laughing tourists bringing
new life to 'a dying community'. As he imagined the riot of
colour against the gold of the sand – the red beach balls, the
striped towels, the gaudy bikinis – he heard the cash registers in
the village shops ringing in an era of bustle and prosperity. Tourists would bring money, and not just to the motel. They would
come to savour an ancient way of life; they would be moved to
buy the work of local craftsmen and mementos of their sojourn

among a simple but noble people. Apart from filling the motel bedrooms, they would provide employment for men and women who had no connection with the motel. The realisation that his aim was nothing less than the public good must have given him a frisson of pleasure that could never have been derived from considerations of personal gain.

The intoxication of his idealism doubled his energy and drive. He advertised widely in Europe and America, and so many tourists came that the motel had to be extended twice within five years. Next he inveigled the Tourist Board into building a scenic road along the mountain overlooking the sea, and when it was built he lined it on both sides with three-room chalets which he let to visitors for the summer months at rents that enabled him to close them without undue concern during the winter. After the chalets came the fishmeal factory, and after the fishmeal factory came the vegetable factory which brought enough spending money to the glen to support the supermarket he had built simultaneously.

The glen folk, seeing that whatever he touched turned to extra cash in their pockets, accorded him the respect which in the past had been reserved for the parish priest. His fame spread. Businessmen on the make and rising politicians came to seek his advice. Journalists from Dublin came to marvel in purple prose at his transformation of the life of a remote rural community from a simple to a cash economy. Unfortunately, not even Brennan could transform the economy of an area without transforming its culture too. At first the changes seemed insignificant, but to the concerned observer they were telling. People spoke less Gaelic and increasingly adopted English, the language of commerce and lucre; they spurned the garrulous story-teller on the hearth for the whip-crack jokes of the television comedian and the slick entertainments at Arty Brennan's motel; and they stopped helping one another in the fields because in their new-found affluence they no longer needed to. Few people saw this. Few people cared. Typically, Brennan saw it, and before a cynic could have said Jack Robinson he had built a folk museum to enshrine and preserve the symbols of a way of life that his works had destroyed.

The folk museum was an immediate success. It was popular with day-trippers who enjoyed the illusion of experiencing the remnants of an ancient and complex culture between lunch and afternoon tea. It was so much more convenient to walk round a centrally heated museum and study scythes, traw-hooks, kibbing sticks and slanes than to go to the trouble of seeking out a farmer who was actually using one of those primordial implements in a wet field or bog. The museum was also popular among the locals, who would visit it with their children on Sunday afternoons to reminisce about a way of life they had once known and whose passing gave them no cause for regret.

Brennan's most grandiose scheme took root in his imagination when he heard an American tourist remark that he would be willing to pay double if only he could live in a peasant cottage without having to endure the inconveniences that make such a dwelling authentic. Brennan immediately envisaged a Holiday Village (he naturally thought in capitals) by the sea, a clachan of 'peasant cottages' with electricity, piped water, gas cooker and fridge, not to mention a turf fire on the open hearth with a wide chimney brace and a big crane from which would hang smoke-blackened pots and pans. The cottages would appear thatched from the outside, but an asbestos roof underneath would keep out the rain, as expert thatchers were now hard to find.

In this way the tourist could nurse the illusion of living the simple life while enjoying all the conveniences to which he was accustomed at home. There would be one or two picturesque trappings to give him a sense of authenticity – a piece of old fishing net hanging over the dresser and perhaps an old cartwheel or broken wheelbarrow by the door. He would receive an attractive colour brochure explaining the mystique of the peasant life, reminding him, for example, that the kitchen hearth was the centre of his cottage; that here the grandfather nodded and told his stories while the woman of the house knitted and rocked the cradle and her weary husband slowly sucked his pipe; that the turf fire must be kept alight at all times; and that for his convenience Brennan could sell him the best of turf which, because of rising labour costs, was regrettably more expensive this year than last.

It was typical of Brennan that the setback over Burke's only convinced him more firmly that he had been born to build the Holiday Village. Hugo was just an obstacle in the path of progress, by no means the first such obstacle he had encountered and overcome.

'We've been invited by the lion to his den,' Hugo said as they both set off in the Land Rover for the motel. 'Should we beard him, I wonder, or should we lionise him?'

'We'll do neither. We'll allow him the lion's share of the food, and when he's sated we'll give a little twist to his tail.'

The motel was a low and rambling concrete structure tacked on to an old stone-built hotel that had been erected in the nineteenth century by an English landlord as a lodge in the wilderness where members of the shootin' and fishin' fraternity could pass a week or two away from the rigours of business and domesticity. It was a quadrangular, two-storey affair built round a small cobbled courtyard on a rise overlooking the sea. As the region was one of Atlantic winds and storms, it had been designed so that the doors opened on to the courtyard while the windows afforded the most splendid views of sea, moor and mountain.

Hugo pulled up outside the front entrance, having ignored the signs pointing to the car park at the rear. From the new ballroom came a shrill wail of rock music, and from one of the lounge bars a chorus of 'Ja, ja, ja' which made the rock music sound soft by comparison. They entered the courtyard of the old hotel with its teak tables and chairs among pot-plants, an enclave of history that for the moment seemed proof against the cacophony of the surrounding motel.

Arty Brennan greeted them in the lobby with a smile that was relaxed and confident. A thin strand of hair had been drawn carefully across his bald crown. His cheeks glowed pink with robust good health, the skin smooth without a trace of stubble. He was wearing an open collared shirt and newly pressed slacks. As he shook hands, he bestowed on them a potent waft of musky deodorant.

'We'll eat in the old hotel restaurant. The new restaurant gets crowded on Saturdays, as you can imagine. But first we'll have a quiet drink, or perhaps two.'

He led them into a lounge bar which he had renamed 'The Hills of Donegal'. From the walls blown-up colour photographs of Errigal, Muckish and Slieve League looked down on a scattering of French and German tourists and two or three intrepid locals who were giving a passable imitation of fishermen in close conversation over pints of stout. They found a table by a window facing a sharp-peaked hill that was not among those commemorated on the walls, and a barmaid came with a tray of drinks – a large whiskey for Hugo, tomato juice and Worcester sauce for

Father Jerry, and Bacardi and Coke for Brennan who told them that Bacardi was all the rage among the young.

While they studied the menu, Brennan made light-hearted small talk about the scarcity of lobsters because of overfishing by the French, and the demands of the business life which kept him awake in bed at night. Father Jerry was polite and Hugo grimly laconic. Brennan put down the menu and spread himself with the air of a man whose sole purpose in life is the creation of good-natured bonhomie. The evening light was fading on the hill and the turf fire at the far end of the bar had begun to blaze brightly. An enlivening buzz of friendly conversation rose and fell behind them. The ear-splitting rock music they had heard as they came in seemed now to belong in a world that was no part of Brennan's creation.

After they had ordered, Brennan conducted them into a small restaurant where a local family was celebrating the father's eight-ieth birthday at a table dominated by a cake with eight red can-dles. They sat at the other end of the room, the sea beneath them dark and grandly mysterious in the waning red of the after-glow. Father Jerry, looking about him, experienced a seductive sense of solidity that had nothing to do with the material success of a man he remembered as an awkward boy running round barefoot in tattered trousers. The thick vegetable soup had a hot, peppery tang that he found superior to the packet soup he and Hugo ate. If the hotel was a lion's den, it was a den of many apartments, and the lion himself was at pains to appear accom-modating and congenial.

'The table is set for four,' Father Jerry remarked. 'Are you expecting another guest?'

'Didn't you know?' Hugo smirked. 'Arty is like you, he always lays out supper for the Devil. He's late this evening by the look of it. What on earth can be keeping him?'

'Actually, as you may have guessed, the missing man is McDaid,' said Brennan.

'Then let's drink a toast to absent friends. To the Devil and McDaid!' Hugo raised his glass while Brennan blew his nose and Father Jerry jabbed a handkerchief up his sleeve with his forefinger.

'Well, speak of You-Know-Who,' Hugo shouted as McDaid appeared at the door.

'You've missed the starters.' Father Jerry sought to be affable.

'I never have a starter,' McDaid replied. 'Nothing but the main course. I believe in solid fodder.'

'Mandamus is a self-starter,' Brennan explained.

'You should have had the avocado,' Hugo said. 'It was almost perfect. Pity it was just a bit hard at the thin end.'

'Let me get you another,' Brennan offered.

'I'll have a whiskey instead.'

'We'll be having wine with the main course,' Brennan promised uncomfortably.

'I never have wine with my meals, always whiskey. Since I'm having steak, I'll have Irish. You're having fish, Father Jerry. You should really have Scotch.'

'I'll have mineral water,' Father Jerry said to Brennan.

'And I'll share a bottle of whiskey with Hugo,' McDaid said in a spirit of willing co-operation.

'That settles it.' Brennan beckoned irritably to the waitress. 'A bottle of Jameson for these two soaks, half a bottle of the house claret for me, and some Perrier for Father Jerry.'

His hand shook the table as he ordered. It was a large, broad hand, heavily clothed in fine red hair that failed to conceal the bulging blue veins beneath.

48

'How much do you want for Burke's?' Brennan asked aggressively as soon as the drinks arrived.

'Burke's is not for sale,' said Hugo. 'When I've reroofed it, I'll have a snug little nest that will stir the imagination of every nubile woman in the parish.'

McDaid guffawed and waited for Brennan to speak.

'If you sell Burke's to me, you'll have enough money to buy a bigger nest. The modern woman expects elbow room, including a bedroom to herself.'

'Burke's is more than a home for me. As a boy I spent my afternoons in the old forge. It has what sentimentalists call a sentimental value.'

'I'm stymied, then. My Holiday Village is a non-starter and the money I've already spent buying up land for it is money down the drain.'

'There must be other sites,' said Hugo.

'Where?'

'Just be patient. Something will turn up.'

'What do you want with a Holiday Village?' Father Jerry asked. 'You've done enough, you should be satisfied.'

'Business must grow. A business that doesn't is earmarked for the receiver.'

Hugo poured himself another whiskey and told McDaid that his steak would have been perfect had it been medium rare, as requested, rather than just a shade overdone.

'I have the money to attract more wealth to the glen but I would like to see local involvement,' Brennan said. 'I've put money in people's pockets. Now I'd like to see them invest some of it in their own future. You are chairman of the parish council, Father Jerry. You could get the parish to back this new venture, perhaps even encourage landowners to provide a site. What I'm

49

doing is not for myself but for the good of the community.'

'I'm against the Holiday Village,' Father Jerry said. 'We've had enough changes here, more than we've been able to absorb in so short a time. There is more money and more of the things that money can buy. Sadly, the quality of life has deteriorated. People have lost their innocence and with it what was left of the local culture.'

'They wouldn't agree!'

'Of course not. The man who's lost his culture is the last to realise it.'

'Ah, you see yourself as a custodian of cultural values.' Brennan laughed sarcastically.

'As a priest, I see myself as the custodian of a culture that makes moral values possible.'

'You're a late convert to peasant culture. You weren't brought up in a poor widow's cottage as I was, you lived in style in the doctor's house in the village. You lived among Corinthians, and now you wish to write self-righteous epistles to the Corinthians like that other convert St Paul. Just remember this: some of us remember enough about the past to know when to say, "Enough".'

'Why don't we forget the past and all that nostalgie de la boue,' Hugo said. 'Let's relax and enjoy the sumptuous present. This is the best spread I've seen since I unexpectedly found myself guest of honour at a cannibal feast in a remote corner of the Pacific over ten years ago. No, don't grimace, Arty. It wasn't at all as you imagine. There was no dancing round a big pot, as you see in the movies. This was much more sedate. They sat quietly round the turning spit, just like the hippies on the Glebe at one of their cannabis feasts.'

'A living culture is a changing thing,' Brennan said to Father Jerry. 'I've enriched the local culture and I'm proud of it.'

'Think of the summer evenings in the glen when we were boys. Young men came to the crossroads to play pitch-and-toss. Now they come to your motel to play bingo.'

'What's wrong with that?'

'There's more skill in pitch-and-toss. Bingo is a game for morons.'

'Cannibalism is going too far,' said Hugo. 'It makes frogs' legs and snails' eggs seem like roast beef and Yorkshire pudding. And remember, there's no Béarnaise sauce – nothing between you and the flesh that horrifies.'

'The loss of culture has led to a weakening of religious feeling,' Father Jerry raised his voice. 'When we were growing up, one or two women would faint at eleven o'clock Mass every Sunday, and two strong men would get up and carry them outside for a breath of fresh air. It was a ritual as regular as the transubstantiation itself. If no one fainted, people felt that there had been a failure of sanctity, that the priest had somehow betrayed his function. When have you last seen a woman faint in church?'

'They fainted simply because they walked long distances from the mountain and because they came to Mass fasting,' Brennan said witheringly. 'Now they come in cars and they eat a hearty breakfast before leaving home.'

'How can you have a spiritual experience on a full stomach?' Father Jerry asked. 'Sanctity abides in the skin and bones of the poor, not in the adipose tissue of the overfed.'

Brennan slapped his thigh and winked at McDaid.

'Cannibalism is only one kind of excess,' Hugo shouted. 'Another is what happened below on the plain while Moses was up the mountain getting his tables of stone. Do you know what went on, Arty?'

'I'm afraid not.'

'That's because you don't wish to know. Every man can find out by looking into his heart. Any man who hasn't doesn't know himself.'

'You should have had the wine,' Brennan said. 'It aids digestion whereas whiskey inflames the imagination and impairs the judgment.'

'Ask me if I'll sell Burke's.'

'I'll do better, I'll offer you full partnership in the venture. The Holiday Village will attract the better class of tourist: university professors, writers and artists in search of simplicity, businessmen in need of a rest cure, and intellectuals who have lost their way. We mustn't be selfish, we mustn't keep our ancient culture to ourselves. We must do our bit to rejuvenate a tired civilisation. We'll offer the Total Experience: we'll pay a few elderly locals to live in the new village to provide a sense of reality – telling stories, singing songs, and generally looking wise. It will be the Total Holiday with Total Immersion. How is that for a slogan? It will be a goldmine for the glen. If you're willing to provide the site, Hugo, I'll split the profits with you fifty-fifty. What do you say?'

'Total Ballsology! Your problem, Brennan, is that you have no gift for theology. What interests me is the origin of moral scruple. Why is cannibalism wrong?'

'It's a great evening altogether,' interjected McDaid. 'For the first time in thirty years we're together round a table – all except Mary Rose herself. If she were here, would we replay the Game? I like to think we're still young enough to play it.'

At the other end of the room the celebrating family began singing 'Happy Birthday' and the white-haired octogenarian burst into tears at the sight of eight red candles burning. Hugo raised his glass to Brennan and in a coarse and gravelly voice sang, 'For he's a jolly good fellow'. McDaid got to his feet to conduct while Brennan and Father Jerry stared stonily at each other across the table.

'That ends the formal proceedings, I hope,' said Brennan when Hugo had finished. 'We'll now go upstairs to my personal lounge to take brandy and coffee in peace.'

'I'm off,' McDaid said. 'I don't have coffee. Nothing but solid packing for the working man.'

'I won't have brandy,' said Hugo. 'But I'm willing to finish the whiskey.'

They entered a small oak-panelled room with an oval table in the centre and a portrait of a bearded Victorian worthy above the fireplace. On the opposite wall hung a blown-up photograph of Arty Brennan steadfastly gazing at the other portrait.

'Is he an ancestor of yours?' Hugo asked. 'I didn't know you had any.'

'He's Sir John Matlock, the man who built the old hotel. I've put a photograph of the Declaration of Irish Independence beneath his picture. It makes a neat political point, I think.'

'It oversimplifies history, a besetting sin in Ireland,' Father Jerry remarked.

'It's important to me. This house was once the symbol of foreign occupation in the glen. Now it's owned by a local lad, the son of a poor widow made good.'

'Plus ça change … Once it was English landlords, now it's tourists from France and Germany and hippies from God knows where.'

Brennan poured coffee. The house claret seemed to have had a mellowing effect on him. He subsided in his chair and gazed up at the portrait of Sir John.

'It's a pity we see so little of each other,' he said affably. 'You and Hugo and Mandamus and myself have a bond that time hasn't broken. We share an unforgettable childhood. Perhaps that's why the three of us have come back here.'

'I came back to slip quietly out of this accursed century,' Father Jerry said. 'It seems that you came back to make my task more difficult.'

Brennan smiled amiably and lit a stumpy cigar.

'I came back to satisfy the demands of my imagination,' he said. 'Here I am the flywheel on which smaller wheels depend.'

Father Jerry had a feeling that Brennan was making a deliberate effort to be friendly. He spoke at length of his early struggles in America and of how he could think only of home once success had finally come to him. Hugo seemed to have fallen asleep, and Father Jerry, who listened without saying much, thought that the men who wreak most havoc in this world, and who deserve to have havoc wreaked on them in the next, are men with a sense of mission. As the clock on the mantelpiece struck one, he prodded Hugo and rose to go.

'You have a strong sense of mission, Arty,' he said. 'It rarely goes with a sense of proportion.'

Brennan smiled understandingly and accompanied them down to the courtyard. The night sky above them was a bulging sail of stars. They stood on the steps of the front entrance while Hugo searched his pockets for the ignition key. The rock music had ceased. The night was quiet, the only noise the back-and-forth drag of the sea. Father Jerry was expecting to hear the wail of a curlew from the shore. He was thinking of human loneliness and the boon of sleep.

'I'll drive,' he said to Hugo when Brennan had left them. 'You've had far too much to drink.'

Hugo climbed into the driver's seat without answering.

'You rather overdid it with your wild talk of cannibalism.

Don't you realise that people may think you're being serious.'

'You think I was making it up?'

'I refuse to think. Some things are unthinkable.'

'As your brother, I deem it my duty to confront you with the full horror of life. Your tourists and hippies are only piped Muzak that doesn't please your ear. Come out of the sanctuary and look at the world as it is. You say I overdid the cannibalism. Well, you overdid the ancient culture bit. Now I know why you came back: to weep over Jerusalem, nothing less. Both you and Brennan are men of extremes. There isn't a ha'p'orth of difference between you.'

Father Jerry felt sleepy. It had been an evening of talk, and he knew that he had talked enough. Hugo was hunched over the steering-wheel, driving with exaggerated care. The road was bumpy and the jouncing headlights picked out clumps of rushes along the verge, and here and there a weathered telegraph pole. The road ran downhill along the edge of the sea cliffs. As they came into the first bend, a stiff-legged wether made as if to cross in front of them.

'Holy Christ! The brakes have gone.' Hugo swerved to the right, away from the railings along the edge.

The Land Rover swayed and the road tilted. For a moment they seemed to balance on two wheels above the sea.

'Hold tight, I'm going to ditch her.'

They were running alongside a bank of peat-moss on the right, still gathering speed as Hugo eased closer with the brake pedal to the floor. He was holding on through the bumping and grating, as if the steering-wheel were a lifebuoy. Then, with a jolt that seemed to electrify the floor, they came to a stop.

'We could have been killed,' Father Jerry said.

'If we'd gone out over the cliff it was goodbye to drink and trogging with women.'

Father Jerry stumbled on to the road and Hugo dragged himself slowly across the seat. He got a torch from the back and crawled in under the vehicle. Father Jerry leant against the wing, staring uncomprehendingly at his brother's upturned feet.

'It's Brennan, the bastard,' Hugo spat.

'Brennan?'

'Someone's tampered with the brakes. The pipes have been cut, come here and see for yourself.'

'Brennan couldn't have done it,' Father Jerry said emphatically.

'He didn't have to. McDaid left an hour before we did. Brennan kept us talking to give him time.'

'It's unbelievable.'

'There's nothing for it now but to walk home.'

They stood dumbly side by side looking down the cliff and listening to the plunging and slapping of the water below. The sound of the sea came from far away. It seemed to Father Jerry that he had his head down a well shaft and that his eardrums were about to explode in a vacuum of silence.

'This is serious. We could have been killed,' he repeated.

'I know.'

'It's now become a matter for the police.'

'Not yet. I'd like to ponder the possibilities for a day or two. The riposte must be swift and telling. It must preclude any possibility of a counterstroke.'

'I don't like that kind of talk.'

'Consider the position. You know who's behind all this but can you prove it?'

'It is not my business to prove it.'

'I've made up my mind. It came to me as a flash of revelation.

56

Now I know what I must do.'

'What must you do?' Father Jerry asked.

'If I told you, you'd be an accomplice before the fact. You're a priest, you must be protected.'

'Hugo, this is wild talk. You are for ever making light of things that are profoundly serious.'

'Far from it. I am nothing if not a moralist,' said Hugo.

Chapter 6

When Father Jerry returned from morning Mass, he found Hugo in the kitchen munching black pudding and stamping his gumboot in time to dance music from the radio.

'I've been thinking,' he announced.

'Have you?' Father Jerry surveyed the mountainous mixture of sausages, bacon rashers, mushrooms and tomatoes on his plate.

'We must take a theologian's view,' Hugo explained. 'We must try to judge Brennan's actions with reference to his intentions. The question is: did he have murder in his heart? Was it his direct intention to kill or create a serious risk of death?'

'The man who cut the brake pipes knew the road home. He knew that it runs downhill for half a mile, parallel with the sea cliff all the way.'

'And still in my mind there's a nagging doubt. Perhaps he merely wished to frighten us. Again, he may have convinced himself that murder would be justified by the "good" consequences that would flow from it. Dead men are not recalcitrant; they wouldn't stand in the way of the Holiday Village. When I know the answer to all these questions, I shall have a clearer idea of the course we should pursue. I would value your opinion, Father Jerry. Can murder ever be morally justified?'

'We are concerned here with a specific attempt at murder. Just ask your conscience. If I'm not mistaken, you'll get an unambiguous answer.'

'You mean that Brennan has broken the Fifth Commandment?'

'The Fifth Commandment is not just for Brennan, it applies to you and me as well.'

'You said that I should go to the police. I've been considering the theological implications of that too.'

Father Jerry waited while Hugo munched a whole sausage which took all of ten seconds.

'We're in a cleft stick, Father Jerry,' he continued. 'Prudence dictates that we pay out more rope and keep mum. Yet silence, you will agree, is one of the nine ways in which a man may participate in another's sin.'

Hugo drew a piece of bacon rind from his mouth and chuckled. Father Jerry left the kitchen and went to his room. He had slept little. While Hugo snored across the landing, he had lain awake pondering the correct course of action. At first he thought he might speak to Canon Hackler, his parish priest. By morning he knew that Dr Sharma was the one confessor in whom he could confide. She lived in London, in a large, empty house in Islington. She had helped him before. During an illness that lasted almost a year she had been his best friend, the only friend he trusted. As he thanked her and said goodbye, she told him to get in touch with her if ever he became troubled again.

After dinner, when he had the house to himself, he took a postcard from his desk and waited until a message had formed:

Dear Dr Sharma,

I am back in the glen where I began. This evening the sky was dark with a window of painfully bright light in the west. I looked hard into the window till my eyes hurt. Then I thought of you and how you used to say, 'Make friends with the inorganic.' At that moment I knew precisely what you meant. I hope you're still wise and thriving. I have a large, empty house here but not as large and empty as your house in Islington.

Blessings and best wishes,

Father Jerry

The following morning he placed the card in an envelope and walked to the village to post it. On the way back he ran into Olga at the parochial house gate, and somehow he drew encouragement from the sight of her. Red-cheeked and wind-blown in a loose-knit pullover and tight trousers, she was carrying what looked like a sheep's skull in her hand.

'This place is alive with forgotten objects, what you call things,' she said.

'Where did you get it?'

'I found it on the hillside between two stones. Here an artist doesn't need imagination. The shapes are right under his nose: rocks, stumps of bog-oak, stunted trees, all battered by bad weather. No gentleness, no kindness. Nothing but force and friction.'

She held up her hand, now gloved in the rain-bleached skull.

'What does it say to you?' she asked.

'Memento mori.'

'All skulls say the same to me: "Look, no eyes".'

Hugo came down the avenue and leant against the pier of the gate.

'A sheep's skull is very acceptable,' he said. 'If you had found a human skull, I'll bet you wouldn't have carried it home.'

'You're Hugo. I've heard about you.'

'Nothing alarming, I hope.'

'Arty Brennan told me that you are Father Jerry's prodigal brother.'

'You mustn't believe everything Brennan says. He's a fox, he may be after your grapes.'

'At least he isn't a talking donkey. He's got brains, he has a new idea every day.'

'Which is it today?' Hugo wondered.

'He's talking of putting speed-boats on the mountain loughs here.'

'That would certainly attract the right kind of tourists – the very rich,' Father Jerry said.

'Surely the loughs are too small for speed-boats.' Hugo smiled amiably at her.

'He's already considered that. He says that the speedboats won't go in a straight line but in circles,' she explained.

'In ever-decreasing circles,' Hugo suggested, 'till they finally disappear up their own spile-holes.'

'Don't mind Hugo,' Father Jerry said.

'Mind how you go with Brennan,' Hugo winked at her. 'He owns everything here. If you don't keep your distance, he'll soon own you.'

'Like Burke's, I'm not for sale. He's told me all about that as well, you see.'

'Your carvings are for sale, and they are your dreams. A man who buys one of your dreams buys a little bit of your life.'

She held up the skull to Hugo, so that the upper jaw was level with his eyes.

'Arty Brennan didn't say you were a tease.'

'I'll tell you a little secret: he's a very retentive man.'

'Retentive? He's generous. Before he left for Dublin this morning, he promised to bring me back some chisels.'

'Maybe he just thinks that heaven is in your bed. Saving your presence, Father Jerry.'

She laughed enigmatically and waved the sheep's skull at them both in farewell.

'Arty Brennan may have found himself a wife at last,' Hugo said when she'd gone.

'At least he's found his match.'

'Why don't you preach a sermon on Sunday against Brennan and all retentive bastards? Say that only the loose of bowel will enter the Kingdom, that the good life is no more than munificence of expulsion.'

Father Jerry walked back to the house. His brother's coarseness and irreverence had become an all-too-predictable irritation. His daily proximity had turned into a challenge to spiritual serenity. However, the news that Brennan had gone to Dublin brought him a sense of relief that was akin to peace.

Brennan returned in time for eleven o'clock Mass on Sunday, and, true to form, he was first at the altar rails for Communion. As he descended the steps to distribute the Host, Father Jerry reminded himself that his ministry in the glen was one of purification, that his duty was to preach the hard, irreducible word through thick and thin. There must be no papering over cracks and no equivocation. He would be unsparing, uncompromising, incorruptible.

Brennan waited with the other communicants. Father Jerry passed without giving him the Host. The other communicants returned to their pews, while Brennan remained kneeling ostentatiously before the altar. After Mass he came to see Father Jerry in the sacristy. His rose-pink cheeks had turned a blotchy red. His fingers twitched as he spoke.

'I demand My Lord and a public apology.'

'Consider yourself lucky, Brennan. The traders were whipped from the temple for less. What you deserve is summary excommunication.'

'You won't get away with it. I'll have you removed from the parish and defrocked to boot.' He stormed off.

Overnight the parish had become a centre of ecclesiastical debate. The parish elders could recall priests who had cursed evil-doers from the altar, priests who ranted and raved about women who wore trousers instead of skirts, and priests who warmed the buttocks of fornicators in ditches with a few well-aimed strokes of their blackthorns. What no one could recall was a priest who had refused a member of his flock Communion, which was tantamount to branding a man a public sinner. Father Jerry differed from other priests in the folk memory. He neither ranted nor raved. He did not even deign to give a reason for his action. His treatment of Brennan was seen by some as a calculated insult and by others as a piece of wilful perversity.

Father Jerry realised that he was on disputed ground. He had acted on impulse, without making a list of pros and cons. As he opened the tabernacle to take out the ciborium with the Host, he simply knew in his heart what he must do. Now he saw it as the most perfect thing he had ever done. It was an act of the utmost integrity, performed without regard to personal consequences; yet, as the days passed, the knowledge that his parish priest and bishop might not agree troubled him with uncertainty and anxiety.

At Mass the following Sunday he prayed fervently as Communion time approached. Brennan came to the altar alone, and again he refused him. The rest of the congregation sat glumly in their seats, determined not to move till Brennan had received the sacrament. Father Jerry lectured them from the altar, accusing them of using the eucharist as a counter in a game of moral blackmail. Blank, immovable faces looked up at him from below. He put the ciborium back in the tabernacle and ended the Mass in a state of agitation.

'You're playing into Brennan's hands,' Hugo told him.

'My conscience is my own. I must do what I think is right, not what I know to be prudent.'

The following day the parish priest, who lived in Corrloch, paid him an unexpected visit. Canon Hackler was a short, heavy man with straight black hair that fell over his ears in shiny strands. He walked awkwardly on splayed feet and his loose-fitting jacket hung down at the sides, prompting his parishioners to wonder if his pockets contained a ballast of stones. He was a sociable, uncomplicated priest with a solid reputation as an administrator and fund-raiser; his nickname, Canon Bingo, was not an unjust summation of his abilities. He smiled benignly as Father Jerry poured him a glass of his favourite malt Scotch, and after the first sip he lay back on the sofa, while the shoulders of his roomy jacket threatened to slide down his arms.

'All my life I've had an ambition to be called Monsignor. When they made me canon, I had hopes of greater things to come. Then I saw younger men promoted, men who'd never done a hand's turn in the vineyard, who'd spent the heat of the day licking stamps in the bishop's palace. Do you ever dream of wearing red socks and –?'

'Not really. I suppose I'm not ambitious.'

'Even a priest with no ambition must watch his p's and q's. He must be holy and humble, and he must be seen to be reasonable. I've heard about the trouble over Brennan. If you're not careful, Jerry, you'll lose the support of your flock. A lost sheep is one thing, a lost shepherd quite another.'

They spoke quietly and seriously for an hour, while Canon Hackler sipped a second bumper of Balvenie. Father Jerry did not dislike the canon. Though he considered him worldly, he admired him for his practical common sense. Now it was apparent that the canon considered him wilful and wildly misguided. At the door he smiled sadly and shook Father Jerry's hand.

'This is really beyond my competence. We've always been friends. I wouldn't like to see you land in trouble.'

It was his way of saying that he would be getting in touch with Bishop Driscoll, a man of quick and irreversible decisions, a man not to be trifled with. Father Jerry had known him as a fellow-student in the seminary, where he had distinguished himself as a sprinter, footballer and speaker in the weekly debates. Though opposites in interests and ambitions, they remained friends, and it was to him that Father Jerry wrote from London asking to be transferred to a parish where he could recuperate quietly from a serious illness.

The expected telephone call came two hours after the canon had left. The bishop sounded friendly. He enquired twice about Father Jerry's health and raised the business of Brennan only after five minutes of light ecclesiastical gossip.

'It isn't something we can discuss over the telephone,' he said. 'Perhaps you wouldn't mind coming to see me tomorrow. We must get it sorted out before Sunday.'

'I can come tomorrow at any time that suits you.'

'I've just had a thought. I'm visiting the parish priest in

Garron on Wednesday. While I'm there, I'll drive in to see you. It's only seventeen miles, and the locus in quo is often the best place to get to grips with a problem.'

Father Jerry devoted the next two days to thinking about tactics and to making the necessary preparations for the episcopal visitation. He hoovered upstairs and down, particularly the bathroom and toilet which had lost some of their sweetness since Hugo's return. He bought half a bottle of brandy in Brennan's supermarket as well as a tub of taramasalata, two slices of quiche Lorraine, and Black Forest gâteau in deference to His Lordship's sweet tooth.

On Wednesday afternoon he went for a walk on the hill to clear his brain and put the final touches to his case against Brennan. When he got back, he found the house engulfed in a steamy smell that intensified as he approached the kitchen.

'What on earth are you cooking?' he almost shouted when he saw a large preserving pan on the range.

'Mutton stew,' Hugo replied. 'I hope His Lordship doesn't insist on lamb.'

'It must be tainted. I've never smelt anything so foul.'

'Then you've never sat round the big pot. To tell you the truth I'm boiling morkin. "Stew for an hour in water," was what the cook book said. "Skim the fat from the liquid and arrange the meat and vegetables in layers in a ten-gallon pot. Salt and pepper to taste. Then add enough of the stewing liquid just to cover …"'

Father Jerry took the lid off the pan and staggered backwards at the sight of a sheep's head bubbling.

'I found a dead ewe on the hill and immediately thought of Olga. I'm boiling the head so that the flesh and skin will come clean away. As a collector, she'll be pleased. After all it's the thought, not the gift, that counts.'

'Take that thing out into the garden this minute. The bishop is due in less than an hour. You'd better go to Burke's for the afternoon. I don't want you here. I've got enough problems already without your madcap antics.'

'Another helping of brawn, my Lord Bishop? For the delicate constitution there's nothing more enticing.' Hugo guffawed as he carried the preserving pan out the back.

When he'd gone, Father Jerry opened the windows and doors and went all over the house with an old thurible incensing every corner to kill any vestige of the stink that might remain. He disliked incensing at the best of times but never before had it made him feel ridiculous.

The bishop looked brisk and businesslike in spite of his red skullcap. He sat purposefully on the sofa and offered Father Jerry a panatella which he took though he would have preferred one of his own filter-tipped cigarettes.

'They're quite mild,' said the bishop, flicking ash without due care and attention.

Father Jerry placed a scallop-shell ashtray to his right and left, poured him a glass of brandy, and waited for him to broach the subject that was uppermost in both their minds. The bishop had decided to start with a game of cat and mouse, however.

'Too much smoking turns the tongue to leather,' he began. 'Too much of anything impairs sensitivity. I've often thought that it would be lovely to smoke one good cigar a day and be satisfied. If you smoked it after dinner, you could look forward to the pleasure all day. Most of us, I suppose, could afford one Havana, but waiting for the right time to smoke it, and looking forward to smoking it, would be too much of a distraction. That's why I smoke panatellas. They're not sufficiently large or strong to intrude on my spiritual life.'

'I often think of us celibates as men who have never smoked,' Father Jerry confided. 'Total abstinence is our strength. It's more difficult to have smoked and given up than never to have smoked at all.'

The bishop gave a pale little smile and gazed at him with profound interest, as if he had said something at once outrageous and original, then he blew an oval smoke ring and changed the subject to dieting and the difficulty of forgoing one's favourite dishes during Lent. He spoke slowly and precisely with a show of self-possession that made Father Jerry recall the seminary debates at which he had so excelled. Suddenly he stopped and said, 'I talk too much. Now it's your turn. I believe you have something to tell me.'

Father Jerry gave him a scrupulous and dispassionate account of his dealings with Brennan, without in any way concealing his view that Brennan was a public sinner who vandalised whatever he touched. The bishop listened with his eyes half-closed and a look of long-suffering on his pallid face. Father Jerry could not make out whether he was a holy man sunk in prayer or merely a worldly man with a painful ulcer.

'You mentioned a "planned accident",' the bishop said without raising his eyelids. 'You assumed (a) that the accident was planned and (b) that it was Brennan who'd planned it. Then you refused him Communion because he was not in a state of grace. How can you make such an assumption?'

'I, too, have a conscience that I must honour.'

The bishop bent his head in the attitude of a weary confessor.

'Did you experience any doubts at all?'

'Not before I acted, only afterwards.'

'Do you still have doubts?'

'Of course I have, from time to time. Absolute certainty was not one of God's gifts to man.'

'St Paul would not agree: "He who has doubts is damned." Romans 14:23. An overscrupulous conscience is as serious a hindrance to sanctity as a lax one. Don't seek to peer into the heart of the rock, and don't turn your back on it either. What you've done is to contrive to get the worst of both worlds, this one and the next.'

'Now you are making assumptions, Bishop.'

'If you insist, I'll leave the next world out of the reckoning and merely remind you that there is such a thing as common-sense morality. You have appointed yourself judge and jury. You have acted imprudently and precipitately. You have got yourself into a quandary, and now you must find a way out of it. As your bishop, I see certain choices for me. Today I shall not dwell on them. Today I have come to advise you as a friend. You must seek a meeting with Mr Brennan and resolve your differences before Sunday. Remember that you are a pastor. Your business is to save souls, not condemn them.'

The bishop listened in impatient silence as Father Jerry went over the difficulties again.

'How is your health these days?' He interrupted before Father Jerry could clinch his argument.

'Much improved.'

'You're fully recovered?'

'Oh, yes. Coming back here after sixteen years in London has been both refreshing and invigorating.'

'At the time I wondered if I was making the right decision. You asked specifically for Glenkeel, and I remember thinking that giving you a parish where you had grown up might give rise to difficulties neither of us could foresee. A prophet is not without honour … Sometimes it is best for a priest to preserve his mystery.'

'Though I was born here, I have no relations in the glen apart from my brother. In a sense I am a stranger.'

'Perhaps that's the trouble. Would you welcome a change, if the opportunity arose?'

'I should like to remain here. There is much work to be done – and much work to be undone.'

He asked the bishop if he would stay to dinner but he had already arranged to eat with Canon Hackler in Corrloch. Nevertheless, Father Jerry managed to prevail on him to have a cup of tea and a slice of the Black Forest gâteau which he ate appreciatively with a little silver fork. As he was leaving, he said, 'When I was a boy, my mother used to say that potatoes were fattening. Now doctors say different. I often wonder if we'll wake up one morning to discover that gâteau is also good for us.'

That evening he went to see Brennan who was still insisting on a public apology.

'What you're seeking is a public humiliation,' Father Jerry told him.

'I've already had mine, thank you.'

'For the sake of peace in the parish I'm willing to let bygones be bygones.'

'You've gone too far to retreat now,' Brennan fumed. 'In refusing me Communion you exceeded your authority. A man who whips traders from his temple must not himself be subject to the judgment of traders. You are answerable to Canon Bingo who in turn is answerable to Bishop Monopoly. Your days here are numbered, my dear Jerry.'

'As your pastor I find your attitude deplorable and

unchristian.'

'You are not my pastor. Fortunately, there are other folds and other shepherds. And I shall be saying as much to the bishop and the canon.'

'I hope for your sake that the other shepherds will be lax enough to overlook the enormity of what you've done here: your factories belching stink and pollution, and then the riff-raff your advertising has attracted – hippies with backpacks defecating as loosely as gulls on every roadside and copulating as shamelessly as donkeys behind every ditch. In all my dealings with you I have been at pains to inform your conscience so that at the last trump you won't get off on a technicality: "Father, forgive him for he knew not what he did." '

Brennan made a loud farting noise with his lips.

'That's what I think of you and your interpretation of scripture! You're not a priest, you're a monomaniac. You're as mad as your brother. It's six of one and half a dozen of the other.'

Father Jerry walked home in the knowledge that he faced defeat. After Sunday he would be moved to another parish; it was obvious that neither the bishop nor the canon had any stomach for adverse publicity. He felt foolish and self-righteous at the same time. It was legitimate to be a fool for Christ's sake, but he knew in his heart that if he'd been a fool it was for the glen's sake. He had not been a wise fool; he had quite simply gone too far.

'It's an impasse,' Hugo pronounced when he had told him about his meeting with Brennan. 'What you need now is a Deus ex machina, unless a little pressure can be brought to bear.'

'Pressure?'

'Perhaps you should first give prayer a chance. If prayer should fail, force may prove efficacious.'

'How can you say such things to me?'

71

'Then I'll say no more.'

'This is my problem and I'm going to solve it my way. I forbid you to act in any capacity on my behalf.'

'As a priest, you can hardly say otherwise.'

'I mean it.'

'We are brothers. We understand each other. Whatever it is you wish for in the depth of your unconscious is done.'

He ground out a laugh that became a cold engine turning over on a winter morning. As he left the room, he said, 'I gave the skull to Olga. She pretended to be surprised but I think she was rather pleased.'

Chapter 7

For the next two days he thought and prayed until prayer became no more than thinking. On Saturday morning he met Olga coming from the shop with a rip-saw which she waved at him half-aggressively.

'You've heard the news?'

'Unlike you, I'm on my way to the village, not returning.'

'Arty Brennan has vanished. Everyone is talking. No one has seen him since Thursday evening.'

'Are you sure he isn't in Dublin humbugging one of his pet politicians?'

'No, his car is in the garage.'

'He's bound to turn up sooner or later.'

'Like a bad halfpenny? Is that how you say it?' She gave him a mischievous smile.

'No, in Brennan's case it would be "like a bad shilling". He's at least twenty-four times as rich as anyone else.'

'McDaid has been to the police to get them to organise a search.'

'So it is true?'

'Oh, yes. In the village they say it's strange how he vanished, just when he had you in a cleft stick, Father.'

'A cleft stick? A cloven hoof perhaps. The ways of God are strange.'

'So that's how you say it? A cloven hoof.'

'I don't know. Wherever he is, I hope he's up to nothing but good.'

In the village he went to three shops and bought a packet of cigarettes in each of them. In one of them he lingered to look at postcards, eager for the hot breath of gossip. The gossips praised the warm weather because it was badly needed, and remained stubbornly silent about the man who was uppermost in his mind. When he got back to the house, Hugo had returned from the garage with the Land Rover, which looked the better for its new wing.

'It's as shiny as a hearse,' his brother commented. 'Now wouldn't it make a lovely freight-car to eternity.'

'Brennan seems to have vanished,' Father Jerry told him. 'The police are organising a search.'

'Has he vanished for good or is he only lying low till the storm blows over? Either way it looks as if your prayers have been answered. Your Deus ex machina has bundled him off in his machine.'

'It's all very odd.'

'Admit it, it's most convenient.'

'I prayed that he should see the light.'

'Perhaps he has. Prayers have been answered before, you know.'

'I hope he is found. Uncertainty can only fuel gossip. People are superstitious, they make all sorts of absurd connections.'

'Do you believe in dreams? Now, I had a dream last night. I saw Brennan bound and gagged in a boat ... My own theory is that he realised he'd gone too far. He didn't want a showdown. He's lying doggo. He'll be back as soon as the theological debate has lost its bite. Father Jerry, you may not be out of the wood yet. It's possible that you've only been granted a respite.'

By the evening the glen was astir with rumour. The police had made a search of the sea cliffs, and the motel manager had had a telephone call from a worried businessman who claimed that Brennan was up to his ears in debt. Soon the village shopkeepers were saying that they had known all along that he'd been robbing one creditor to pay another, an old dodge that never yet survived a loss of confidence. Everyone had his own mite of insight to contribute. By Sunday morning the judgment of the village elders was that Brennan had come to realise that the game was up and, rather than face bankruptcy and humiliation, had quite simply absconded.

During Mass Father Jerry prayed for his congregation. His prayers were swiftly answered. A record number of people took Communion. He rang the parish priest and the bishop to tell them that the crisis was over. The bishop suggested that it would be wise to assume that Brennan was still alive, and charitable to offer Mass for his good estate. Father Jerry agreed, though in his heart he hoped that he would never set eyes on Brennan again.

That evening, after Hugo had gone to the motel to pick up the latest gossip, he tried to settle down to a book. He felt excited. The words kept swimming before his eyes; the sentences on the page were not those that formed in his mind. He wandered into the kitchen and made himself a salad sandwich before going upstairs to fetch a newspaper from Hugo's room. On the night table lay a casebound book as heavy as a ledger, with feint-ruled pages that crackled when he turned them. Hugo had begun writing what looked like a diary:

July 6th

'Where are you taking me?' Arty Bradley asked.

'To a little island where you'll be monarch of all you survey,' I replied.

He was lying on his side in the bows. I was taking no chances, I had him bound hand and foot.

'You won't get away with it, I'll see to it that you don't.'

I resented his self-confidence because it planted a germ of doubt in my mind. I forced myself to listen to the monotonous putter of the outboard and the hiss of the water which seemed to come up through the floor boards. I knew that he was watching me, trying to read his fate in my face. I stared stonily at the play of moonlight on the oily water, pretending that the moon had powers of hypnotism that could not be broken by anything he cared or dared to say. I lapsed into a reverie without thought, from which I did not wake until a dark hump rose out of the sea on the port bow. As I throttled back, I imagined Father Johnnie and Helga warm and dreaming in their separate beds, and I told myself that I must surely be mad to motor ten miles down a rocky coast in the small hours with no one but a sworn enemy for company. The landing place was on the landward side. Treading on the white shingle in the moonlight was like walking on auk's eggs baked hard by a tropical sun.

'What do you expect me to do here?' I was pleased that he now sounded aggressive rather than self-confident.

'Eat raw rabbit meat and think about how to escape.'

'You expect me to run after the rabbits?' The note of contemptuous sarcasm in his voice was forced.

'I don't expect you to shake salt on their tails. In that old sack you will find a handful of snares together with certain other little luxuries – seven cans of corned beef, a knife and fork, and

76

four bottles of Bacardi. I forgot the coke. You will agree that I don't do things by halves. No expense has been spared. For your added convenience, and because the grass is so sparse, I have packed a roll of two-ply toilet paper from the best supermarket I know. I'm sorry I haven't been able to get you a musket and shot. There really wasn't time. And, alas, there are no goats to supply milk, meat, and hide for an umbrella. Sorry it isn't the warm Pacific. You'll have to make do with Atlantic breezes to cool your heels.'

The humpback of the island rose dark and bald above us. A chilly breeze from the west uncoiled a strand of hair over his crown. I got behind him and dragged him up the beach, away from the shingle and the boat. Then I untied his hands so that he could undo the shackles on his ankles after I had gone.

'I'll have the law on you for this when I get back,' he said.

'It's a problem I hadn't considered. Perhaps you won't be coming back.'

'You haven't thought this out. There are certain things you haven't taken into account.'

I could see that he was rattled. He wanted to keep me talking, he didn't want to be left alone.

'Don't succumb to self-pity,' I said. 'Think of your sojourn here as a challenge to your ingenuity and your big chance to find out if you are universal man. Look on the bright side. Your slumbers won't be disturbed by hippies chanting mantras in the night!'

As I hurried down to the boat, he had already begun to undo the rope that bound his legs. I pushed her out and jumped aboard.

'Look out for footprints,' I called. 'Beware of visiting cannibals in canoes. I'll be back within a week to see how you're doing, and I'll bring your Man Friday – it's only fair.'

'You mad bastard, I'll sue you for this,' he shouted.

'Guard against spongy gums, loose teeth, foul breath and purple blotches. All that spells "scarby", better known as scurvy. 'Bye for now.'

The splutter of the engine drowned his feeble obscenities. As the shingle receded, I was surprised to find that I felt sorry for him.

On the way back I became so excited that I could have written a poem. The rhythm of it kept thudding in my mind with a hollow sound that made me think of waves breaking against an empty barrel. I could have sworn that I was on the brink of something. Then I realised that the poem wasn't mine but someone else's:

We made an expedition;
We met a host and quelled it;
We forced a strong position,
And killed the men who held it.

The moon had begun to lose her light in the dawn. The castellated cliffs on my port side had acquired

Father Jerry slowly reread the incomplete entry, seeking what he could only describe as a sense of purchase. It read like fiction, yet undeniably it could have been a record of actual events. In his study he took down a copy of *Robinson Crusoe* and found the page on which the hero discovers a footprint in the sand. The words were simple and vivid. He clearly saw a single footprint and, though the text was silent, he heard shouts that made him shrink within his skin. Greedily, he read on until he came to a description of what the narrator called 'a dreadful sight':

> The place was covered with human bones, the ground dyed with their blood, great pieces of flesh left here and there, half-eaten, mangled, and scorched … I saw three skulls, five hands, and the bones of three or four legs and feet …

These events were fictional, yet they vibrated with all the horror he had come to associate with Hugo's diseased imagination. In a sense they were more real for being horrific. With Hugo there was no knowing and no certainty. Father Jerry could confront him with a knowledge of what he had read or he could sit tight and observe until his brother gave something of his true intentions away. St Thomas would ask to see the Bacardi bottles and the tins of corned beef. In dealing with a man like Hugo scepticism was a virtue that any prudent person would cultivate.

The next day he was called to the mountains to visit a boy who was said to be suffering from an incurable disease. The distressed mother greeted him at the door and led him to the sick room where the boy was sleeping. Her husband had died the previous winter and the boy was her only son. Father Jerry sat by the bedside while the widow knelt and prayed. The boy opened his eyes. He was slightly deaf, he found it difficult to focus, and his speech was slurred. Father Jerry held his hand and the mother recounted what the specialist at the hospital had said. The small bedroom was stuffy. The sunny afternoon outside the window seemed to belong in a perfect world elsewhere.

'Will he get better?' she asked at the door.

'That's not for me to say. I'll pray for him. I hope that prayer will be enough.'

He wanted to escape the scrutiny of her imploring eyes. In his flurry he did not turn the car but drove farther into the mountains, away from the houses and patches of tilled land towards a bleak terrain of sheep pastures and rough heather. He felt uncomfortable for having given her hope where he had seen none, and oppressed by the knowledge of what he had read in his brother's diary. He wanted to get away from human kind, to lose himself in a landscape trodden only by sheep and wild fowl.

He had come to a sloping glen with a narrow stream running down to a beach of white stones. A rocky promontory jutted half-way across a little inlet, forming a natural sea wall and hiding from view the wider bay to the west. Beyond the promontory rose a crooked sea stack which fishermen had nicknamed the Devil's Pintle and which was overlooked by two sheer, grey-seamed cliffs, one to the north and the other to the south. Glenshask once supported eight or nine families who lived by sheep-farming and fishing. Now it was a place of empty houses, overgrown roads and bare fields with broken walls between them.

He took his father's shotgun from the car and walked up a green slope to a deserted hamlet of roofless cottages built of whitish stone. Between the houses ran a grassy lane peppered here and there with black droppings where sheep had sheltered at night from the wind. With the gun on his shoulder he went from house to house, peering into windows and doorways at smooth-flagged floors and empty chimney corners. Now and again he ran his fingers over the stonework which was clean, mossless and sharp-edged as if it had come straight from the mason's chisel.

For him Glenshask was a place of pilgrimage. He came here

to escape from the works of man, yet strangely it was the marks of human habitation – the ruined houses, the low byres, and the grassy slopes bearing the balks of ancient lazy-beds – that bestowed on this hallowed spot what he could only describe as a spiritual value.

He walked down to the beach from the houses with his eye on the tip of the Devil's Pintle rising coldly above the grey promontory. He climbed the slope above the beach and hesitated on the crest. Below him was a man he recognised, sitting on a rock with his arms locked round his shins. Father Jerry dropped to his knees, then slowly eased forward till he found himself lying prone on the grass. He brought up the unloaded shotgun and found the man's head in the sights. He cocked the safety catch and waited. If he pulled the trigger, the firing pin would go 'Click!' and the man would continue looking out over the water at the hump-backed island in the west. He got to his feet and made his way down the slope to where the bulky man was sitting.

'Don't you know it's still the close season?' Hugo turned and grinned as he drew level.

'I was in the mountains on a sick-call. It was a lovely afternoon, so I decided to keep going north.'

'For a sick-call a stole would be more seemly than a gun.'

'It was Father's. I carry it, as he did, because I like the feel of the stock.'

'You're a role-player. You play so many roles that only a theatre critic could keep up with you.'

'I thought you were at Burke's. What brings you out here?'

'Curiosity. I wanted to pace a patch of ground where Brennan's ox-foot hasn't trodden. Man defiles and desecrates. It's a marvel to find a little oasis where his works are only a memory. Here even the Devil has gone out of business, as you can see from the tuft of moss on the tip of his pintle. Take a good look round. No hippies, no fishmeal factories, no supermarket, no motels.'

'You're telling me what I like to hear. Are you telling me the truth?'

Father Jerry stood gazing at the humpbacked island which was undoubtedly the one described in Hugo's diary. Hugo got to his feet and faced him with the light of mischief in his eyes.

'I've got news for you. This place is only a half-way house, a kind of Purgatory. Heaven is in Glencrow to the north of us, on the other side of that hill. There's no road to shorten the journey, only a sheep-track, and when you come to the end of it, you look down into a heathery glen with only one ruined cottage. If Glenshask is a sanctum, Glencrow is a sanctum sanctorum; and if you don't mind walking in my footsteps, I'll lead you there.'

'Not today, thank you. I'm going back the way I came.'

'Back to Brennan's Gehenna! Or do you carry it about with you?'

Below them the Devil's Pintle with its surface of blackened age, sprang out of the water. At its base lay two submerged rocks from which dark fronds of seaweed reached out towards the land, wavering tentacles searching blindly in the ebb and flow.

'Do you want a lift home?' he asked Hugo.

'Home? This is home,' Hugo smiled. 'I'll linger for another while. Don't wait for me, I've got my boat.'

Father Jerry made his way down the slope towards an old quarry where he had parked his car. The narrow moor road stretched emptily in front of him, leading back to the larger glen and a world he at least found comprehensible, even though he had rejected it. He had come out here to escape from that world for an hour. Today he had found an alien place that wakened within him a presence he could describe only as that of a stranger.

He drove slowly in third gear with his mind on the hump-backed island crouching rodentlike in the afternoon sun.

'The alert conscience weighs accurately and reacts quickly,' he said aloud. 'But any judgment of conscience that precedes action must have its basis in something approaching certainty. All I know is hearsay and supposition. When I act, it must be from faith, not doubt. In the meantime I must pray for guidance and clarity, remaining alive to every hint and nuance. If I ride with my back to the engine, I shall see my bridges only after I've crossed them.'

In the morning Hugo said that he was going to town on business. As soon as he had gone, Father Jerry drove to Smug Rone Pier where his brother kept his boat. He had decided to make an expedition; he felt puffed and excited, as if he were entering a race that must on no account be lost. He relaxed somewhat as he nosed out through the narrow inlet. The strong smell of salt and sea all round dispelled the sense of enclosure with which he had begun the day.

A heat haze hung over the water, and behind him in the east the mountain tops melted into a low sky. The day could not have been more suitable for what he had planned. First, he would go south to the Sound and troll lazily and purposelessly for an hour. Then he would go out wide and swing north to Scariff Island, concealed from the shore by the haze. The realisation that he was bent on a mission of mercy gave him a sense of peace, yet the knowledge that he was intent on concealment made his sense of peace less than perfect. After an hour he had caught five young pollack and a codling. He munched an apple, then headed north.

When he had put the bay behind him, he kept within sight of

the cliffs and the shore because his navigational powers were far from sure. After what seemed an eternity, a dark outline loomed through the haze, farther from the land and longer in shape than he had expected. As he approached, the island emerged from a light veil of luminous vapour and became a grey-green hogsback with a selvage of black rocks opening on the landward side into the little cove that Hugo had described in his diary. He cut the engine and rowed in slowly. With raised oars, he sat waiting for a sound or movement.

'Brennan,' he shouted. 'Brennan, are you there?'

He scanned the rocks and listened, reluctant to draw closer. He received his answer, a shriek from a cormorant as it rose from a whitened rock to his left.

He rowed round to the seaward side, keeping a watchful eye on the shore. The island looked weathered and bare, stilled in a timeless silence. At the narrow end a stony beach formed a door-mat before a wall of round, black boulders that looked as if they had been heaped in a hurry to block a concealed entrance. It would have been possible to moor the boat and climb up through the boulders but again he rejected the idea of going ashore. He returned to the landward side and waited. Glenshask and the Devil's Pintle formed a vague outline in the haze behind him. Convinced at last that he would find no one on the island, he beached the boat and made his way up an uneven shingle strewn with dried seaweed that crackled underfoot. It was an eerie and unsettling place in which to be alone, and when he spotted a heap of clothes on a rock less than ten yards ahead, it seemed to him that they had materialised before his very eyes. He glanced over his shoulder at the boat, and again at the neatly folded clothes. It was like discovering a footprint in a place where no footprint should be. The jacket and trousers were undoubtedly

Brennan's. What he experienced as he touched them was not so much unease as revulsion.

'Brennan,' he shouted again. 'Brennan, do you hear me?'

He spent an hour exploring the island, looking for empty Bacardi bottles or anything else that might substantiate Hugo's narrative, but the clothes were the only indication that someone else, possibly Brennan, had been there before him. There were no rabbits either, nothing but heaps of brittle sea wrack and the whitened bones of birds. He returned to the shingle and went through the pockets of the jacket and trousers which were empty except for two white pebbles the size of goose eggs. He rolled the clothes into a neat bundle and hid them behind a rock at the upper end of the cove. Then he hurried down the rough shingle, pushed out the boat, and jumped aboard while it was still moving. He could not say why he had left the clothes behind. All he wanted was to get home or better still wake up and realise that the events described in Hugo's diary were indeed a dream.

He spent the afternoon in his vegetable garden trying to collect his thoughts. He realised that most priests, indeed most people, would now go to the police. Yet all he could do was walk round his runner beans in a state of tense hesitation, weighing conflicting responsibilities and asking himself whether his loathing of Brennan and all his works had vitiated the affective side of his conscience, making recognition of the good nothing more than a remote and intellectual process. To break silence would incriminate his brother, perhaps wrongly; and to maintain silence was tantamount to condoning what was possibly a criminal act. It was a dilemma from which there was no riddance. *Conscientia perplexa* was what his professor of moral theology had called it. No matter what he did he would take on the burden of a bad conscience, an abiding awareness of personal imperfection.

85

After dinner he sat in his study listening for the hum of the Land Rover in the driveway. He flicked through a book on ethics, too anxious to put his mind to the endless distinctions and classifications. He went to his desk and with painful deliberation wrote another postcard:

Dear Dr Sharma,

I brought back two egg-sized beach pebbles from a bare island, one rough and grainy, the other smooth. The grainy one is less cold to the touch, and when I turn it over under the lamp it emits little pinpoints of white light. The smooth one is ellipsoidal; the grainy one spherical with a little omphalos on one side which I caress with the pad of my thumb.

Tonight I placed them on my desk with a red-cheeked apple in between. The apple came alive, though in the bowl among other apples it had looked quite lifeless. I took a bite from its rosy side and it became an ugly and accusing skull between the two mutely perfect stones. When I munched it to the core, the space between the stones was empty and gaping. I did not fill it again. This is not a dream. The stones are in my trouser pockets. I have touched them once again to make sure.

Kind regards,

Father Jerry

With a sense of stillness he read what he had written. The words had come slowly across a void. They were not what he wished to say, yet the act of putting them on paper had had a calming effect on his mind. What he needed was certainty because he already had the desire to act honourably and the wish to overcome a threatening evil. He would cross-question Hugo again; and his judgment, when it came, would be definite and unambiguous, taking account of all possibilities and all the circumstances.

Meanwhile his postcard would land in Dr Sharma's letter-box together with promotional mail from pharmaceutical companies and gas and electricity bills. He had first sought her help at a time when the world had become for him a place of terrifying darkness, when he had despaired of ever again seeing a glint of hope-inspiring light. He had been working as a curate in north London, in an area of decaying Georgian buildings and pinched noses that seemed to skewer him in the street. He had met her first at the hospital where she worked as a consultant. When she discovered where he lived, she invited him to her house in Islington one weekend for tea. She sat opposite him in a black-and-gold sari, a sheet of finely woven cotton that enfolded her lean, brown body so that only her face and sandalled feet remained exposed.

'Your life has been invaded by the past,' she said. 'Those boyhood friends you speak of – Brennan, Hugo, McDaid and Mary Rose – belong in a richer life whose passing you can't accept. The relationships you formed then affected you in a way you are still trying to apprehend, and now the memory of that time has encroached on the present like an angry sea that meets with no solid resistance.'

For six months she listened to the tedious litany of his anxieties, mainly at the hospital and now and again at her home. She had told him that he was her favourite patient, and he trusted her as he would a confessor or spiritual director. They discussed oriental philosophy and Christian theology, and one day she told him a Hindu proverb that burst on him in a flood of sunshine: 'If you have two loaves of bread, give one to the poor. Sell the other – and buy hyacinths for your soul.' He did not for a moment believe that it was her proverb that cured him, but the thought of the hyacinths had released a kind of peace within him, a singing that he could barely hear, or hear only by listening carefully.

Gradually he came out of his sickness, sloughing off the too-tight skin that had bound his wounded self. She had told him that she could not give him back his old self, and that he accepted with a mixture of relief and regret. His new self was more outward-looking and less sensitive than the old. The poet in him had died, the poet who had been making him unhappy, misanthropic and ultimately less than human.

'Will I write poetry again?' he had asked her.

'I don't know. It depends on why you wrote it in the first place.'

'To achieve some sort of equilibrium between myself and the world, I suppose.'

'You may never write a poem again, you may never need to.'

He felt wistful at the thought of what he had lost. The cure was a trick, a piece of mechanical manipulation, and Dr Sharma was an optician placing different 'lenses' before his eyes and asking him, 'Is that more comfortable?' She was too clever to deny his imagination and its demons. Instead she had found a means of accommodating them. Now he was detached from the struggle, his desires no longer hot and clamouring, and his thoughts had acquired the disembodied quality of thoughts that do not root in the evil-smelling tilth of the heart.

'You had withdrawn from the physical world,' she told him on his last visit. 'You've been away. Now that you're back you must not allow yourself to be abducted again. Touch, touch, touch. Familiarise yourself with the textures and contours of things.'

She offered him her hand and he held it for a long time without speaking. When he told her that he would never forget the debt he owed her, she said that she would always be pleased to hear from him if he should ever feel the need to write to her.

Again he placed the beach stones on the table and, closing his eyes, touched them gently with his fingertips. When he heard the crunch of wheels on gravel, he hid them under some papers in the drawer of his writing desk. He went into the hallway to meet Hugo whose face registered extreme excitement.

'Have you heard the latest about Brennan?' he asked.

'He's alive and well and playing host at the motel?'

'His body has been washed ashore. A sheep farmer from the mountain found him wedged between two rocks in the shadow of the Devil's Pintle. He was naked apart from his underpants, and he didn't look in the least like a man who'd been dead ten days.'

'What did they say at the motel?'

'They were like beagles on the scent, every man with his own theory, even men who normally leave thinking and talking to their wives. McDaid was the exception; throughout the evening he smoked like a chimney and said nothing. The great question was where our friend had spent the last ten days. He'd grown a beard, you see, which means that he couldn't have been dead.'

'What did *you* say?'

'I looked into my pint and muttered to the man beside me, "There's more to this than meets the eye." I'm the only man who knows the truth. I had a dream over a week ago and I wrote it down. It's nothing short of clairvoyance and I'm nothing short of a genius.'

Hugo ran upstairs and returned with the casebound diary.

89

'It's all there. Read it and see.'

Father Jerry studied the entry for July 6th, then handed back the book to his excited brother.

'Who is the narrator?' he asked.

'Who else but me? I wrote it down exactly as I dreamt it, every word.'

'You dreamt that you marooned Brennan on Scariff Island, leaving him with enough food and drink for a week?'

'In my dream it was a humpbacked island full of rabbits. Brennan appeared as Robinson Crusoe but I knew all along that he was our friend in fancy dress. I told him to keep a weather eye out for cannibals, and as the island receded, it took on the shape of a young rabbit petrified by fear. Now that's something I forgot to record in my diary. You can never boil a day down to five hundred words, and a dream is a thousand days in one.' Hugo spoke eagerly, his big face flushed under a spreading beard.

'You left him food?'

'Only corned beef. I told him to eat grass if he wanted to avoid scurvy.'

'Did you leave him goose eggs?'

'The nearest thing to eggs I left him was a packet of Birds Eye custard.'

'You didn't mention that in your diary.'

'Again, I forgot.'

'Now perhaps you can forget your dream and tell me what really happened.'

'This is how I see it, reconstructing the events I've recorded. Brennan realised that his creditors were getting restless. He wasn't man enough to face them, so he decided to go into hiding to give himself time to think. He got McDaid to run him out to Scariff Island. After a week he felt lonely and made the mistake of trying to swim ashore. Or perhaps he headed for the mainland knowing that he'd never make it. Suicide arranged to look like accidental death.'

'It doesn't hang together. If Brennan wished to abscond, surely he'd have left the country with whatever ready cash he could muster. No one in his right mind would willingly spend ten days on a bare island living on tinned food. It seems to me that he was taken there by force and that he drowned while trying to escape.'

'Of course, we're assuming that my dream is true. It's possible that he may have been hiding in Glenshask or Glencrow.'

'Wherever he's been, he will have left traces of his stay. If he swam ashore from Scariff, his clothes will still be on the island. Do you intend making a trip to verify your dream?'

Hugo studied his brother's face before exposing his teeth in an ambiguous grin.

'I don't think so. The man is dead. Your problem is solved. There's nothing more to do and nothing more to say.'

'You're sure you're not being less than frank with me?'

'Less than frank?'

'Do you know more than you're letting on?'

'I know only what I've dreamt, and I've shared my dream with you. Consider yourself privileged. I don't propose to share it with the police.'

'I think you should destroy your diary. It's open to misinterpretation to say the very least.'

'Dreams are wish fulfilment, I believe. It's no fault of mine if now and again my dreams come true. If all of them came true, I should be worried. As a man of moral character, I couldn't afford to sleep.'

Hugo laughed gleefully as he went off to bed. Within five

minutes he was back, still full of his own ingenuity.

'I've thought of a defence,' he said. 'My diary is not a diary but a novel in the form of a diary. All good diaries aspire to the condition of the novel, and mine is no exception.'

Father Jerry sat pondering until the fire in the grate had died and the lights in the neighbours' houses had gone out. Three years ago he had lived through a nightmare of misshapen monsters which, with Dr Sharma's help, he had come to realise had been his own creation, calling into question his capacity for objective experience.

'Now you are hesitant and unbelieving,' she had said. 'You are on the way to recovery but you still lack the unconsidered faith we all need in order to face each day. Naturally, you would like to think that your perceptions are as valid as anyone else's. Don't worry, the core of your personality will reform, and you will once again be able to accept your experience in spite of other people's "knowledge" of its subjectivity.

He went to his writing desk and took out the two white beach stones. He placed them on the table and rubbed the smooth one and then the grainy one with the forefinger of his right hand. Finally he took a stone in each hand and rubbed them simultaneously with the pads of his thumbs.

'Hugo's dreams are my nightmares,' he said. 'He thrives among the monsters that almost wrecked my life.'

Chapter 8

In the village Father Jerry could sense an atmosphere of excited speculation. The pathologist who had carried out the post-mortem said that Brennan had been dead no more than two days before his body was found. His lungs were full of salt-water. Apparently he had drowned following a heart attack while in the sea. The local doctor hinted at deeper mysteries. Brennan, he said, had been drinking heavily before he died; his blood contained twice the amount of alcohol required to impair an average man's balance and judgment. The local police carried out a search of the north coast and Scariff Island but no trace of his clothes or any other belongings was found.

In the shops and pubs every shred of evidence and every theory, no matter how outlandish, was weighed and tested. After the second day nothing new remained to be said. The village elders resumed the available facts and concluded that Brennan had taken his own life while his judgment had been impaired by financial worries. He knew that his business was on the verge of collapse, and the knowledge had proved too much for his self-esteem. He had deliberately bequeathed everyone a mystery to cover up what he must have seen as a sordid and inglorious end.

Olga did not share their certainty.

'Brennan came to see me the day before he disappeared,' she said. 'He asked me to show him my work and he promised to exhibit my best pieces in his craft shop at the motel. He wanted me to carve things with a local significance, using motifs from the megalithic remains here. He was excited and full of good ideas. He was thinking about the future. Dying was far from his thoughts.'

'Then something must have happened after you spoke, a reverse in business perhaps. He had a finger in many pies, not all of them his own.'

'He didn't commit suicide, I'm sure of that. Only a man who has lost sight of the world outside himself would want to end his life.'

'What are you trying to tell me, Olga?'

'Something is wrong. Do you think there was bad play?'

'Foul play? I don't know.'

'What *do* you think.'

'Like most people, I'm not sure. I've heard the verdict of the medical men. The police have made a search and have found nothing. What should I think?'

'Don't close your eyes just because you can't see clearly. One thing is certain: his death caused no grief. When he was alive, people thought they admired him. They found out when he died that they had only envied him.'

Father Jerry smiled at her rueful humour and said goodbye. As he walked up the avenue, he kept hearing her question: 'What *do* you think?'

'I did what I could,' he answered aloud. 'I cross-examined Hugo again and again and prayed unavailingly for moral certainty – the certitudo moralis of the textbooks. Now I am plagued by doubts of conscience. Did I demand too much certainty?

94

Surely all judgments of conscience are necessarily based on incomplete knowledge of the facts. Aren't these doubts only to be expected after any judgment where the facts are not clear. I was never in doubt about the moral norms, only about their application in this particular case.'

He felt pleased that there was little time for self-scrutiny; he had to devote the morning to preparing the funeral address. His first draft, critical and perhaps a shade splenetic, told the unvarnished truth about Arty Brennan, but the truth, he decided, was for another time and place. His second draft was circumspect and precise, dwelling on Brennan's 'good works' while ignoring his destruction of a culture with a 2,000-year history behind it. When he had finished, he read it aloud, standing by the north window with the Glebe and the hippies' tents under his eye.

The following morning he sprayed the coffin with holy water from a brass aspergillum that Brennan had donated to the church, knowing in his heart that these obsequies would best be performed by Canon Bingo or a priest with an instinctive understanding of men who weren't interested in two and two unless they made ten and made it quickly. Before reading the collect, he prayed for Christian humility, then listened in disbelief to his own voice and a beloved prayer that had become both bizarre and incongruous:

O God, whose property is ever to have mercy and to spare, we humbly beseech Thee on behalf of the soul of Thy servant Arthur, whom Thou hast called out of this world, that Thou wouldst not deliver him into the hands of the enemy, nor forget him for ever, but command that he be taken up by Thy holy angels and borne to our home in paradise, that having put his hope and trust in Thee, he may not undergo the pains of hell, but may come to the possession of eternal joys.

He struggled to count Brennan's good and forget his bad, if only for an hour, yet he knew that the good would moulder and the bad would live in the hearts of men who had traded an ancient and spiritually enriching culture for the material conveniences of a cash economy. Even in death Brennan was victorious. What he had so blindly destroyed could never be rebuilt.

For the address he had chosen a text from St Luke's account of the Resurrection: 'Why seek ye the living among the dead? He is not here, but is risen.' He waited in the pulpit for perfect silence, knowing that Canon Hackler and two other priests were seated in the sanctuary behind him; that every eye was on him; that every ear was straining to catch even one delicious hint of personal animus against the deceased. He spoke quietly, with each word carefully weighed and none that might be construed as ambiguous or insincere. While his mind ran on the incisive first draft in his hip-pocket, he could see in the faces below a gratified recognition of what was just and appropriate to the occasion. He refrained from telling them that Arty Brennan had turned their glen into a cheap peep-show for vulgar tourists who came to stare at them as if they were clowns in a circus. Instead his words had caused the here-and-now to recede before their eyes. He had given them a glimpse of a landscape that he himself had yet to see.

After the funeral he invited the other priests to the parochial house for lunch. Canon Hackler congratulated him on an address which he described as 'generous in its sympathy and sincere in its every expression'.

'The words came only after a great struggle,' Father Jerry admitted. 'I had to listen hard to catch them.'

'I know what you mean,' said the canon. 'Sincerity is a matter of style, little more than an absence of cliche. It is the art of leaving the wrong notes out.'

'I didn't mean that at all,' said Father Jerry peevishly.

'His death has got us all off the hook – you and me and the bishop. At the very least we owe him a couple of Masses, and as scrupulous men we shall say them. It is more than his debtors will do for him now.'

Father Jerry looked into the canon's large, self-satisfied face and poured him another hefty Scotch. He had no wish to say even one more word about Brennan to anyone except himself. When the other priests had left, he stood by the window overlooking the Glebe and read the alternative address which he'd been carrying in his hip pocket since morning. He kept reading it over and over throughout the evening, as if reading could obliterate the sense of personal defilement that tortured him in his soul. He was still reading when Hugo returned from his nightly tipple at the motel. Father Jerry handed his brother the typewritten sheets and watched his flushed cheeks and moving eyes as he scanned the uncompromising lines. He had stretched out fully in the armchair, a heavy man with a heavy face struggling against the torpor of overindulgence.

'It's the real address, the one I didn't – the one I couldn't – give,' Father Jerry explained.

Hugo got to his feet and with his back to the fireplace read a paragraph in a voice that bore an uncanny resemblance to his brother's:

I remember from boyhood how two fiddlers came into the old hotel one morning and spent a long summer day making music. They stopped only for bread and soup and a pint of stout to slake their thirst, and they didn't get as much as a penny for their playing. They didn't expect payment; they played to give delight and to take delight in their art. Now, thirty years later, if you were on your deathbed and longing to hear a last reel, you wouldn't find a fiddler to play it unless you resined his palm with money. It was not the least of Arty Brennan's achievements that he showed us the place of culture in a cash economy – at least those aspects of culture, such as music and dancing, that can be seen and heard and paid for at a box office or gate. As we count the parts of our local heritage which we have lost, we should echo the deceased and say in self-justification: 'What has no price tag has no value.'

Hugo sat down and shook his head.

'It's no good,' he said. 'It's only a cantle of the truth, not the full round. Why lift one corner of the veil? Better to live in mystery as Brennan died.'

He handed Father Jerry the sheets and said good night. At the door he looked back and slowly tapped his forehead with his finger.

'Forget the dead, they're in safe keeping. They can't escape by swimming ashore. Now the living are still in the running. You heard the funeral bell today. It had never been tolled more loudly. McDaid was determined to give his hero a hero's send-off.'

'In my view he overdid it. He pulled so hard that he cracked the bell. I'll be giving him a piece of my mind in the morning.'

'As I listened to the final stroke and the bell going "Bling!", I couldn't help feeling that McDaid had made a statement.'

'You never rest, Hugo, do you?'

'We're a restless species. McDaid is one of us. Think about it, Father.' Hugo laughed derisively as he closed the door.

Part II

Olga

Chapter 9

He was back on the island again, the sea all round him and the night so dark that he could not make out his hands. He got down on his knees and groped along the sloping ground on every side. He was in the centre of the hogs-back, he lacked the confidence to walk. He wanted to get back to the place where he had beached the boat and left his clothes in a neat pile on a rock. The noise of the sea grew louder with the rising wind, and the shingle rattled as the waves ran back. What if they should carry his boat down the shore and break it into splinters on the reef beyond? He began crawling slowly down the slope in the direction of the rattle, which had become the noise a savage might make as he gargled in the morning. Suddenly the gargling came from behind. All round him waves were breaking and stones rolling back and forth in the night. From under the waves came a distant ringing and a gravelly voice that said, 'Doe to the book, quench the candle but do not toll the bell.'

The sun was shining through the parted curtains when he woke. It was barely six o'clock. The hills in the east merged luminously in the morning haze and the hollow of the glen gleamed bright with reflections. The Glebe was quiet. Within the ring of green and brown tents no one moved. To the west a row of white seagulls dozed on the roof of the fishmeal factory. Nothing had changed. Not really. Brennan's business had been put into receivership, and the receiver was anxious to sell it as a going concern rather than in bits and pieces. A businessman with money to burn would buy it for a song. The motel, the fishmeal factory and the hippies were here to stay. The idea of Brennan was in the very air he breathed. All his death had achieved was that the glen had been spared, at least for the moment, that anathema of anathemas, the Holiday Village.

Father Jerry dressed and stole downstairs so as not to wake Hugo who was gargling obscenely as he snored. The scented morning air was cool in spite of the sunshine. The glen was soundless; in the fields not a cow or bullock stirred. He leant against the gate pier as a naked woman appeared at the bend of the road. She was coming towards him, jogging rather than running. Now he could see her thighs moving up and down and her rounded breasts bouncing with a shadow in between. He turned his head and gazed across the glen at the face of the north mountain, a solid, unyielding mass that was solid and unyielding in every weather. He tested the ground beneath him with his heel. The hippies didn't know the word 'enough'. They fornicated and smoked pot; they got drunk and stole their neighbours' hard-won turf. All that was nothing compared with jogging naked, every nook and appendage on display. As he waited, he refused to look again in her direction. He kept his eyes firmly fixed on the purple of the mountain and thought of Brennan still active while the whole glen slept.

'Good morning, Father Jerry.' Olga gave a breathless laugh.

She stood before him in a cream-coloured tracksuit with her hands on her hips and her hair tied neatly in a pony-tail behind.

Her cheeks glowed red and her breasts still heaved as she breathed. Her tracksuit was tight-fitting, her body firm and strong.

'You're up early.' He was determined to show no emotion.

'I ate a heavy supper and decided to work it off before breakfast. Wood carving keeps me fit but unfortunately it doesn't exercise the legs.'

Her tracksuit was almost flesh-coloured. Her legs were long like a frog's.

'The morning is the best time for jogging,' he said vaguely.

'It's the coolest time, and there's no one around to stare at you.'

'If you don't wish to attract attention, you should find yourself a less spectacular tracksuit.' He smiled amiably to conceal any nuance of censure.

'This isn't a tracksuit, it's a leotard. I bought it in Munich in a sale and never wore it till this morning.'

'You could dye it black.'

'Ah, you'd like me to jog like a nun. 'Bye for now.'

She left him with a mocking laugh. He watched the easy rhythm of her jogging and told himself that she was too unworldly to intend offence. He walked up the avenue without looking back. In his study was a photograph of sixty-three young men in clerical suits and round white collars that had been taken on his ordination day. Most of them were practical, rough-and-ready men with little gift for reflection, destined to fit easily into a world of parish bazaars, jumble sales and bingo. They had come from small farms and small towns, and those who weren't close to the soil were close to the common people. Though they had studied theology and canon law, they drew their spiritual strength from the simple beliefs of their unquestioning parents. Canon Hackler was such a man, and so was the bishop. They went about their business as would a conscientious solicitor. Religion was a matter of doing things and getting things done. It had little to do with the solitary life of the spirit and the spirit's craving for exaltation and joy.

He sat at his writing desk by the window and after a moment's thought wrote three paragraphs on a plain postcard:

Dear Dr Sharma,

Late yesterday the sky was heavy and dark with a judas of piercing light in the west. I stared into the judas long and stubbornly but no glint of light entered my mind. I seemed to fall into a slumber and when I woke the pinpoint of light had faded into watery grey.

Nature is alien, you once said to me. Nothing in the universe is meant for man. The mountain will never come to Mohammed, and Mohammed is besotted with its permanency and solidity. He is truly and utterly alone.

I grope for the shape of things in the dark, seeking knowledge that still eludes me. I'd like to hear from you. A paragraph on a postcard would do.

Father Jerry

After breakfast he walked up the hill to the cottage where Mandamus McDaid lived alone.

'I've come about the bell,' he said.

'She'll never ring again,' said McDaid. 'I had a look at her yesterday. The crack is over six inches long.'

'What caused the crack?'

'Metal fatigue. I was ringing out poor old Arty Brennan, and somehow I got carried away. It was the last pull that did it. The sound that came from above my head was the last sound that bell will ever make on earth. The bell died with Arty, there's no denying it.'

'It isn't the first bell that lost its voice here,' Father Jerry said sharply. 'I'll get a bell-founder from Dublin to look at it. Believe me, it will ring again.'

'I know about bells because they're in the family. My father was sexton and so was my grandfather. That bell cracked before, way back in Grandfather's time. It was only a hairline crack, and brazing put it right again. This time it's different. The bell is buggered. It will never wake the living in their beds any more.'

They were standing in McDaid's back yard surrounded by pecking hens. McDaid looked unnaturally clean shaven and clear-skinned, and his piercing blue eyes seemed to reflect the purity of the morning sky. He looked down at Father Jerry who wondered if the other man experienced subtleties of the spirit denied to himself.

'We need a new bell,' McDaid went on. 'I've been talking to one or two members of the parish council –'

'Behind my back?'

'Gossip, like wonders, will never cease. It always sprouts best when someone's back is turned.'

McDaid's eyes lit up with mischievous humour. Then the light in them faded and he seemed to look inwards as if he were alone.

'A new bell is out of the question. The old one must ring again with the same old tone.'

'Then I'm out of a job. What's broken is broken and what's dead is dead. There's no turning back the clock. You're the opposite of Arty Brennan, Father. Now he was for ever putting the hands of the clock forward when everyone's back was turned.'

'Arty Brennan is dead, may he rest in peace.'

'He's dead and he isn't dead. He left an empty space behind him that no one else will fill. As long as we feel it inside us, he's still alive. I had great hopes when Hugo came back. We were all together again, all except Mary Rose. I thought something outlandish was bound to happen. Little did I know.'

'What did you think might happen?'

'I was thinking about the Game.'

'We're grown men now, we've put away childish things.'

'There was nothing childish about the Game. We were grown men at twelve and didn't know it.'

'I don't like all this talk about things that are dead and buried. We were children. We behaved like children. We lived in a world of adults, all we knew was imitation.'

'Now *we* are the adults,' said McDaid. 'Who do we imitate now? You're a priest, so I know what you'll say. Nothing's changed, life is still a game.'

'Not for me. I'm serious in everything I do and say.'

'Then say something that will surprise me, Father. Something that comes from you alone.'

'I'll think about it,' said Father Jerry. 'I could serve you old wine in new bottles.'

'I want something fresh or something that sounds fresh. Since Arty Brennan died, I've had nothing but old hat.'

He strolled back slowly to the parochial house and realised from the smell in the hallway that Hugo had been boiling morkin. He found him seated at the head of the kitchen table with a sheep's skull at the other end. He was staring into the empty eye sockets, an old cotton rag in one hand and a bottle of linseed oil in the other.

'What on earth are you up to?'

'I found another dead sheep on the hill. The carcass was practically intact apart from the eyes which had been pecked out by gulls. I cut off the head and brought it back for Olga. I know she'd prefer a skull that's been whitened by wind and sun but it's surprising what spit and polish can do in a fraction of the time.'

'She'll think you're cuckoo.'

'On the contrary, she may see it as a little love offering. I've been telling her that it was once the custom here to place a row of glass buoys on the top of one's dresser to go with the willow-pattern chargers and the bowls. Buoys are made of plastic now and the willow-pattern chargers have found their way to the antique shop. A row of sheep's skulls is surely an imaginative substitute.'

'It's possible that she may not appreciate your macabre sense of humour. I don't like to see you making fun of her.'

'Olga can look after herself. I've seen her in the village pubs. The face of childish innocence she turns to you is not the one she reveals in the company of drinking men. I'm telling you for your own good, I wouldn't like to see you get hurt.'

With a cryptic laugh Hugo draped the dirty rag over the sheep's skull to make a crinkled headscarf.

'What are you trying to tell me?'

'You're an innocent when it comes to dealing with women like Olga. If you have any plans to convert her, forget them. Some of us don't pray for her conversion. We like her as she is.'

Father Jerry fought back rising anger because he knew that anger was precisely what Hugo wished to arouse.

'Nothing is to be gained from idle talk,' he said slowly. 'I should like you to realise that I can't have you boiling sheep's heads in the parochial house.'

'What's up? Surely you're not expecting another visitation from the bish?'

'If you must boil morkin, as you call it, do it at Burke's. There

107

are no other houses near and there are fewer people calling.'

As Father Jerry went to the door, Hugo leant forward and said, 'Bub-bub-oh!' to the sheep's skull on the table. 'You'll find a sack of old clothes under the stairs,' he called. 'McDaid said you might like to have them for your next jumble sale.'

'He knows perfectly well that I never hold jumble sales, raffles or bingo evenings.'

'Perhaps he thinks it's time you did.'

Father Jerry emptied the contents of the sack on the floor: a tweed jacket, twill trousers and a checked shirt.

'Have you looked in the bag?' he called to Hugo.

'I'm afraid not. I already have two good suits I never wear.'

'You'd better come and see for yourself.'

Hugo picked up the jacket and pulled it on over his sweater.

'A snug fit but not my style.' He tugged contemptuously at the sleeve.

'They're Brennan's clothes, don't you see?'

'Well spotted,' said Hugo. 'They could be the clothes he left behind on the island – assuming that my dream is true.'

'How did McDaid come by them, and why didn't he give them to the police?'

'Perhaps he wanted you to have them for old times' sake. You could offload them on a wandering tramp – if you don't want to see them worn in the glen, that is.'

'I was talking to McDaid just now and he never once mentioned Arty Brennan's clothes.'

'Neither did he mention him to me. "Give these old duds to Father Jerry, they'll do for jumble," was all he said. Then he walked off, leaving me holding the bag. He's not himself these days. He thinks of nothing but Olga. He's even taken to shaving every morning instead of once a week.'

108

'I find him unfathomable.'

'He's full of dark imaginings. He's a man who thinks Satanic thoughts.'

Hugo bundled the clothes into the bag as Father Jerry climbed the stairs.

'I'll keep them as a souvenir,' he called after him. 'I may even donate them to the folk museum.'

Father Jerry pondered the problem his brother had set him. If he should take Brennan's clothes to the police, then McDaid and Hugo might be forced to speak. If they said too much, he would face exposure of his previous silence and the scandal to the faithful that was bound to ensue. It was a matter of the lesser evil, not the greater good. There was no easy way out of the predicament. The wicked flee when no man pursues. They carry their Gehenna on their backs.

He stood by the north window of his bedroom, looking down on a windy sea with waves rising against the cliff faces across the bay and falling back in white rivulets that sent a mist of bright spume up into the clear air. Below the road a dark reef ran down beneath the water which in the sunlight gave momentary glimpses of brilliant green among the patches of breaking white above it. He watched the spot where he knew the rock lay hidden. A little swirl became a stronger swirl, then the water went dead again. He stood for two or three minutes without taking his eyes off the spot. Suddenly the water rose in an upward spout, as if four waves had converged from different directions with four strong winds behind them. They rose in a single column, spread into a mist-white mushroom at the top, and spilt back until the water lay flat above the hidden rock again.

He gazed for half an hour with his watch in his hand, seeking vainly for a trace of a pattern. Perhaps there was no pattern.

What he was seeing was the working of the innocent universe: water swirling and rising, water falling and spray scattering, being swallowed up again in a greater, all-absorbing body. What he sought was life unseen, life before the human eye and mind had a chance to distort it.

'Bye for now.'

He heard her voice again as she took off down the road, leaving him standing in the gateway looking after her. He had seen what he had no wish to see. Wisdom after the event. She had come here, she said, to practise her art. She was still a child. In some mysterious way she reminded him of his twin-sister Carmel.

The thought disturbed him for a reason he could not fathom. Carmel had died without having lived. She had never roamed the hills with him and Hugo because their mother had insisted that she stay at home to read and recite and practise on the tune-defying piano. Mother was determined to make a lady of her only daughter, while Father suppressed his concern that she might turn her into 'a right little madam'. Carmel had provided Mother with a young life to shape and guide, and he and Hugo had been free to explore the countryside, provided they did not tell their mother what they'd been exploring.

After Carmel's death life in the house became a litany of fate-ful prognostications. Mother kept reminding him of his weak chest and asthma, of the need to avoid chills and wettings, of the perils inherent in all the games a boy might wish to play. Mean-while, Father hummed philosophically, or drummed on the table with his fingers. Hugo, being Hugo, escaped the smothering of a love made over-possessive by disappointment.

Had Carmel lived, his own life might have been different. Had she lived , she would probably have grown away from him. He would have neither sought nor seen her in a stranger.

110

Chapter 10

Olga came to see him the following afternoon as he was making notes for Sunday's sermon. Between her hands she bore a squat object wrapped in a bath towel which she placed in front of him on the table.

'It's for you,' she said.

She rearranged the towel so that the object became a statue draped in purple for Holy Week.

'Don't you want to find out what it is?'

He pulled the corner of the towel until it slid off the object and revealed a wood carving of a kneeling woman, her long hair falling forward over her knees. He placed the carving in the centre of the table and walked round it with his hands behind his back. The woman's face was hidden by her hair. Her knees became buttocks and her heels became knees as he moved.

'What am I supposed to see?' he asked.

'I invite you to see what you must.'

'To me it says one word: "weeping".'

'Surely it says more.'

'Not to me.'

'Then live with it for a week. It may speak again.'

111

'I see a weeping woman who is weeping from every angle. This woman was born to weep, she could be Mary Magdalene.'

She picked up a book from the table where he had been working and sat in the armchair with her long legs close together, the hard, white knees protruding from the dark, tight skirt. Now she looked serious and remote, no longer present. As she flicked through the pages, her face lengthened and the corners of her mouth turned down. Inside her shirt collar a triangle of flesh had taken on an unhealthy tinge. She stared at the title page. She looked quite dead, as if the blood had been sucked from her veins. He noticed that the skin at the base of her neck had stolen some of the colour from her light-green shirt. He ran his hand caressingly over the head of the weeping woman.

'Why were you reading about grace?' she asked.

'For my sermon on Sunday.'

'Grace and God's salvific will. What's that? Don't tell me now. I'll come to listen to what you preach, though not necessarily to practise it.'

'You can sell this carving for money.'

'And give it to the poor? I want you to have it.'

'Thank you, Olga. It's very kind of you. Is the crack between the woman's knees deliberate?'

'Yes and no. The wood was cracked before I started carving and already looked like knees.'

'So it was an accident.'

'Wood is alive and moving. It swells and contracts, it even breathes. It isn't stable and dead like a lump of plastic. If it cracks, so be it. It cracks because cracking is in its character.'

As she bent over the book again, her hair fell forward until he could see nothing of her face except a thin, straight nose. The day he had come upon Hugo in Glenshask sitting above the

Devil's Pintle, he had stood by a river for an hour watching the flow of water over a brown boulder. Observed from upstream, the boulder seemed to rise like the neck of a horse from the river bed. The water ran up the neck in an overflowing mane, then curled before falling sideways into the frothing pool below. He moved downstream expecting to observe the face of a horse from the front. The face became a woman's with a cascade of rippling hair obscuring one side of it. Something like steam was rising from below. Blown foam gleamed in sunlight. He moved up and down, observing the horse's neck behind and the woman's face in front. As he walked away, he knew that what he had seen contained a germ of undisclosed truth that would continue to vex and haunt him.

'You're quiet today,' he said to Olga.

'It's one of my Dom Days. The sun is shining outside but in my mind it's drizzling. Dom was my husband. Still is, I suppose.'

'Tell me about him.'

She put down the book and lit one of her strong, sharp cigarettes.

'I met him in Munich one summer while he was still a student in Dublin. I was barely sixteen. My father and mother had died the previous year. I thought him handsome and amusing, and when he began writing to me, I wrote back. The following summer he invited me to Dublin. He had taken a degree in civil engineering, and at the end of the holiday he returned with me to Germany. He got a job but not a good one. We got married and rented a small flat. Though we both worked, we were always short of money. He'd never get anywhere in Germany, he said. The language was against him; he'd always be someone's assistant, he'd never call the shots. I came back to Dublin with him

113

and he got a job which, from the first day, he felt was beneath him. Then he applied for a posh job in the civil service and got turned down because he didn't know Gaelic, or so he said. Another language problem, this time in his own country. He started coming home late from the pub and sleeping on the sofa after dinner. He had always looked a bit boyish and soft. He put on weight and his cheeks began to sag, though he was barely thirty. The accident happened on a train coming back from Howth. There were three of us: Dom and myself and Dom's best friend. The two of them had been drinking. Dom got obstreperous. He began jabbing at his friend with his umbrella. The train swayed, his friend ducked, and the tip of the umbrella went into my eye. He came every day and sat by my bed in the hospital with his big drooping cheeks, saying, "I'll never touch another drop. I'll never put a glass to my lips again, I swear." I lost the eye. It was like losing my parents all over again. Our marriage went from bad to worse. I began to lose my self-confidence. I gave up wood carving. Then I saw an advertisement in one of the papers: "Cottage in secluded glen overlooking Atlantic". I went to the library and found a paragraph about Glenkeel in an old gazetteer. It didn't tell me much but the last sentence flared in my mind: "There's a remarkable echo in the mountains." I kept repeating it all the way home. Dom was at work, so I wrote him a note saying that I'd gone back to Munich, and warning him not to follow. Now I call myself Olga Petersen. Olga Madagan is dead. The thought of her makes me shrink. I still haven't found my freedom, though. Sometimes I wake up in the morning and know immediately that it's going to be a Dom Day; that I'll be imprisoned inside myself; that I'll lack the inspiration to start anything new. I spend Dom Days sharpening my chisels and polishing – mechanical work that doesn't require me to be fully present. Dom Days are heavy and acid, completely lacking in balance and finish.'

'Everyone has what you call Dom Days, days that are a long contemplation of life's trammels.'

'Dom never had Dom Days, and neither does Hugo. I see him as another Dom, a blind man who wants us all to play blind-man's buff. I tell him that I've come here to be quiet. It's some-thing that he's incapable of taking in.'

'You mean he keeps pestering you?'

'He keeps giving me skulls, sheep's skulls. He thinks it's funny but it's creepy and unsettling.'

From the catch in her voice he sensed that she was on the verge of tears. He wanted to go to her and offer comfort and understanding. He remained rigid in his chair on the far side of the table.

'Many people are like Hugo. They stumble on what they take to be a joke and then keep repeating it because it's the only joke they know. Hugo does these things because he doesn't know bet-ter. When he comes in this evening, I'll tell him to leave you alone.'

'Please don't. I wouldn't want him to know that it's important.'

She raised her face to him, her nose thin and sensitive, so finely chiselled compared with Hugo's hacked old parsnip.

'In the village they say he's eaten human flesh,' she went on.

'Like all travellers, Hugo is a raconteur. His stories are meant to shock. If you don't want to hear them, pretend that you've heard them before.'

'I heard one of the neighbours say, "Hugo is not the full shil-ling." Did he mean that he's bananas?' she asked seriously.

'Perhaps he meant to say that he's only eighteen shillings in the pound. In other words, not good value for money.'

He was trying to make her smile but all he got from her was a look of pained incomprehension.

'I sometimes think he's evil.' She spoke the words slowly so that each word bore the same stress as the others. He concentrated his gaze on the dark eye that did not dance, and drummed on the table with his fingertips.

'You don't know him as well as I do. He's a repertory actor and a fairground showman. The freedom you seek from Dom Days he finds behind one of his gaudy funfair masks.'

She went to the window and stood with her back to him, the flow of her hair arrested by the stately evening sunlight. He could have touched a tress without her knowing, it was so abundant. She suddenly turned and smiled at him.

'Did you have a golden age, Father Jerry? Or a period you look back on as a golden age?'

'In the seminary perhaps. It was an enclosed community and therefore gave the appearance of being comprehensible.'

'I had no golden age, thanks to Dom. I went straight from the shackles of childhood to the shackles of adulthood. Everyone should have at least three years of untrammelled immaturity.'

'Surely you're not too late. Look at Hugo and McDaid. Their golden age has lasted all of forty years.' He tried to tease her.

'You're different from other priests I've known. You, too, have your masks, different ones from Hugo.'

When she'd gone, he walked round the table surveying the figure of the weeping woman. He caressed the polished head with his fingertips, and the hair down to her knees, then placed the nail of his forefinger in the cleft between the knees. Once more the hair became a woman's back and the knees a pair of dainty buttocks.

'Olga is a maker of little mysteries,' he said aloud. 'No number of little mysteries will ever make a great one.'

He carried the carving upstairs to his room and placed it in the bottom of the wardrobe, as it was not a work fit for Hugo's inflammable eye. He crossed the landing and entered his brother's bedroom. As usual the casebound diary lay open on the night table. He read two or three entries about the problems of reroofing an old house single-handed, then found a longer entry concerning a girl called Helga:

July 30th

Helga goes to pubs for the company of drinking men. They put their arms round her waist and tickle her bottom. She laughs in their faces, winds them with bear hugs, then downs her stout and goes home alone. She never goes drinking except in full battle-dress – white baggy trousers and brown-and-green jacket with two pockets in front where she keeps her purse and cigarettes, and stuffs her fists. For the pub she sweeps up her hair and wears a flat cap like a man, and when her jacket pockets are bulging, she's got four breasts.

'In for the last knockings, Helga?' we shout.

'Knockings, what's that?' she calls back. 'I'll have a pint instead.'

She doesn't sponge, she stands her round. She makes no distinction between young men and old. She's a man's man's woman, a tomboy through and through.

McDowd comes to the pub every evening now. He's cleaner and younger-looking, and he's started making jokes. You can tell by his step that he walks on air. The poor man is in a bad way. Yesterday I lay with him under the lee of a rock watching her comb the shore for driftwood. He knew I had my eye on her and

I knew that he had his eye on her too, but each of us pretended to be looking at rain showers passing down the bay. McDowd was lying on his side, his long legs stretched, with his trousers tucked into white socks. He took his pipe from his gob and blew a puff of rank smoke across my face.

'It's a great pipe you've got there,' I said.

'It's bigger than yours.' He pretended to look into the offing.

'Is it a pipe of peace?'

Helga straightened and turned, offering us two juicy grape-fruit. They bounced up and down in perfect unison as she walked.

'If it were a pipe of peace, I wouldn't smoke it,' he replied. 'There's always something to trouble a man. There's never any peace, not even on Sunday.'

Helga was stooping with her back to us, tying a piece of rope to the thin end of a tree trunk.

'When you see Helga in slacks and high leather boots, what do you notice?' I thought I'd give him a little test.

'I'm not telling you.'

'She's ever so slightly bow-legged. She gives me a sense of massed armies marching, trampling everything into the ground.'

'That does something for you?'

'It's impressive.'

McDowd turned to me, his face serious and hard. I could see the blue of the sea reflected in the unnatural blue of his eyes.

'When I see Helga,' he said, 'I think of soft chocolates.'

'I don't think she'd appreciate that.'

'Then you don't have to tell her.'

Helga put the rope over her shoulder and, leaning forward, began dragging the tree trunk after her.

'She'll do herself an injury if she isn't careful,' I said.

'She'd give a weak man a hernia watching her. Now a strong man would offer to take the strain.'

She came towards us up the path with her head down and her hair unkempt from the breeze. I got up and offered her a hand, because at that moment all I wanted was to be her chosen help-mate. She looked a cool refusal. She was about to pass when McDowd got up and said, 'We'll both give you a hand, and you can stand back and be gaffer.' That seemed to please her. She stretched out between us in the shelter of the rock and lit one of her sexy French cigarettes. We both put away our pipes, content to share the slipstream of her Gauloise. McDowd was lying behind her, peering over her shoulder down the shadowy cleft inside her blouse, a randy man with one thing on his mind, totally lacking in sexual delicacy. As I was facing her, I could see his slack mouth and his eyes leaping in their sockets. I had a fair idea of what he was going through, lying there so close to her and at the same time so far from home. He drew even closer, slowly and silently, as if trying to ease an ache on the sly. She must have felt his tobacco breath on her neck because she turned on her back, and we both leant on one elbow looking down at her. Her eyes were closed and in her face was a serenity that challenged the urgency of all animal appetite.

'You're no great shakes as conversationalists, are you?' she said.

'Conversation, did you say? All you need is love,' McDowd advised.

'I've always wanted to know what the men here talk about as they lie under rocks looking out to sea. Now that you're both together, perhaps you could give me a demonstration.'

'Ah, very difficult,' said McDowd. 'We're two hot-blooded men in the prime of life. How can we pretend that you're not

119

sandwiched between us? It's asking too much of straining flesh.'

'This morning I saw you mowing the field below the cottage and you left a square uncut in the middle. Now why did you do that? Is it an old superstition?' she enquired.

'I came on a corncrake's nest and I didn't want to disturb her little family.'

'I am impressed, Mandamus. You have a warm heart after all.'

Her breasts rose as she inhaled. Pure blue smoke poured from her nostrils, flowering between me and McDowd. I could see that he was excited. He looked as if he could eat her. His lips were wet.

'I was only being selfish.' He pretended to be self-effacing. 'I'm fond of the corncrake. You and Hugo may hear her call this evening but I'll know that it's me she's praising.'

'Crex-crex! Crex-crex!' Olga mimicked. 'Praise Mandamus, O my soul: and forget not all his benefits.'

'You yourself will have cause to praise me. I robbed a wild bees' nest this morning and kept the honey for your tea.' McDowd almost cooed in her ear.

'The bees will go hungry when winter comes,' I said casually.

'Perhaps I shouldn't accept it.' She glanced quizzically from one to the other of us.

'Only you can decide. It's a matter of fine moral judgment.'

'If you accept, you'll be doing good,' McDowd said. 'I promise not to rob any more bees' nests today.'

'I'll accept it then. I believe in doing good,' she smiled.

'I'll bring you the honey in time for tea. It's better than any honey you've ever had from a pot.'

'We've talked about the corncrake and wild honey. What would you two talk about if I wasn't here.'

'The past,' I replied before McDowd could catch her ear again.

'The past is Mary Rose,' explained McDowd. 'She grew up with Arty Bradley, Father Johnnie, Hugo and myself, then she left for London and married a millionaire. You should have known her. There was no girl like her, not till you came to the glen.'

'Do I look like her?'

'You think like her,' I said. 'Now, she was a daring girl.'

McDowd bent over her and whispered in her ear. I missed the first sentence but I heard the second.

'Heaven is in your breeks,' he said.

'I refuse to believe it.' She smiled through an ethereal smoke screen.

'I'd like to prove it, but for that I need your permission.'

'Proof is for scientists. As an artist, I'm willing to take your word for it.' She ended the rally with a smash. 'Now I want to be gaffer,' she said, getting to her feet.

I had wanted the three of us to lie under the rock for the whole afternoon, making slow conversation with neither envy nor animosity in our hearts, postponing all resolution, and delighting in the delicious tension between not knowing and the desire to know. It was not to be. McDowd had broken the spell. No sexual finesse, that's his problem. I once said to Helga, 'Heaven is in your bed', and she didn't bat an eyelid. It was the word 'breeks' that made her bridle. I could see by the way she threw back her head.

McDowd and I carried the log between us up the slope. We laid it against her barn gable and waited for her to speak. He listened to her breathing as she thanked us, and suddenly he knew that thanks was all he'd get. I could see the blank

121

disappointment in his face as she closed the door on us.

'You should buy her a pair of braces for her britches,' I said. 'She's for ever hitching them up.'

'Isn't that the beauty of them, the sense of inner space they give you?'

'There are men who wouldn't welcome inner space,' I reminded him.

'It doesn't worry me. Her breeks may look like flour bags, but as Father Johnnie might say, if he had a mind like mine, "One night in them, O Lord, is better than a thousand." '

McDowd doesn't like me and I'm not overfond of him. Helga smiles on him, though it's possible that she may be flirting to make me jealous. She is not a woman but womankind. She could have carved her own figure, it's so trim; made by the Devil himself to model tight skirts and skimpy shirts. Instead she comes to the pub in flour bags so capacious that McDowd and myself could get lost in them simultaneously. And what of Father Johnnie? Surely there's room in them for him. He'll be the last (apart from Helga) to know that he's besotted. Men who make morality their business often lose the yearning for moral perfection, while those with a gift for immorality are sometimes driven by a vision of the *via negativa*. You need to have made the dunghill to appreciate the full beauty of the rose that grows on it.

Father Jerry read the entry twice before going downstairs to resume his note-making on grace and God's salvific will. Olga was a woman with a soul that must be saved. In all his conversations with her he was aware of an alternative dialogue, of the things he should be saying to enliven her awareness of the exalted life. He had decided to proceed by indirection and thus preserve his influence and her good opinion. St Paul would have laid it on the line and lost her. From the beginning he had realised that what was required was a man with an instinctive understanding of women.

Hugo had misread her of course. She was serious and strong-minded, full of sharp angles and edges. With her there would be no communion, either physical or spiritual, no enfolding warmth, only a chilly calm. She was the antithesis of Dr Sharma who was as warm-hearted as a mother, open-handed and tender, full of concern with no wish to coerce. That evening, after much heart-searching, he tackled Hugo over dinner.

'I want to marry Olga,' Hugo said. 'And marry her I shall.'

Father Jerry could have told him that she was already married but he took the view that, if he did, he would be breaking a confidence.

'Olga wants to be left in peace. She's an artist who puts her art before all mere conveniences.'

Hugo gave a laugh of cold ridicule.

'Then you must put in a good word for me next time you see her. In the village they think she practises her art on you. They snigger and quip about "Father Jerry's romance".'

'Idle gossip.'

'Smoke without fire? Someone saw her reading an odd sort of book on the beach the other day. *The Sin of Father O'Mara* I think it was. And last week she said to me right out of the blue, "Can a man who lacks a religious sensibility experience sexual ecstacy? Sex is a sacrament, it's wasted on the ungodly." '

'Olga is a young woman who is far from friends and home. I see myself in loco parentis. Whenever she needs help or advice I shall be here to give it.'

'The neighbours see her as a mysterious woman full of tricks and artifice. She's unleashed the communal imagination; her visits to the parochial house have become the germ of all fantasy and gossip here. Someone kissed her dark eye in the pub one night and later swore that it was icy cold. "Like the tip of the Devil's pintle," was how he put it.'

'All this is beneath the contempt of any intelligent man. Olga is serious and hard-working. She does her best to fit into the life here. She even comes to Mass on Sunday.'

'She doesn't take Communion.'

'Neither do you, I've noticed.'

'I've eaten *human* flesh, that's enormity enough.'

'You blaspheme against the Mass and against God Himself. Is there anything in life, or even within yourself, that you hold sacred?'

'Nothing. Everything's for sale and also everybody. I'm for sale, you're for sale, and so is Olga. Believe it or not, even Burke's has a price.'

'If you believe that, you're lost.'

'One thing could redeem me: a woman's love. She wouldn't have to be perfect. Olga would do.'

'Love doesn't just make do. Such a marriage would be no more than a business contract.'

'You talk to me as if I were a teenager. I'm a middle-aged man who's seen enough of life to have learnt detachment. I've decided to marry Olga but, sadly, when I try to talk to her she talks only about you.'

'Perhaps we've talked enough.' Father Jerry went to the door.

'We may both lose her,' Hugo grinned. 'The man with the best chance is McDaid. He's head over heels, and I heard this afternoon that she's employed him to do odd jobs about the cottage. She's a superior woman. It's possible that she might wish for an inferior.'

124

'You parade your so-called detachment,' Father Jerry said. 'It's nothing more than a profound lack of seriousness.'

Throughout the evening he kept pondering Hugo's blasphemous reference to the Mass. That night he kept dreaming the same dream and waking up every half-hour. He was alone on the island in late autumn and the ground was bare and cold. Below him lay the shingle strewn with severed feet and hands and whitened bones from feasts long forgotten. The sun sank and night fell. The Devil's Pintle melted and shrank into darkness visible. In vain he waited for the moon to rise. He lay on his back on the hard ground, his head filled with the rattle of bones being dragged over pebbles by an ebbing tide.

Chapter 11

Canon Hackler called just before noon. He settled himself on the sofa with vulturine inelegance and spoke briefly of the bishop's passion for panatellas, causing Father Jerry to wonder what was really on his mind. As the clock on the mantelpiece chimed twelve, he poured the canon a glass of Balvenie. He had been waiting patiently for the clock to chime because he judged that to offer him Scotch before noon might imply that he was fond of it. The canon sipped his favourite malt and sneezed four times in succession, making a sound that seemed to say *Eheu fugaces!*

'Bless you, Canon,' Father Jerry said aloud, though to himself he murmured *Carpe diem.*

The canon blew his nose and fished a battered envelope from an inside pocket.

'I never pay any attention to anonymous letters,' he said, 'but I think that this is one you should see. In every parish there are mischief-makers. Sometimes it is prudent to attend to what they say before someone else does.'

Father Jerry read slowly with an expression which he hoped was suitably blank. The letter was written in capitals and in black ink. There was no address at the top and no signature at the bottom. It said:

Dear Canon,

I write out of Christian concern, not mischief. Father Jerry McSharry in all innocence plays with fire. A handsome young German woman called Olga visits him daily and spends her evenings in the company of drinking men in pubs. Her wood carvings of naked women are immodest and could be considered inflammatory. If the scandalous speculation and gossip which she attracts should prove to have a foundation in truth, the parochial house and the priesthood may well be dragged into disrepute. Father McSharry in his sanctity is unaware of all this. Perhaps it would be a kindness to bring it to his attention.

Yours in Jesus Christ,

Concerned Parishioner

With a smile of resignation Father Jerry handed him back the letter.

'Well, you have brought it to my attention, as the anonymous letter-writer suggested.'

'I am not for a moment accusing you …'

'Like most anonymous letters, it contains a germ of truth. My nearest neighbour is a young German woman called Olga, and she does indeed call in here from time to time. I know that she is a wood carver and for all I know she may visit the village pubs. More than that I can't say.'

'Who could have written such a letter?' the canon wondered.

'Not many people here: the schoolmaster, the postman, the doctor, the lightkeeper, and possibly the police sergeant. I prefer to leave conjecture to gossips.'

'I thought you should see it, that's all.'

The canon dragged himself to the edge of the sofa and after two attempts got to his feet.

'The bishop is coming next week. This is just a visit, not a visitation.'

'What's on his mind?' Father Jerry asked.

'Income and expenditure. We've always paid our way in this parish but we must do better. I think it's time you organised some bingo, Jerry.'

'You know I don't approve of bingo. I'll announce a retiring collection next Sunday instead.'

'Tithes are like teeth, I always say. They should be extracted painlessly. For painless extraction Mr Bingo is your only anaesthetist.' The canon's face expanded in a smile of self-satisfaction.

Father Jerry watched him drive off, then washed his glass and put the Balvenie back in the cabinet. For a moment he gazed at the bottle, which was more delicate in shape than any Scotch bottle he'd ever seen. Beset by Hugo's wayward aggressiveness, by the smug prurience of the letter-writer, and by the canon's obsession with bingo, he wondered why the sense of exaltation he sought came so rarely. Perhaps he was in the wrong place at the wrong time. Or perhaps the inner peace he craved was to be found in the seclusion of a monastery rather than in the glasshouse of parish life.

The canon was to be envied. When in doubt he could consult his budget to see if he were on target. Less businesslike priests had it harder. They had no projections, no critical path charts for guidance; no log; no compass with which to make a dead reckoning. How many souls have I saved today? How many sinners have I forestalled in their desire to sin? Am I on schedule or behind schedule, O Lord? He pulled himself up short. He had caught himself out again. Whenever he felt weary and over-wrought, he tended to measure his ministry against the canon's. It was perhaps a harmless piece of self-deception. Harmless? He went back to the cabinet and gazed again at the almost feminine form of the Balvenie bottle. More self-deception. The things that threatened his spiritual life had little to do with either the canon or Highland malt.

He went upstairs, remembering that Hugo wrote his diary in black ink. He read a page in praise of vehicles with four-wheel drive and a paragraph about the effects of sexual frustration on the human metabolism. Then he lit on a longer entry which must have been written the previous night:

August 2nd
It was barely six in the morning when I reached the Crag of Cats on the hill. McDowd was up before me, zigzagging suspiciously on the slope with a little black bag the size of a doctor's satchel in his hand. From where I crouched, the satchel looked like a handbag and McDowd looked like a woman – a woman in man's clothing with all the alertness of a woman who considers it pos-sible that she is being observed. As he disappeared over the crest, I bounded up the hillside and jouked before I came to the rim. Slowly, I raised my head. The flat, green plateau was empty, and by the look of the grazing sheep no one had recently disturbed them. He had disappeared, it seemed, into thin mountain air.

I turned my head to make sure he wasn't behind me and spied a blast of pure blue pipe smoke rising from behind a dry-stone wall on my left. He was obviously jouking too, perhaps hiding whatever treasure he had been carrying in his satchel. I retreated behind a boulder and waited. For what seemed like an hour I lay on my belly with my chin on my forearm and watched the blue

129

smoke rising in little puffs of contentment over the grey coping of the wall. Then, as I was beginning to run out of patience, I saw the back of his cap and the stoop of his shoulders as he set off across the plain towards the next hill. He was still carrying the satchel and walking so jauntily that I wondered if it had become lighter after his lengthy sojourn behind the wall.

I waited till he had disappeared over the next crest before going to investigate. I made a complicated detour in case I myself was being observed, then I leant over the wall as if by accident and looked down on nothing more incriminating than two spent matches. Like his late master, a worrier and a retentive man. The knowledge gave me confidence, and the confidence enlivened my natural sense of superiority. Why this should be I have no idea. I hadn't discovered his Achilles' heel, and neither had I discovered what he was carrying in his satchel. An outrageous thought occurred to me which I banished immediately from my mind.

Imitating his springy step and meditating the while on the loose-bowelled heroes of history, I set off after him. Beyond the next hill was another little plain, so I decided to keep to the river for cover, as it ran in a deep groove with banks that rose above my head. I made my way upstream, and when I'd reached the second plateau, I peered over the edge of the bank. Again, the dextrous McDowd seemed to have disappeared. And again, I scanned the landscape, scrutinising every shadow in the low sun. Something stirred close to the ground less than two hundred yards away. A man turned on his side as if seeking a more comfortable position. McDowd wasn't lying on the ground. He was stretched out fully on the Termon Stone.

For a long time I watched his moving arms and still legs, wondering what on earth he could be up to. I began walking towards him in a semicircle, keeping downwind of him in case he had

130

keen sniffers. Even my enemies will agree that I'm a skilled bog-trotter. I'm sure-footed and light-stepping, a master of fieldcraft who can recognise a quagmire before he puts his foot in it.

I stood behind him, peering over his shoulder, and he never once sniffed or looked round. He was working a chisel and hammer, carving what looked like hieroglyphics on the Termon Stone and grunting shamelessly with every tap.

'God bless the work since the Devil isn't in the business of blessing.'

He didn't jump but his left leg gave a little twitch as if he had struck the patella instead of the chisel with his hammer.

'I'm trying my hand at lettering,' he grinned. 'I hope you approve.'

He sat up so that I could read the inscription he had just finished.

Arty Bradley 1941–86

Many's the good Rub he had here

'It's a neat job,' I said, just to be friendly.

'We should exhume poor Arty and bury him under the Termon Stone. The only sex he ever had was with Mary Rose on this hard and springless bed.'

'Surely a man who lived as he did in New York couldn't have wanted for life's necessaries. The sex he had here may have been good but it wasn't enough to last a lifetime.'

'He told me so himself: "The only sex I ever had was on the Termon Stone." I suppose the same must be true of Father Johnnie.'

'I'm not my brother's confessor, I wouldn't know.'

'Arty had the Rub here, and so had Father Johnnie. Arty got the lion's share, while you and I looked on.'

'Mary Rose had the lioness's share, even more than the lion.'

McDowd leant forward over the lettering and blew the dust out of the serifs.

'It was a golden age,' I said to encourage him. 'Sex every day before the permissive society was invented.'

'Pity it wasn't real sex. Even Arty was too young to ejaculate.'

'I've had sex on every continent and sex between continents, but the sex I remember before falling asleep at night is the sex I saw on the Termon Stone.'

'Maybe that's why none of us got married. You're a bachelor and I'm a bachelor. Arty was a bachelor, and so is Father John-nie. It must be disturbing for a priest to remember the things that you and I remember every day.'

I had no wish to comment on the casuistries of the priestly conscience, so I got out my tobacco pouch and filled my pipe. His face was close to mine, a face of bone. McDowd is a man of bone; beneath the skin is as little flesh as bone requires to survive. Now, Arty Bradley was a man of flesh and fat. In the pot of a certain tribe I've lived among, I know which of the two would elicit the more positive Pavlovian reaction. Yet McDowd to me is the more interesting man. Cannibalism is not my métier. I'm a white man, I play the white man's game.

'Some good came of it all,' I said amicably. 'Mary Rose, from what I hear, is happy with her millionaire. I'm pleased that she got value for money – or money for value. It's no more than she deserved.'

'When Helga came, my first thought was to get her to play the Game. I soon realised that things weren't all that simple. Father Johnnie had cried off the sports list. Then poor old Arty died. Now there's only you and me.'

I pretended not to be listening, and to lend verisimilitude to my pretence I relit my pipe with a loud smacking of the lips and an indrawing of cheeks.

'There's no going back,' McDowd went on. 'The Game has taken a serious turn. Now it can only be a twosome.'

'Precisely my sentiments,' I said coolly.

'Two things remain to be seen. How did Arty Bradley meet his end? Who will lie with Helga on the Termon Stone? They are two questions I think about every day.'

'Will thinking solve them?'

'Thinking solves nothing and neither does play-acting.'

I knocked out my pipe on the edge of the Termon Stone and blew loudly through the stem. The dottle that flew from the bowl whizzed by his ear with the force of grapeshot, and he didn't so much as blink. He saw it as a declaration of war, and I couldn't tell him that it was unintentional. As a man who has lived in savage societies, I have learnt never to qualify a declaration.

'The weather is holding up well,' I said, getting to my feet.

'The outlook, they tell me, is uncertain.'

I left him to admire his lettering and walked back along the semicircle which I had already trodden. I wondered if I should tell Father Johnnie about McDowd's obsession with prepubertal sex on the Termon Stone, and then I wondered if Father Johnnie would thank me for telling him. Perhaps not. He doesn't take Matthew 18:9 with the customary pinch of salt. He is a man who has cut large chunks of his life out of his thoughts.

By the time I had reached the Crag of Cats again, I had more or less forgotten about McDowd. I sat on the Crag looking down at Helga sawing a dead branch off a tree in her back garden. She came here, she says, to practise her art. Art or jumped-up craft? And is that all? Only a refugee would seek out this wind-scoured outpost. Is she fleeing from justice or injustice? Or resting after a surfeit of carnality? The answers to these questions don't matter to me, but they should to Father Johnnie. No one knows her. He's mistaken if he thinks that he does.

Of course he is protected from life by the closed system within which he operates. What he knows as 'the life of the spirit' is a life of imprisonment within fifteen centuries of systematisation. It makes for smugness and self-satisfaction; the belief that there are no new questions and no new answers. If I were my brother's keeper, I should make a breach in the mile-high wall that surrounds the garden of his soul, so that he might experience, just for a moment, the sting of the world's winds.

Already I can hear his dismissive laugh, a laugh of self-complacency. I once reminded him that ancient Christian custom permitted a hermit to live in spiritual marriage with a holy woman. He gave me a look of blank condescension, impervious to the needle-point of irony. Does he see our Helga as his *virgo subintroducta?* And if so, how long can he remain *virgo intacta?*

Father Jerry went over the entry again. He studied the hand in which it was written, heavy and blunt with a hint of impatience in the joining strokes. The black ink and tight spacing gave the pages a cramped, inelegant look that reminded him of the anonymous letter, yet he could not be sure. Though Hugo was wayward and unpredictable, he was not an enemy.

A knock at the front door brought him out on to the landing. He paused at the head of the stairs, as the heavy door opened below.

'Father Jerry,' she called.

He held his breath.

'Father Jerry, are you there?'

He listened to her footsteps on the hallway tiles, unsure of

134

himself and of his reason for wishing to be alone. Then the front door closed and she was gone. He went to his room and sat on the edge of the bed, waiting for the fluttering in his chest to subside. A cyclist passed on his way home from the village. A woman in a checked apron shooed two hens from a potato patch. A black dog skulked between the tents on the Glebe. The sea below his window lay calm and blue. The cyclist, the woman and the dog were no longer there. Only the sea remained, dreamy and somnolent, as if it were a painting by an artist who could convey just one mood at a time. The whole world seemed to have become a still life. What lay before his eyes mocked him by changing from 'real' to 'not real' and back again.

He lay on his back with his eyes closed. The Game ... the Termon Stone ... Mary Rose. It seemed inconceivable that McDaid and Hugo should keep such faded memories so urgently alive. What neither of them realised was that he himself had known Mary Rose in London.

He had come fresh to the city from university to find her already established within a circle of genial friends. He met her by accident and fell in love with her all over again. They began going out together. Life flowed round him unseen. He knew no one and cared for nothing except her. During the day he worked in a library, living among book stacks and books, or rather among authors' names and book titles, while she enjoyed the enveloping life of the hospital and the sorority of nurses, which gave her a sense of belonging in which he could not share.

They met whenever she was free, sometimes in the evening and sometimes at weekends, filling the Sunday afternoons with visits to public parks, historic buildings, art galleries and museums. He had little money; he spent hours planning their expeditions and working out the cost of travel to the last penny.

'You're a born rubberneck,' she said. 'You can't see a listed building without wanting to know what's inside it. Why don't we spend an afternoon doing nothing for a change?'

The thought filled him with alarm. He wanted to release her from the world of doctors, patients and nurses but he had no equivalent world to offer her. He knew that the stone and mortar of the buildings they visited were a cold substitute for the human warmth of the hospital wards, and already she was envisaging a kind of life that he did not want and could not hope to provide.

'I don't hanker after an Adam fireplace or an ogee arch,' she said. 'What I'd like is a suburban semi with lattice windows, central heating, a television lounge and wall-to-wall carpets. I'm sick of cold and gloomy bedsitters. I don't know how you can bear to live in yours.'

Occasionally he would spend a night at her flat but she'd never agree to stay the night in his 'horsebox of a room'. He grew uneasy. He was afraid that he might lose her, yet he knew that in trying to hold on to her he was in danger of losing what he saw as his own distinctive centre. She was wilful and demanding, greedy for every experience. She seemed at once younger and older than himself. They had arguments that left them raw and smarting. The physical pleasure that followed their reconciliations only reinforced the sense of personal defeat that had drained them both of sweetness and spontaneity.

At last she suggested that they stop meeting for a month, 'just to see how we'll feel at the end of it'. When he rang again, she told him that she had fallen in love with a building contractor who had been 'admitted to casualty after a car accident'.

'So you've found your suburban semi?' he joked.

'It's more than a semi,' she said seriously. 'It's as big as a Palladian villa.'

After a year of what he could only describe as mourning, he entered a seminary and found a frozen peace for which he was grateful. Now Hugo's obsession with Olga was only a coarser version of his own unachievable love. Both Hugo and McDaid still romanticised Mary Rose. How could they know that the vivacious schoolgirl for whom no jape was too daring had grown into a practical, tough-minded woman who knew what she wanted and did not look back once she'd seen it?

Hugo did not return that evening, and Father Jerry lay awake listening for his footsteps. His mind was a ground-sea of perpetual motion made ugly by the play of winter light. He thought about Mary Rose, the Termon Stone and the Game, and he said to himself as he fell asleep, 'Lucky the man who can foretell the effects of things.'

He had hardly finished the sentence when he found himself driving into the mountains in thickening dusk. He was covering ground, trying to keep up with Hugo who was perched high in the Land Rover thirty yards in front. They came to a fork in the road. Hugo turned left and Father Jerry took the other route because he wanted to get to Glenshask before his brother. They were both on the same mission, and now, as night set in, he could not recall what the mission might be. He drove with demonic concentration, as if nothing mattered but to greet his brother on his arrival. Then he saw a chain of lights emerging from the side of the mountain on his right. He stopped the car. The lights kept pouring out to make a gleaming necklace that circled the foot of the mountain. He realised that what he was seeing was a diabolical mirage, an endless train coming out of a tunnel to beguile his eye so that Hugo would reach Glenshask before him. He moved off again, the headlights now slicing through the slanting rain. He was approaching the place where the roads rejoined. As the Land Rover shot out in front of him, he slammed on the brakes. His car skidded. The Land Rover overturned and burst into flames. He jumped out to pull Hugo to safety and froze as he saw his own face behind the closed window. The heat was overpowering. From a safe distance he watched his own death agony until Hugo came up from behind and led him away. When the flames had died down, they went back to the Land Rover and Hugo wrenched open the door with a crowbar. A pile of charred bones fell out at his feet. He stooped and in trying to collect them burned his hand.

'Can these bones relive?' he asked.

'No, no, no.' Hugo pulled him roughly away. 'We must hurry, we're late already. Best to leave them for McDaid to chew over when they cool.'

In the morning he found that Hugo's bed had not been slept in. Though he did not believe in dreams, he decided to skip breakfast and see if McDaid was at home. He found him in Olga's garden, sharpening a scythe. Though it was a weekday, he looked scrubbed and clean-shaven, the beaten bronze of his face forming a mask in which only the darting eyes spoke of life and movement.

'When are we getting the new bell, Father?' he asked.

'We're not getting a new bell, I said. We'll have the old one repaired.'

'When?'

'In the fullness of time.'

'It's on everyone's mind. I'm the sexton and naturally I get asked questions.'

'Then refer your questioners to me.'

'I liked ringing the bell. God spoke through the bell. Now He's silent.'

'If you wish to talk to Him, come to church more often.'

'When I want to talk to God, I go out to Glencrow. There you can have a quiet conversation with no one except the water fowl to butt in. You should go out there on retreat, Father. It's a very spiritual place.'

'I never go further north than Glenshask.'

'You can see Scariff Island from Glenshask. Now that's a lonely spot if you were marooned on it. Nothing to hear except the shingle rattling and nothing to see but the Devil's Pintle raising its head above the land.'

Father Jerry met his glance. The self-confident mockery in McDaid's blue eyes gave away no hint of his meaning.

'The Devil doesn't have a pintle of his own,' Father Jerry said. 'He doesn't need one. He has negotiated a lien on the pintle of every living man.'

McDaid slowly opened his mouth as if to laugh. His lower jaw swam sideways and his lower lip went slack. Father Jerry looked stern and McDaid's eyes danced a quick jig of disbelief.

When he got back to the house, he found Hugo in the kitchen tucking into one of his gargantuan breakfasts, the piled plate crowned with a double loin chop that in outline resembled a frizzled crab.

'Where on earth have you been?'

'Keeping vigil in the open. I miss the jungle here. I find a hissing cistern a bit suburban when I wake up in the middle of the night.'

'You could have told me you would be spending the night elsewhere. I was convinced that you'd had an accident, or worse.'

'I'm not accident-prone, though I may be the cause of accident-proneness in other men.'

'Where did you spend the night?'

'On Scariff Island. I motored down just before sunset. I'd have been back earlier if the outboard hadn't given trouble.'

'What made you do such a thing?'

'I wanted to find out how it was. There are some things a man really needs to know. I felt the same about sex once. Now I can put it from my mind – the island, I mean. I'm still finding out about the other.'

'Did you sleep?'

'I didn't go there to sleep, I went to listen. It wasn't in the least like the jungle. I heard no sound I didn't recognise.'

'You're satisfied, then?'

'Not entirely. I can't figure out why Brennan should want to leave it in such a hurry. I could spend my life there alone, if someone drop-shipped a hamper once a week.'

'Has it ever occurred to you that you may have a screw loose?'

'It has occurred to me that my vision is better than yours. I see what there is to see. It's a pity that I myself am not perceived so accurately.'

Chapter 12

The bishop arrived shortly after midday, looking taller, more military and more self-possessed than last time. Sipping his brandy and smoking a panatella, he deployed his well-known gift for oblique but insistent questioning. It was the kind of gift that a man given to self-questioning and self-denial would use sparingly.

'As I drove through the village, the Protestant church clock struck twelve. Our bell was silent. It pleased me to see the people in the street pause to say the Angelus, and I couldn't help smiling at the way we rely on the Opposition to remind us to pray.'

'I'm trying to get the old bell brazed. Understandably, the bell-founders would prefer to sell me a new one.'

'Why not buy a new bell and trade in the old one for smelting?' the bishop suggested softly.

'In a sense there is merit in having no bell. A bell is a symbol of health. "Sound as a bell" is a well-known phrase. Here in this glen we are no longer sound. We're recovering from the effects of twenty years of vandalism. The bell, I'm convinced, cracked for a reason that had nothing to do with metal fatigue.'

'We mustn't impute to God such crudely mechanical

intervention. Bells do crack from time to time, and bells that crack must be replaced.'

Father Jerry took him up to his bedroom to show him the view from the north window. He pointed out the fishmeal factory with its cloud of shrieking seagulls, and then the hippies' tents on the Glebe below.

'When you look down over the Glebe, what do you see, Bishop?'

'A circle of tents. Rather picturesque, I must say.'

'You don't notice the smouldering fires?'

'Yes, now that you've mentioned them.'

'I see the refuse pit that smoked day and night outside Jerusalem.'

'Gehenna? Surely that's a bit far-fetched.' The bishop laughed.

'Here Gehenna is a living presence. I breathe its smoke and smell its stinking refuse on the way to Mass every morning. At night I dream about it, and when I wake, it lies open before my bedroom window.'

'Ge-Hinnom ... Gehenna,' the bishop murmured. 'You're out of step with the times, my dear Jerry. Hell has become an embarrassment that requires a great deal of theological ingenuity to explain away. But look at those seagulls. They're rather beautiful, in spite of all you say.'

'When I was a boy, I used to think of them following the plough or looking whiter than white among grazing sheep in a field. My father and I used to watch them on mountain loughs, coming and going and crying as they rose. He used to say that they were more romantic than Shelley's skylark and Keats's nightingale. Here they've become gluttonous scavengers grown fat on pollution. And like the hippies, they don't care where they defecate.'

The bishop gazed down on the sleeping sea below them, a flat

142

expanse of blue with zigzag paths of viridescence and curling selvages of white that formed a living, wandering picture of perfection and peace on earth.

'I love this glen,' he said. 'As you approach it over the moor, you feel that you are about to shed all worldly impedimenta, that you will come back a leaner and truer man. It is a place where you don't have to be a saint to keep yourself unspotted from the world.'

'The World is already here, I'm telling you. And with the World has come the circus of the Flesh and the Ringmaster himself who shall be nameless in your presence.'

The bishop blew a smoke ring. It floated delicately upwards, an expanding halo that yet remained too small for his head.

'I thought the Ringmaster had absconded,' he smiled. 'You were luckier than most. Not everyone who jousts with the Ringmaster can claim victory.'

He wondered if the bishop were making fun of him. His face was expressionless, his grey eyes fixed on the squiggles of green that melted into the blue of the palimpsest in front of them.

'Are you happy in your ministry, Jerry?' He spoke directly to the sea while he puffed.

'I have found more peace here than in London. There is more time for meditation –'

'You've recovered from your illness?'

'I've never felt better.'

'You're making a name for yourself as a confessor. Canon Hackler tells me that certain devout women from his end of the parish come to you rather than him for confession. He said you were the new Curé d'Ars.'

'The canon likes to jest about these things.'

'The Curé d'Ars was just the man for nineteenth-century France. Today we value above all the socially active priest with a

143

socially active conscience. The canon is such a man, but he is only human. In his heart of hearts he would like to be a gifted confessor too.'

'We're men of different methods, the canon and I, but we work well together, I like to think.'

'The canon is a practical man who never gets bogged down in detail. We need such men to bridge the gap between the Church and the World. We must never forget that double-entry book-keeping was invented by a monk.'

The bishop gave a little laugh that was at once affable and admonitory. Neither the fishmeal factory nor the hippie camp could shake him in his determination to be himself. He wheeled with military correctitude and led the way down the stairs. In the hallway he brushed a flake of ash from the front of his soutane and, with a smoothness that was almost surreptitious, drew a little red skullcap from his pocket.

'It looks like rain. You should have brought your cappa magna,' Father Jerry smiled.

'I'm a modern bishop, I don't possess one. I've got a mac in the back of the car.'

'A black one, I hope?'

The bishop adjusted his skullcap and pretended not to have heard.

'The spiritual life reminds me of swimming in the sea,' he confided. 'In swimming hydrodynamics is all. A good swimmer makes the destructive element work for him. He propels himself with the minimum of energy. He knows when to glide, when to rest, and when to breathe. In a true sense the water is his ally. The spiritual life has its dynamics too. The World is the water in which we must sink or swim. I'd like you to think about that, Jerry. We must all strive to see with an eye that isn't ours.'

As he took the bishop's proffered hand, Father Jerry said that Canon Hackler was the best swimmer he knew.

That evening Hugo told him that he would be going to Dublin at the weekend to collect his missing trunk.

'It's the one that contains my diaries,' he enthused. 'It turned up miraculously in Tilbury, thanks to your prayers, I'm sure. I'll be a different man once I've got my diaries back. You must read them. They're even franker than Pepys's. The best entries begin "And so to bed".'

Father Jerry remembered that Olga had not called on him for over a week. He decided to drop in on her, in the hope that talking to her might calm his almost Manichaean fear of the world and worldly bishops. She was in the back yard killing a young chicken in a manner that he could describe only as unusual. The chicken was stretched on the ground with a broomstick across its neck. She was standing on the broomstick gazing down at the open beak and the weakly fluttering wings. She looked aggressive and formidable, her long legs far apart.

'I'm sorry,' she said. 'You weren't meant to see this.'

'I'll come back when you're less busy.'

'No, please go inside. I shan't be long.'

He waited in the kitchen which was somewhat bare. She came in for a knife and went out again. Then she returned without the knife and told him that her method of killing pullets might be unconventional but that she found it less obnoxious than twisting their necks. She led him into a little workshop next to the kitchen where a carving of two dolphins stood on a table.

'I found a lovely piece of elm quite by accident. When I looked at it, I saw two leaping dolphins waiting for a hand to release them.'

'What lovely grain.' He stood beside her caressing their backs.

'The wood dictated everything. They came as a gift from nowhere.'

'They're twins, and at the same time they're not identical.'

'One is called Hugo. I haven't yet found a name for the other.'

She gave a little laugh which he took to be critical and left him to examine her chisels while she made tea. With the tea she gave him a slice of home-made cake and sat by the open window in the low sunlight of evening.

'I'm going up to Dublin at the weekend to sell some of my pieces. This cottage doesn't pay for itself, which is a pity. I need a rich patron who would love me for my carvings, not myself.'

She smiled and leant forward with the sun on her neck. For a moment she looked very young and vulnerable. Then she sat upright again, confident and self-reliant. Golden sunlight enriched the sheen of her fine, straight hair.

'You're taking the coach, I suppose?'

'I'm getting a lift with Hugo. If things go well, I'll buy a second-hand car before the winter. Then I'll be really independent. That's my aim.'

He was annoyed that Hugo hadn't told him, and he felt less than happy with himself for being annoyed.

'I dislike having to go to Dublin, it's so squalid and joyless; it has even more bureaucrats than Bonn. And making sure that I don't bump into my husband gives me that feeling of being on the run. It's lovely coming back, though. This glen's a haven, it's so far away from what people call the world.'

'As Prospero said to Miranda, "'Tis new to thee."'

She leant back and closed her eyes. A piece of thistledown floated in through the window and played before her immobile face. He watched its rise and fall, and then its gentle drift down

146

inside her blouse. She opened her eyes and looked at him in surprise.

'I was on the verge of sleep,' she said, getting up. 'It's this heavy sea air. As you say, it's new to me.'

He rose abruptly and thanked her for the tea. On the way home he breathed deeply and evenly, filling his lungs with air that was clean and strong. She had left him with a sense of not knowing and not being able to know. The life she led was simple. She spent most of the day carving and for exercise went for long walks on the hill. He saw her in the distance every day, and in another sense he saw her every day for the first time. She had stirred the communal imagination, as Hugo put it. She was not an ordinary woman; her mind did not run on ordinary things.

'Olga is fleeing from the world,' he said. 'Yet for me she is the world. Like most people who wish to escape from the world, she is merely seeking to escape from herself.'

He said nothing about Olga to Hugo. Instead he kept an eye on Hugo's diary. With growing excitement he went into his brother's room every morning only to find the words 'No thought, no action' written against the date of the previous day. What Father Jerry sought was something akin to objectivity, a view through a narrow, deep-set window that would bestow on him a sense of wholeness and completion and the will to act.

On Friday morning Hugo had an early breakfast. As Father Jerry returned from Mass, the Land Rover was parked by the gate with Olga's carvings in boxes in the back. She and Hugo came out of the parochial house and down the avenue together. She was wearing a black blouse; a long, tight-fitting skirt with blue and black vertical stripes; white stockings and black shoes. It occurred to him that he had never seen any woman dressed so strikingly before.

147

'We're off,' Hugo said. 'And don't worry, we won't do anything you wouldn't do yourself.'

'What shall we bring you back?' Olga asked.

'A case of vintage altar wine?' Hugo suggested. He was smiling broadly out of a dark beard that could have done with trimming.

'No, thank you. I've got everything I need here – in fact more than I strictly need.'

He watched her climb into the Land Rover and visualised her in the back yard with a gasping pullet between her feet. Today she looked so elegant that she was not just remote but absent. Yet it was not a conventional elegance; it was a public declaration, a criticism of the very idea of elegance as something to be put on and taken off. He went straight to Hugo's bedroom and, with an interest that in a layman might have verged on the prurient, read the entry for the previous day:

August 19th

In my pursuit of Helga I neglect my diary and McDowd. Two weeks ago she'd barely talk to me. Things have changed; she's accepted my offer of a lift to Dublin, as if she'd clean forgotten those sheep's skulls and the time I goosed her too violently in the pub. Why this sudden *volte-face?* Has McDowd fouled her bed? Has the Holy Man said a prayer for me? Or does she find my Land Rover irresistible? It doesn't matter. She's taken up permanent residence inside my head. She's a physical woman with a muscular way of thinking. As you talk to her, you can feel your mind expand. She's aware of the danger of being loved for the wrong reasons. She deliberately wears those loose-fitting flour bags to enable you to concentrate more fully on what she's saying. Or perhaps she wants to go easy on Father Johnnie. It must be hell for him, being so close to her and not being able to think what's on his mind.

Pity about the carving. She talks of nothing else and, worse, she thinks about nothing else. Yesterday she called me in to see her latest masterpiece, a pair of sleek dolphins in a spin.

'They're called Johnnie and Hugo,' she said, 'but don't tell Father Johnnie.'

'I can't vouch for His Reverence but I'm flattered. Dolphins are intelligent. I hope you don't do them an injustice.'

'Which is Father Johnnie and which is you?' she teased.

'Father Johnnie is the one leaping up with his nose in the air. I'm the one going down, about to re-enter the water. Am I right?'

'You only see yourself in contrast to your brother.'

'We *are* dissimilar. I'm heavy, he's light. I've got a broad face and a bushy head, broad shoulders and a thick waist. He's got thin, aquiline features and fine, sleek hair. He's a near-vegetarian who eats frugally and I'm what he calls "a carnalising carnivore". He's full of quick movements, he never sits still. I can sit in my room for half an hour without moving a muscle. He's a reader who doesn't think and I'm a thinker who doesn't read.'

'I don't see you like that at all. To me you are similar to the point of dissimilarity, quite a different thing.'

'Which of us do you prefer? The one going up or the one going down?'

'You mustn't assume that you're the one going down.'

'You haven't answered my question.'

'I like you both. There's more of you to see and there's more of him to understand.'

She covered the carving with her apron, and I thought of closing time and the barmaid putting a towel over the beer pumps. She's a superior woman. I can tell that I have my work cut out. Though McDowd has the best opportunity, she may come to see him as her paid servant, not her *cavaliere servente*. So my real rival may be the holy celibate who would if only he could. How can I let him know that he is standing in my way without putting bad thoughts in his oh so sanctified head?

He weighed each word slowly as he read. Hugo had fictionalised Olga and McDaid; he had created an alternative reality with a solidity and coherence that he knew to be illusory. Reading the diary day after day gave him a sense of personal depth which he could only attribute to the experience of observing his own character being re-created by a stranger.

He spent the afternoon pottering in his vegetable garden because he couldn't settle down to a book. The house was empty. All life within its walls had ceased. He was bound by a feeling of not quite knowing what to do. On Saturday morning he went through the diary again from start to finish. So much was missing, including any mention of the night Hugo had spent on the island alone. The things that moved him to write seemed as random and arbitrary as life itself. He paused at a paragraph which he had not noted before:

It has become clear to me that I must take Helga to Scariff Island. Certain things can only be experienced at first hand. I've told her about the hogsback and the rattling shingle which is best heard on a wild night. She showed no interest, and that I took as a criticism. If she spent a night till morning on the island with me, she would come back a changed woman. She seeks an elemental experience. I know I am the man who will provide it.

He felt a desire to see the island again for himself; to go over the ground, examining stones, bones and bladder-wrack. Though he did not know what he expected to find, he had a sense of exhilaration as he readied Hugo's boat.

All the way down he faced a salty breeze that subdued the heat of the sun on his head. He sat at the tiller, open-collared and in shirt-sleeves, watching the polishing action of the breeze on the water, which seemed dull and heavy with a skin of warts and wrinkles. Whenever a gannet plummeted, he visualised death beneath the skin, but for the most part he was aware of little more than a sense of peace that came from being alone and unobserved under an open sky.

He beached the boat on the white shingle, above which rose two pinnacles of rock with a narrow gully in between. He picked his way up the slope to the highest point and looked back to the mainland where the north-facing cliffs stood dark and sheer. Then, wheeling quickly, he scanned an empty sea of stippled light stretching to the horizon in the south. The ground was strewn with crisp, sun-dried wrack that had been blown ashore during the winter and now crunched loudly underfoot. Though he knew that he was alone, he had a feeling that he was being observed, which obliterated the sense of peace he had enjoyed on the water. Among the wrack on the high ground were the whitened bones of sea birds but there were no bones among the beach stones below. His sense of unease could be explained only by the fact that the things he saw and the sounds he heard were those he had seen and heard before as he read through Hugo's diary.

He made his way back to the boat with his hands in his trouser pockets touching the stones he had found on his last visit. It seemed to him that he was a prisoner of his brother's imagination, that he was being jostled by spectres that were not of his own creation. He took the stones and flung one over each shoulder. Now they were somewhere behind him, lost in a field of white.

He started the engine and headed south-east in the direction of Glenshask. Gradually, the Devil's Pintle took shape before him, dark, asymmetrical and weirdly obtrusive. He circled slowly, keeping clear of the submerged rocks that surrounded its base. It towered above him, rising in irregular layers with vertical and horizontal fissures that gave an impression of unmortared brickwork. The narrow base and the wider circumference of the projecting top gave the whole structure a look of bluntness, brutishness and ugliness combined. Hugo once told him that he had put his hand in one of the crevices in its side but Father Jerry did not believe him. Its power over his brother must surely come from its unequivocal demand to be seen as an unknown part in a comprehensible whole. On that day in Glenshask he and Hugo had seen it rising from behind the rocky spit, half-hidden by the land with only the blunt tip visible, an unmistakably alien presence in a landscape that was itself almost homely. Again and again it drew his eye. The effect on him then was immediate. It was one of utter disbelief.

He headed for home with a feeling that he was escaping from unknown territory. Both the island and the tor represented in some unfathomable way areas of life that were outside his waking experience, yet they had gripped his imagination as places which touched on the secret life that Hugo's diary adumbrated but did not explore. As he went over in his mind the events that Hugo had described, it occurred to him that in trying to understand his brother he was trying to understand himself.

Chapter 13

When Hugo returned on Monday afternoon, he uttered one word: 'Lost'.

'You mean your journey was in vain?'

'Not in every sense. I got my trunk back all right but not my diaries.'

'Surely they'll turn up.'

'Not unless the man who's nicked them is a fool. There were things in my diaries that would shame civilisation as we know it. They were a rain forest of forbidden knowledge.'

'You may be better off without them.'

'You don't understand. They weren't just idle rumination. I recorded without comment; I was present only in my choice of what was worth recording. They were my defence against mean-inglessness; they made my life real.'

'I'm sure it's a loss you'll get over. Most of one's life is only fill-ing. You're bound to remember whatever is important.'

'Remembering's no good, it's unconscious forgery. I can never resurrect the same events, and the events I do resurrect will be falsified. They'll never again be seen in the light I shone on them in my diary. What I've lost is a whole history of departed selves.'

He saw little of Hugo in the weeks that followed. Most mornings he had already left for Burke's by the time he returned from Mass. He did not come back for lunch, and in the evenings he had dinner with Olga. Father Jerry ate alone and wondered if he should call on her since she no longer came to see him. One afternoon he went to Burke's to see how his brother was getting on. He had finished his work on the roof and had repointed the stonework of the east gable. Father Jerry found him on his knees in one of the bedrooms, replacing joists and floor boards that had gone soft from dry rot.

'Never take on an old house,' Hugo said. 'There's enough work here to keep a jack of all trades going for a twelvemonth.'

'It will be a snug little nest when you've finished.'

'It takes two to make a nest. Do you think Olga has an instinct for nidification?'

'She's already married. I thought you knew.'

'She's less wary of me now than she was. Maybe one day she'll come up that lane with a piece of straw dangling from her beak. Now that's the sign I'm waiting for. When I get it, you'll be the first to know.'

He left his brother to his sawing and hammering and wandered down the lane between the sycamores. At the gate he met Olga who smiled warmly as he spoke. She was wearing half-length wellingtons, black trousers and a red shirt, the tail of which hung out from under her white pullover at the back. She looked strong and healthy, young and self-confident.

'I haven't seen you for ages,' she said. 'I must call on you some time for one of our chats. Do you still lay out milk and biscuits for two?'

'Always.'

'Does anyone come?' She smiled pleasantly.

'Rarely, but that doesn't matter.'

'Let me be your visitor, then.' She walked away up the lane to the house with the tail of her shirt flapping over her buttocks.

On the way back he got caught in a shower and sought shelter under a blackthorn bush. At a bend in the road three girls with heavy backpacks were taking pictures of one another in the rain. He listened to their laughter as they approached and wondered if they were speaking German or Dutch. It was raining heavily. Their trousers clung to their legs and their hair looked straight and bedraggled. They passed without looking his way. Their laughter echoed with youthful energy and joy, reminding him of the hunger for experience he had found so exasperating in Mary Rose. He felt dry, brittle and old – or, worse still, middle-aged.

When he arrived home, he went to the wardrobe and took out Olga's carving of the weeping woman. He placed it on the table and sat down in front of it, as if waiting for it to speak. Outside Dr Sharma's consulting room a sculpture of a naked female figure had faced the wall. As he climbed the stairs to the landing, the statue would tower over him; and afterwards, as she listened to his ramblings, it would overshadow his very feelings and thoughts. One day, as he reached the landing, he found the female figure facing him with a smile playing on her marble lips. Suddenly he felt weightless. The black raven within him seemed to fly out of the window into the sun, bearing with her a whole woeful world of umbrageous connections.

'I feel better today,' he said to Dr Sharma.

'You look better. The clouds have lifted. Soon you won't have to remember to smile when you hear a joke.'

'Why have you moved the statue on the landing?' he asked.

155

'I didn't. It must have been the cleaner.'

'Then the statue has no significance.'

'None. Do you think it should?'

'Somehow I had come to believe that you put it facing the wall while the patient is unwell and that you turn it round again only when he gets better.'

Dr Sharma laughed and sat on the couch beside him.

'What do you feel now?'

'A sense of release, and relief from the weight of circular thoughts. I feel like a dove that's been let out of its cote with a message in its bill. I can't read the message. I don't know what it says, only that sooner or later I shall meet someone who will have need of it.'

At dinner he felt shivery. He lit a fire in the study, thinking that he should have changed after the wetting he'd got earlier in the day. He sat at the table pretending to read and make notes. At last he got up and wrote a postcard to Dr Sharma. Then he wrote a second and finally a third:

Dear Dr Sharma,

September 3rd; 10.45 p.m. A faded half-moon hangs low in the sky between the dark outlines of two trees, a piece of parchment with faint squiggles, a worn-out palimpsest, wafer-thin. Above the moon in a clearing between clouds is a single star, coldly steadfast, a piercing point of light.

Father Jerry

Dear Dr Sharma,

September 3rd; 11.04 p.m. The star has lost its brilliance, stolen by the tugging moon, now a cutting-wheel with a rim that slices. The moon has come closer; the star has retreated to a great

156

distance from all that is human and warm.

Father Jerry

Dear Dr Sharma,
September 3rd; 11.36 p.m. No star. No moon. No trees. Total
darkness. Total night. Tomorrow the sun will rise before breakfast. Cold collation.

Father Jerry

The following morning he shivered in the sunlight on the
way to church. He said Mass before a congregation of six – five
old women from the village and one middle-aged bachelor
who shaved his head for fear he might inspire lust in young
women. After breakfast he took to his bed with two hot-water
bottles to keep warm. He felt joyless and weak. He lay on his
back listening to the lisp of the tide between the rocks and
looking up at the trap-door in the ceiling. Now and again he
thought of the girls with backpacks taking pictures of one
another in the rain.

Hugo was at Burke's. He was alone in the parochial house, a
solid structure of stone that overlooked the village and the low
townlands by the sea. As a boy he had come to this house to do
odd jobs for Father Muldoon. Then it was a place of prayer and
meditation, of scholarship and spiritual serenity. He remembered the glass-fronted bookcases, the chiming clock, the walking sticks in the hallway, the semicircular hearth rug, and the
pipe rack on the leather-topped writing desk. When Father Muldoon died, other priests came and left their mark. One put in a
new fireplace. Another modernised the kitchen and threw out
the pinewood dresser. His own predecessor replaced the lovely
wrought-iron gate with a crude cattle-grid simply because he

157

couldn't be bothered to get out of his car to shut the gate behind him. These men were vandals and like all good vandals they did not destroy, they prettified.

He had returned determined to re-create the parochial house of Father Muldoon's time. He bought walking sticks and a chiming clock with a glass case; pipes and a pipe rack though he himself did not smoke a pipe; and a semicircular hearth rug of many colours. On his first evening, as he viewed the empty rooms and gazed at the empty bookshelves, he realised that this house had been at the centre of his vocation from the beginning, representing, as it did, a reclusive life of study and contemplation. He furnished the rooms and filled the bookshelves, but somehow it remained an empty house. The sense of mystery had evaporated, leaving him with an abiding awareness of his own shortcomings as a priest.

During his first month in the glen, he used to stand for hours by his bedroom window looking across the inlet at the sombre cliffs beyond, a black embankment with spilling foam making white veins down rock faces. Outside the blunt-headed bluff stood a single sea stack that resembled the ruined gable of a fallen house. That scene had impressed itself on his imagination. He knew every cleft and promontory. It had become his most valued 'possession'. In a sense it was the only solid and changeless thing that remained, the antithesis of his life which had become a treacherous quagmire.

Even his childhood lacked shape and commodiousness. Asthma dogged him as a boy, causing him to wheeze at night as if his windpipe were an aeolian harp. He would sit by the open window in the dark, gasping for air while Hugo snored, miserable with guilt because of the strain his illness placed on his hard-pressed mother. Sometimes he had to stay in bed for two or three days in succession, knowing that Hugo was roaming the fields and enjoying the robust games played by Brennan, McDaid and Mary Rose.

One evening he was alone in the house after a weakening fit of asthma when he suddenly remembered a thrush's nest in the old lane that ran up the side of the hill. Again and again he visualised the spotted, sky-blue eggs, wondering if they had hatched during his illness. It was his nest, and he had been careful to keep it a secret from Hugo. He dragged himself out of bed and stole up the lane, stooping between the ditches in case he should be spotted. His heart gave a sideways flutter as the mother left the nest, shooting past his face in the dusk. Afraid to breathe, he peered into a round hole in the moss and counted four little fledglings, tender balls of fluff with wide, greedy beaks. He looked up and down the lane, suddenly alert. Then he looked up the hill, and at the very top, standing on a rock, was Hugo. He felt weak at the knees and stooped to cough, pretending to spit out an irritation in his throat. He climbed the hill with his hands on his knees to give Hugo the impression that he was still weak.

'You've found a nest.' Hugo smiled knowledgeably.

'I thought I might find one but there's nothing in the old lane this year.'

'I must have a look myself.'

'Would you like my hoop and rod?' he asked in desperation.

'I've got two hoops already and there are more rods growing than I'll ever cut.'

'If you like, I'll give you my rabbit.'

'Why are you offering me all your things?'

'It's my asthma. I've been so poorly all week that I haven't been able to enjoy them.'

Hugo laughed into the sky, picked up a stone and with brute force hurled it down into the lane. Three days later Jerry found the torn nest and the dead fledglings near the spot where the stone had landed. He didn't mention it to Hugo and he tried not to think about it, because in his heart he knew that if he had not looked for the nest in the first place the nestlings might have survived. Hugo was not a mystery then. He was like any robust and uncaring boy.

He kept thinking of his brother throughout the afternoon, seeking in vain after reason and motivation. Towards evening Hugo returned from Burke's and brought him up a cup of tea.

'What have you done with Brennan's clothes?' Father Jerry asked as he took the cup which came without its saucer.

'Nothing. They're hanging with my own clothes in my wardrobe.'

'What do you intend doing with them?'

'I could give them to the poor or I could put them on our next bonfire. To be honest I haven't given the matter my most profound thought.'

'Is it a matter that requires profound thought?'

'At the very least it requires stubborn thought.'

'I suggest you get rid of them. The parochial house is hardly the place for them.'

'If you say so, I can only believe you. A knowledge of canon law is not one of my attainments.'

He slept little that night and in the morning he did not feel well enough to say Mass. The day passed in a haze of drowsiness. Several times he dreamt that a black raven had perched on his shoulder with a swish of dirty wings. He called for Dr Sharma to put her to flight and Dr Sharma told him that nothing but feverish activity on his own part, preferably physical labour,

160

would banish her. The raven began pecking at his head, trying to drink his brains. He woke in terror with the conviction that his illness in all its horrifying unreality had returned.

At dusk Olga brought him a bowl of vegetable soup and sat by the bedside recounting the village gossip. In the shadowy room her face had lengthened. Then her hair fell forward, obscuring her neck and cheeks. After she left he fell asleep again. He knew that it was dark outside, and he was standing on a windswept platform waiting for a train. There was no timetable, no indicator, no station-master, and no one knew when the train would arrive.

'Where is it going?' he asked an old man when at last it pulled in.

'It doesn't matter. It's the last train. There will never be another.'

The train was crowded. He ran up and down the platform in the throng. Finally, he managed to get into the guard's van and found himself alone in the dark with Olga. The glow of her Gauloise provided the only light. The train was gathering speed. An ill-lit station flashed by, and then another.

'It's fast,' Olga said, as the swaying of the carriage flung her body against his. Her distended belly bounced up and down, rubbing against his own, a quagbelly threatening spillage.

'The child is Hugo's but it's yours too. Sin of lust. Sin of Father O'Mara,' she whispered.

As they rattled over points, she put her arms round his waist to keep her balance. Then came an announcement in the unmistakable accents of the Preacher: 'This is a non-stop service, there is no getting off at Paisley. The landscape through which we are passing is the landscape of eternity. Consider yourselves on the endless edge of things. In the words of a later and less quotable

161

preacher, "There is nowhere to go for further enlightenment or explanation." '

With a lunge that almost toppled Olga he made to open the door.

'Pull, don't push,' she advised. 'The door of the guard's van opens in.'

He yanked and yanked until it became obvious that the door had been double-locked. Then Olga put her arms round him again and pressed her belly against his. Now she was eternally pregnant and present. Her Gauloise glowed but did not burn. He was overcome with grief; a senseless, bottomless grief, the grief of his illness persisting for ever. No *jouissance*, no desire except one: death, the ultimate good, denied for all eternity. A phrase came to mind, doxology and great amen, and he could not recall where he had heard it. Tears ran down his cheeks. He pushed Olga unceremoniously away.

The house was in darkness when he woke. He became aware of the stuttering of the sea. The stuttering ceased. He heard a laugh, a smothered, conspiratorial laugh that could only have come from Hugo's bedroom. He got up and switched on the landing light, then went back to bed and lay awake in the dark with his door open. In his mind he went over everything that Olga had ever said to him, and he acknowledged a grief quite distinct from that of his dream. After half an hour she came out of Hugo's room and switched off the light before stealing down the stairs. In the morning he knocked on Hugo's door and told him never to invite her to the parochial house again.

'Why?' Hugo asked, his beard sticking up over the rim of the blanket.

'She was with you in this room last night.'

'You're quick to jump to conclusions. We had a drink and a

162

chat, then between us we finished the crossword. There was no hanky and no panky, no jiggery and no pokery. We didn't commit fornication, if that's what you want to know.'

'This is a parochial house, not a night club. If you invite Olga in here again, you will have to find yourself bed and board elsewhere.'

'You're a hard man, Father. You're hard on everyone except yourself.'

Hugo pulled the bedclothes up over his head and emitted a long, vibrant snore.

Chapter 14

In the afternoon he felt strong enough to get up. Neither he nor Hugo mentioned Olga, and she did not come to the parochial house again. Though he did his best to avoid her, he could not keep from thinking about her. She had blurred the clarity of his image of her. Like her wood carving of the weeping woman, she had become shadowed and ambiguous, full of dark and unacknowledgeable promptings. Perhaps it was not her fault. What he had seen in her was not an errant human being but a refined reflection, a woman who had sprung fully armed from his head.

He would turn his back and not look over his shoulder. Some things in life were best forgotten. The world of memory and desire was seductive and transforming, and simply had to be transcended. Hugo was immersed in that world, a warm equatorial lake of floating weeds and algae. Better to live in the icy blue waters of the Arctic that enliven every body cell with an awareness of discomfort and animate the mind itself with a knowledge of mind-in-body.

One evening a week later, as he was laying out milk and biscuits for two, a sharp double-knock at the door made him think of her. He paused in the hallway, waiting for another knock. The middle-aged man who looked up at him took him by surprise. He was short, bald and stocky, and a shade too neatly dressed for the country.

'I'm John Delgany,' he said. 'I was passing and I thought I'd introduce myself.'

Father Jerry invited him into the study and offered him a seat but not a glass of milk. His suspicion that his visitor was none other than Brennan redux was soon confirmed.

'I've just bought the late Mr Brennan's business. I thought it would be a good idea if we talked.'

'Did you buy it as a businessman or as a philanthropist performing a corporal work of mercy?'

'As a businessman, of course. As a shrewd one, I hope. The receiver made me an offer I couldn't refuse. I'm arranging a government grant and with a bit of luck we'll get a loan from the EEC. All in all the future looks bright.'

'As you may have heard, I was not among Brennan's most ardent admirers. I've always thought, and still do, that he did irreparable harm here.'

'I've been told about your differences. What I had hoped was that you and I might reason together and try to see things as they are. Unlike Mr Brennan, I'm a stranger here. I start with a clean slate and the hope that I can rely on the support of the community and especially of its leaders.'

Father Jerry launched into a ten-minute lecture to which Mr Delgany listened in cheerful silence.

'Not all priests think as you do,' he said as he rose to go. 'I've already spoken to Canon Hackler, a most practical and far-sighted man. I think we see eye to eye.'

Canon Hackler 'looked in' the following evening. Ostensibly,

165

he had come to enquire about his curate's health, and indeed he devoted fifteen minutes to recounting his own experiences of wettings and sudden chills. Father Jerry poured him the obligatory bumper of Balvenie while trying to divine the true purpose of his visit. First the canon spoke about the bell and how it had aroused the interest of the bishop. While he realised that it was primarily Father Jerry's concern, he could not help feeling that the bishop would hold the parish priest responsible for any lack of urgency in replacing it. At last he came to Mr Delgany's visit and his own belief that priests must show leadership in all matters affecting the material welfare of the parish.

'We must keep our young men at home where we can keep an eye on them. In this case spiritual salvation depends on material good. As a man who began his ministry in a sinful city, you're bound to agree.'

'I've seen more ungodliness on the Glebe than I ever saw in London.'

Canon Hackler did not reply; his mind was on higher things. Mr Delgany's talent for business had obviously reminded him of the need for sound financial management in the Church. He discoursed at length and with elephantine flatulence on the merits of bingo as opposed to charity dances in fund raising, and he recommended that Father Jerry start a weekly bingo evening in the motel. He had raised the possibility with Mr Delgany whose attitude could not have been more helpful. Father Jerry was sympathetically non-committal. He praised Mr Delgany for his sartorial elegance and he agreed that bingo, though less enlivening, was a more innocent pastime than dancing which was the kind of thing they did in sinful cities.

Canon Hackler put down his glass with a force that betrayed extreme irritation, and picked up his hat by the brim. In the hallway he turned and gave his curate a long look of steadfast scrutiny.

'You look tired. Perhaps you need a rest.'

'I'm feeling much better now, thank you.'

'If you ever wish for a change of parish, do tell me. A word in the bishop's ear never goes unheard.'

'It's very kind of you. I've already told the bishop that I'm happy here, serving my people as I think they should be served.'

'Serving is more than praying, which in a sense is only self-exploration. We live in the world and we must give the world its due. We must look outwards with a readiness to make compacts and compromises, to beat the Devil at his own game.'

Alone in his study again, Father Jerry dropped into his softest armchair. He did not reject the world for reasons of theology or philosophy, he simply did not believe in it. The only reality that had any meaning for him was the reality within. Even his interest in Hugo's diary arose from his conviction that he could make it into a vehicle for self-realisation. Canon Hackler would not, and could not, understand. Like most churchmen he saw the world as a straying cow that must be caught and milked. And if the cow turned out to be a bull, he would not be deterred in his milking. His fellow-clergy deemed him a success and eagerly sought his advice at chapter. Father Jerry thought different. The more he saw of other priests, the more he inclined to think with Nietzsche that 'There has been only one Christian and He died on the cross.'

On Friday morning Hugo came down the stairs in a black jacket and trousers. Bearded and somewhat obese, he looked like a dishevelled patriarch of Constantinople.

'I'm taking Olga to Dublin for the weekend,' he said.

167

'Again and so soon?'

'I must see about my missing diaries. Without them I'm a gelding.'

'You're soberly dressed.'

'I was hoping you'd like the cut of my jib. The jacket is Brennan's and so are the trousers. I dyed them at Burke's thinking that you might appreciate the symbolism. Understandably, the trousers are a bit tight at the crotch. Only an innocent would expect wonders from the lost-property office.'

'It's a jape you may live to regret.'

'The colour scheme is not ideal for separates. Sadly, we must make do. Life is an accident. There is so little that is planned and pondered. Now, if Brennan could have foreseen the use to which his ensemble would be put, he would have chosen a fabric of a different colour. A suit of white cotton would have dyed beautifully. Nothing is perfect. God who ordains, bless His soul, has such an extraordinary sense of imperfection.'

Father Jerry watched him drive down the avenue. His brother saw life as a game of moral choices. The choices, of course, were for other people, never for himself. He was a puppeteer who pulled strings, whose greatest delight lay in prediction and anticipation. Recently, he'd been taciturn and preoccupied. He spent whole evenings with Olga and recorded nothing in his diary except detailed and rather tedious accounts of the work of renovation at Burke's. Father Jerry was surprised, therefore, to find an entry about Olga that had been written the previous night:

September 15th

I write in haste, my thoughts leapfrogging my hand. To Dublin with Helga in the morning. Another opportunity; another train

I must not miss. I've seen a lot of her in the last few weeks, and in a sense I've seen nothing. What does she want? Or should I say, 'What doesn't she want?' It's all beyond me. Is it Father Johnnie who's on her mind? I know that she's on his. McDowd is out of the running; now it's a battle between siblings. It's a battle he can't win without losing more than he can give up unscathed. He's a holy man with unholy preoccupations. My aim must be to sharpen his self-awareness; to get him to question his calcified morality, to give a sermon that relates to something other than itself. The only morality that keeps you alive and alert is one you have to make up as you go along. There I am his manifest superior. In my library (I mean my rucksack) are no sacred texts. No Bible. No *Summa*. Nothing given. Nothing received. My life is a Thermopylae. New swordsmen come out to meet me in the pass every morning, and I am the last Spartan standing. I suppose I should be grateful.

Helga doesn't know me. She's too troubled in herself to get to know me. She seems to like me now. For all I know she may love me but deep within her is something dark that holds her back. Yesterday I took her to see the Termon Stone and recounted the story of the Game. I made her read the inscription: 'Arty Bradley 1941–86. Many's the good Rub he had here'. It was early morning. We stood with our backs to the east looking down at our shadows on the oblong rock, twelve feet by six and two feet high, flat on top and covered with greyish lichen. I felt that we had shared a moment of mystery. I was about to tell her why we called it the Termon Stone when suddenly she turned and walked away.

'How is Father Johnnie?' she asked when I caught up with her.

'Fighting demons like Columcille before him.' 'Is he still angry?'

'Of course not. Anger is for lesser mortals like you and me. As a priest, he mustn't let the sun go down on his.'

'He was kind to me. I can't help feeling that I've disappointed him.'

'Then you must go into his confessional in the dark and tell him you haven't sinned with me. Tell him that the only sins we've committed are those in his own inflamed imagination.'

Again she walked away and this time I did not follow. When she came back, I returned to the Termon Stone and the unchanging ritual of the Game. She listened only for a minute before interrupting.

'Is Father Johnnie an artist or a scientist?' she asked.

'He's an artist to judge by the length of his fingers. They're so long and thin that they could have been painted by El Greco.'

'To me he's a scientist, perhaps a pathologist.'

'You mean he deals in diseased souls?'

'I once watched him eating a sea trout. He held the knife and fork so that they were almost vertical and he made an incision along the lateral line before stripping the trout of its skin.'

'Was he wearing a white smock or a black cassock at the time?'

'It was an operation of the utmost delicacy. He picked the backbone clean and then folded the skin over it, as if he wished to pretend to himself that he had not eaten.'

'It doesn't surprise me. As a boy he used to blow eggs. O he was a queer one, Fol dol the di do.'

I could see that my conversation was not having the desired effect. Perhaps a visit to Scariff Island would do the trick, I thought. I've made up my mind. I'll choose a calm day with a warm sun. We'll sit on the hogsback and grill two sea trout on a spit. I'll hold my knife vertically and make an incision along the lateral line with chirurgical delicacy, and she'll say to me, 'Hugo,

170

you're a scientist. Now at last I can love you.'

There is so much I want to tell her but the time is not ripe. If I showed her the knobbly sea stack now, she'd think me crude. Yet some time I must tell her that when I was a boy I knew it as the Stake. Then one day an old fisherman told me its secret name and it became my pillar of cloud by day and my pillar of fire by night – in the Ivory Coast, New Guinea and the Amazonian jungle. How can she understand these things? How can I make myself clear?

She's a haunted woman. In Dublin she never feels safe. Once we lost our way heading north for the N4. Another motorist who saw my plight rolled down his window at some traffic lights and asked me if I wanted help. When I told him where I was heading, he said, 'Follow me'. We followed him for five minutes. Then we got caught at the next set of lights, though he got through. Further along he pulled in and waited. That did it. Helga panicked. I could hear her heart pounding as she made me take a quick left. I had no idea what had come over her, until she told me that our 'guide' was the spitting image of her husband Dom.'

He closed his eyes, aware of nothing but a man and a woman alone in a speeding vehicle. Again he examined the hurried hand, half-regretting that he'd returned the anonymous letter to Canon Hackler. Dr Sharma had once said to him, 'Unbeknown to yourself you are seeking to discover your place in the sexual universe. Though celibate by choice and perhaps by inclination, you do have a place. You can't ignore women and neither can they ignore you.' Dr Sharma was herself unmarried. She was the only woman he'd ever met who seemed entirely free of sexual compulsion. A wise virgin? Better still, a vestal virgin who tended no hearth but her own.

171

He looked round the room. The large bed was unmade, and on a chair in the corner lay an untidy pile of vests and under-pants. On the carpet by the bed was a heap of old newspapers and an odd sock. Nothing was in its place because nothing had a place – except the faded photograph of their dead mother that stood accusingly on the mantelpiece between an empty tobacco tin and a bottle of black ink. He gazed at the picture, trying to recall something of her physical presence. He was rewarded with a memory of rustling underwear and a vague warmth that smelt of cloves. The curtains of the open window moved. Fine dust floated in a slanting sunbeam that seemed to spring up from beneath the wardrobe.

He opened the door of the wardrobe, wondering if Hugo had really dyed Brennan's clothes. In the bottom, between two pairs of brogues, stood a wood carving that caused him to blink in bafflement. He picked it up and half-reluctantly turned it over in his hands. It was a grotesque piece of work, about two feet high, crudely executed and utterly lacking in proportion: the skull of a sheep on an emaciated body with protuberant breasts and but-tocks. The arms of the sheep-woman extended outwards, while the legs bent at the knees as if she were about to leap off the blocklike base. In the skull were two gaping eye-sockets and between her legs hung a ridged mound that looked like an open sporran. The ugliness that the figure communicated was at once inside and outside himself. Within a volume of less than a cubic foot it embodied all the loathsomeness of Brennan's glen, which had now become a cold and leaden faecalith in his bowels.

He put the figurine back in the wardrobe and firmly closed the door. What he had seen was the work of an artist who was living through a nightmare with her grip on daylight and sanity insecure. He went to his own bedroom and uncovered the carving of the weeping woman, so fine and lovingly done, so full of the expression of human vulnerability in a cold and indifferent world. He placed it on the windowsill and caressed the head and hair down to her knees. Clearly Olga, in a mood of disenchantment and cynicism, had carved different artifacts for different men.

Below the window the sea had become an eternity of dark blue fading into the pellucid blue of the sky. The day was bright and windless, the outline of the hills sharp and clear. What he wished for was the spiritual austerity of Savonarola, the passion of Luther, and the intellectual clarity of Aquinas. He carried the carving of the weeping woman out to the garage and laid it on a plank on the concrete floor. Then he took an axe belonging to Hugo and split the kneeling figure down the centre along the natural crack in the wood. He made a fire in the study with sticks and paper and put one half of the mutilated carving in the centre of the flames. He sat in the armchair and watched it burn until all that remained was a fistful of floury ash. After a while he carried the other half upstairs to his room, wrapped it in a sheet, and put it back in the bottom of the wardrobe.

Just before lunch a messenger from the widow in the mountains came to tell him that her son had taken a turn for the worse. Pleased to be called out in a time of trouble, he drove up the glen as the afternoon began to mellow into evening. The car breasted the hills, the breeze grew fresher and more pungent. He was pushing forward into a stern landscape out of sight of the sea and the more populous townlands by the shore. The narrow roads had passing places, the starkly weathered houses stood alone at the end of lanes. He had left Brennan's base legacy behind in the west. The symbols of the old culture, which Brennan had enshrined in his folk museum, formed part of life's living fabric here. He felt close to nature and the nature poetry of the early Irish monks and anchorites. After visiting the boy he would drive further east into the mountains where he would be alone with a few sheep, with rocks and stones.

The widow met him at the gate, her face drawn and pale. She grasped his hand and thanked him for coming so promptly. He followed her into the narrow bedroom where the form of the boy was barely discernible under the covers of the sagging bed. Father Jerry touched his forehead and held his hand. The boy opened his eyes and made a brave attempt to smile.

'How are we feeling today?' he asked.

'My legs and arms are weak, and my back feels weak when I try to turn on my side.'

'We'll say a prayer. We'll all ask God to make you better.'

In the boy's eyes was a faraway look, as if his mind was on a country only he could see. With pity rather than hope in his heart, Father Jerry knelt by the bedside. The widow knelt next to him with her face buried in the bedclothes.

'We won't pray aloud, we'll pray silently in our hearts,' he said. 'That way we won't be distracted.'

When they had prayed for ten minutes, he gave the boy Communion. It was his first Communion, and he made it in the knowledge that it might also be his last. The boy's earnest devotion had a profound effect on him. He remembered his first Mass after ordination and the sense of awe with which he approached the Consecration. As he paused before breathing the words that would change bread into Body and Blood, his mouth went dry, so intense was his feeling of unworthiness. In the beginning each Mass was a peacemaking, bringing joy, serenity and a shedding of earthly connections. Now the sense of freshness, of daily renewal, had gone. An older priest had told him in confession,

'It's only natural. After twenty years of marriage a middle-aged husband and wife don't experience the same emotions as they experienced on their honeymoon.'

When the boy had finished his prayers of thanksgiving, he asked if the evening sun was shining on the brae. Father Jerry went to the little window and told him that the brae was covered with grasscocks that looked like giant mushrooms in the golden light.

'Will I ever run up the brae with a hoop and stick again?' the boy asked.

'Of course you will. Pray and be patient. Give yourself a little more time.'

The boy fell asleep and Father Jerry sat by the bed holding his hand while the mother knelt and prayed. He stopped thinking about the boy and began going over the most memorable events in his own spiritual life. He had sunk into a kind of trance where he floated freely beyond the pull of this world and the next. Suddenly the boy raised himself on one elbow.

'Look, my back is strong again. My strength returned in a rush this minute.'

'Good,' said Father Jerry. 'Didn't I tell you it would.'

'When did it come back?' His mother crossed herself.

'When I heard the cuckoo calling from the trees on the other side of the river.'

'Are you sure you heard the cuckoo?' Father Jerry asked.

'She called twice, then she stopped and called just one more time.'

'I heard no cuckoo,' said his mother. 'She left last month. By now she's probably half-way to Africa.'

'The cuckoo didn't call for you and me,' Father Jerry told her. 'She called specially for Sean, she made him better.'

The widow grasped his hand with tears in her eyes. Then she leant across the bed and hugged her son. Father Jerry began making ready to go. The boy was smiling and the mother was wiping away her tears.

'Take care of yourself now,' he said to the boy. 'Say your prayers morning and evening, and don't say a word to anyone about what has happened.'

He had decided not to go farther into the mountains that evening. He went straight to the car and headed for home, driving down into the glen with the setting sun beneath him shooting spokes of light at the hilltops north and south. His mind was a glassy lake unsullied by the merest reflection. He heard himself say, 'Joshua went into the desert, a day's journey ...' and he wondered how he had come to say it.

Before him the parochial house stood white and gleaming on an eminence overlooking the Glebe. Traditionally, it was a house of truth, the nerve centre of all spiritual and intellectual life here. Now it had lost its primacy to the sprawling motel with its bustle, noise and glitter. Its primacy must be reinstated. The parochial house was built on rock; it could and must stand firm against the capricious winds of chance and change.

The wheel of history had swung full circle. Fourteen hundred years ago St Columcille had come to the glen and banished the demons that had made this mist-enshrouded place their home, hurling them down the ledge called the Devils' Slide into the engulfing sea below. The demons had returned, and the Devils' Slide still hung above the sea, an enduring reminder of that first uncompromising expulsion. He parked the car at the gate and set off down the footpath to the Glebe. When he reached the height above the tents, he joined his hands and bent his head in an attitude of single-minded prayer. He would banish the

176

hippies from the glen as his great predecessor had banished the demons of his day. He would ask for one more miracle, just to dispel all doubt. He closed his eyes and visualised the hippies and their tents being whipped up to the top of the bluff by a sulphurous whirlwind that singed the trodden grass of the Glebe. Then he saw the Devils' Slide emitting a cloud of steam from the friction of sizzling bottoms slithering down into the sea far below.

He opened his eyes. Nothing moved in the shadows of the unruffled tents. The mountain on the other side of the Glebe stood fixed and solid. It was not a mountain that would ever come to him. He made his way towards a tent in which a man and a woman were lying with their legs protruding beneath the half-closed flap. They were rubbing their legs together more and more furiously, as if their whole preoccupation was the achievement of a soundless crescendo. He walked on. Perhaps it was just as well that man had to work out his own salvation without any hope of visible intervention by God in his affairs. With the exercise of divine power would surely come a new kind of human doubt and also a most terrible responsibility. God knew better. He had come and gone. Emmaus no more.

When he reached the shore, he sat on a rock and took off his shoes and socks. With his feet in the water and the waves making froth round his ankles, he looked into the thickening afterglow. The ocean was vast enough to wash five continents of the very last stain of humanity. The Council of Trent had described God as an infinite ocean of joy, at least that was what he'd read in a book during his illness in London.

'Where is this Ocean so that I may immerse in it?' he'd shouted at Dr Sharma. 'The day I set eyes on it I shall call out, "Thalassa, thalassa" for all the world to hear. And cursed be anyone who says, "Blessed are they who have not seen and still call out, 'Thalassa'." '

Dr Sharma never said a word. Now the memory of a despair that could explode in such blasphemy made him shudder. He dabbled his feet and looked across the shadowy bay with a sense of gratitude.

On the way home he said, 'St Columcille fought demons in this misty glen and defeated them. Were his demons like my hippies, not real ones but only those that raised commotion in his breast?'

Chapter 15

Sunday passed quietly. He fought the temptation to reread Hugo's diary and instead dipped into St Augustine's *Confessions* and Conrad's *Falk*. Though he tried hard, neither saint nor novelist was sufficiently potent to make him forget the unreason and disorder that impelled his brother. Hugo's all-consuming need was to misinterpret, to polish the mirrors of distortion, and to body forth the phantasmagoria of a life of mere animal urgings. Monday and Tuesday came and went without any word from Hugo. On Wednesday afternoon he rang and said that he was still in Dublin.

'I've got bad news for you,' he warned. 'Olga's body was fished out of the Liffey at low tide this morning. I thought I should tell you before the press get hold of the story.'

'I don't believe it.' He couldn't be sure if his brother was drunk but he knew that in all likelihood he wasn't entirely sober. He kept gabbling incoherently, he seemed to have lost the thread of his story.

'How did it happen?' Father Jerry kept repeating.

'Olga was not what she seemed,' Hugo answered at last. 'She didn't come to Dublin just to sell her carvings. She ran a little business on the side, entertaining rich clients in a bedroom in a certain posh hotel.'

'When did you find that out?'

'Only this morning. We were supposed to come back on Monday. She never turned up. I've spent two days looking for her. The police say her death was no accident. A punter probably strangled her and dumped her body in the river.'

Father Jerry spent the afternoon in the garden, sitting on a plank on which he'd spread out onions to dry. He peeled one of the onions with a penknife and ate layer after layer until all that remained was a greenish little bulb. He twirled it in his fingers and cut it longitudinally. An onion was an onion to the core. At first he felt anger. Towards evening he realised that what he felt most keenly was the grief of loss. He had seen her as friend and truth-teller. In their conversations she spoke so directly that he often pondered her words afterwards on his own.

'You don't believe in progress,' she had teased.

'Not material progress that cuts a swathe of destruction through an ancient and hard-won culture.'

'You'd like everything to stand still?'

'I'd accept natural change, not forced growth under plastic. The landscape is the touchstone. Anything that defiles it defiles the hearts and minds of men.'

'Our nature is to seek. We need change to provide the illusion of thriving and winning. We're all cyclists, we must keep pedalling. It's only our velocity that prevents us falling to the ground.'

'We had something precious here, a culture with an umbilical cord that enabled us to draw sustenance from a life-enriching past. We have cut the cord and thrown away a thousand years of irrecoverable experience that did not live in books but in our bones.'

'Arty Brennan saw the past as a prison-house from which he provided the means of escape. He left people with a vision they can never forget. Brennan lives. He's indestructible.'

'His works live. They remind us daily of how he rewrote the past and recoloured the pastness of the present. For that I can never forgive him.'

'He had the same upbringing as you. He rejected his childhood, while you fell in love with yours. He looked forward. You look back, seeking to reflect and understand. You resent his achievement because it makes reflection and understanding more difficult. Your vision is purely personal. His was a vision that embraced his neighbour.'

'Pity he wasn't a priest.'

'He would have made a caring priest. In loving himself he contrived to love his neighbour. It wasn't in his nature to love himself alone.'

'You have a high opinion of him.'

'Yes, I have.'

'We mustn't canonise him, at least not yet.'

She turned to go, then paused and looked back.

'You are obsessed with the symbols of a vanished life: scythes, turf-spades, spinning-wheels, butter pats, churns. Is it that you find some extraordinary spiritual value in your childhood?'

'It's more than that. It's an involuntary and perhaps irrational allegiance that can neither be inculcated nor explained. In the things in which we are most characteristically ourselves we are alone.'

'I thought you were a teacher. If you can't explain, I shall have to seek enlightenment elsewhere.'

She enjoyed poking fun at him, while disclosing nothing of herself except the play of a lively intelligence. Her death had humbled him. He had been insensitive and obtuse, too preoccupied with his own life to see her as she was, a woman with a need that she could neither acknowledge nor communicate.

He went to his bedroom and gazed at the mutilated carving. It was neither a turf-spade nor a scythe but a piece of elmwood polished smooth on one side and hacked coarsely on the other. Now nothing could restore it. He felt deeply ashamed of himself.

'I must have been an innocent,' Hugo said when he returned. 'Now, as I look back, it all seems so obvious. She tried to tell me but I didn't hear. "I can understand sex being given for love and I can understand it being given for money," she used to say. "I can even understand it not being given for either love or money. What I can't understand is the hippies on the Glebe. They give sex for sex." '

'You drove her to Dublin several times. Surely you must have had some inkling.'

'In the city we went our separate ways. I used to drop her off at a craft shop and arrange to meet her again in a pub near Grafton Street on Monday morning. She was always on time until last weekend. What she'd told me about her past – about her childhood in Munich and her marriage to a violent engineer called Dom – was all a sham. She was born of German parents in Dublin and she'd never been married. She'd spent some years on the Continent. She'd lived in Canada and Australia, a restless soul.'

'What could have brought her here?'

'Perhaps she was weary of her trade. She wanted to be an artist but she needed a reliable source of income. *Give me chastity and continence as soon as I can afford them* was her motto.'

'Did you see the body?'

'I identified it.'

'Did she look different in death?'

'If you mean, "Did she look dead?", the answer is yes.'

'I meant, "Did she seem at peace?"'

'How can you be so self-satisfied?' Hugo raged. 'You failed her, admit it. I failed her, and I know it. She was reaching out towards you and you turned your back. She saw you as her only hope and you saw her as a sexual threat. You're willing to save souls within the confines of the confessional but the red-light district is a no-go area. In industry your policy would be called restrictive practice.'

At the best of times Hugo was irascible and unpredictable. In his present mood he was incommunicado. Canon Hackler called after dinner, full of self-esteem and self-righteousness. Without waiting to be asked, he spread himself generously on the sofa that Father Jerry had vacated. Father Jerry offered him a cigarette, having decided to make him wait for his Balvenie.

'There's been gossip.'

'There's never bingo without gossip,' Father Jerry reminded him.

'You know what I mean. People are talking about the German girl.'

'It's a sad story.'

'You must feel it more than most, you knew her well.'

'She was my nearest neighbour. I tried to help her in every way I could.'

'They say she attended Mass from time to time. You can understand why people feel confused. Did she receive the Holy Sacrament?'

'No, but she always seemed charitable and well disposed.'

'Did she come to you for confession?'

'No.'

'That at least is something. It would have been serious if she had been receiving the sacraments sacrilegiously.'

'As I look back, I realise that she may have come here to make a break with the past. She may even have been seeking spiritual help. At the time, of course, I had no idea.'

'It's a lesson to all of us. A priest can never be too careful in his relationships with women.'

'She never said or did anything improper in my company. She loved the glen, and everyone who knew her liked her.'

'Unfortunately, there is the possibility of scandal. You can imagine the kind of thing that most people will think and some people will say.'

'That I'd made friends with a wicked woman? We must remember that Christ consorted with sinners.'

'But He took care not to cause scandal except to Pharisees.'

'The Pharisees are always with us. They hold high office in the Church.'

'That's a dangerous thought. Authority rests on humble acceptance. A good priest is a good listener.'

'If you feel uneasy about my conduct, Canon, I can only assure you that there was nothing prurient or improper in it.'

'The thought of impropriety never entered my head. I'm not here to judge, I merely wish to forestall the likelihood of wrong judgment. I met your brother as I came in. I hadn't realised he still lives with you.'

'Oh, yes.'

'He knew the German girl, of course?'

'They were friends, though not what the newspapers call "intimate".'

'You're satisfied that is so?'

'I'll put it like this: I'm as certain as I can be in the circumstances.'

'There is always doubt, and rumour feeds on it. You must understand my concern. I think it might be better if your brother lived elsewhere.'

'At the moment he's distressed. When he gets over the shock, I'll speak to him.'

'And I shall speak to the bishop. It is my duty, you understand.'

'Of course.'

'I shall say no more than is necessary. It is best that he should hear of this from me than from another, possibly less scrupulous, source.'

Canon Hackler raised his eyes to the ceiling and drummed with his fingers on his short, fat thighs. Father Jerry got up and went to the sideboard.

'I'm afraid I'm out of Balvenie.' It was a white lie but justified in the circumstances, he thought. 'Would you care for a drop of Irish instead?'

'No, thank you, I must be going. There's always work in the vineyard, even at the eleventh hour.'

He raised himself awkwardly from the sofa with the help of both hands. At the door he grasped Father Jerry by the sleeve and said, 'Don't feel disheartened, I pray for you every day.' Father Jerry watched him waddle to the car with his fists deep in his jacket pockets, a wide, ungainly barge bearing heavy cargo. After he'd settled himself in the driver's seat, he rolled down the window.

'I'll look in again next week,' he called. 'There's much to talk about and much to ponder: bingo, the bell and Mr Delgany's plans for the glen. If I know anything, he's even more dynamic than Arty Brennan. I'll try to get here a little earlier. Who knows, I may even have time for a Balvenie.'

Father Jerry spent an hour considering how to evict Hugo without severing diplomatic relations and starting an unholy war that would only provide further fodder for gossip. His brother had become more volatile and at the same time more saturnine. Olga's death had extinguished not only light but also joy, desire, ambition, faith, hope and charity itself. He went to his bedroom and read the latest entry in the diary:

September 23rd
In death she looked foreign, an exile who'd lost her way. She was wearing slim, black trousers and a white, silk shirt that clung transparently to her breasts. Her face looked fuller and her head smaller. Her hair had been flattened into strips, reminding me of Carmel. Knowing the past that she had concealed, I looked down at her body, seeing her finally and for the first time. I kept thinking of the day she lay under the lee of a rock between me and McDowd, so remote and so superior to both of us. Sadly, I never saw her as she saw herself. I saw her hair, lips and hips. I had neither eye nor ear for the woman who was trying to escape from them. As the doctor pulled the sheet over her face again, I had a sense of completion that filled me with self-loathing. On the way back to my hotel I passed a factory with a tall chimney, the white smoke thinning before vanishing into clear air. O most insatiate and luxurious woman! All I could think of was two lives wasted. She should have said, 'Hugo, I have a secret I can't share. If you knew it, you'd run a mile from me.' 'Try me,' I would have replied. And having said it, I wouldn't have reneged. She gave more of herself to Father Johnnie than to me. She bared her

bosom to the blind because she knew it to be a fruitless exercise. I was too extreme for her. When she looked at me, she saw a rough-hewn savage instead of the savage moralist that I am. She could have carved me down to size and polished me till I shone. She could have shaved off my beard. Anything would have been better than this.

I did a rough carving of a sheep-woman which was a portrait of both of us in one. I spent a day at Burke's trying to get it right. I had meant her to polish it. She was proud, proud, proud. No weakness, no need of sympathy. She preferred to live her tragedy alone. She came out of nowhere like a mushroom after a warm night. Was she less original than I thought? She failed to realise that the Helga I saw would have freed from the past the Helga she herself knew. She rejected me because I did not give back the desired reflection.

I'm sick of Burke's. It's only a Wendy House. She's pulled out the carpet from under it.

'Your prayers have been answered,' Hugo informed him two days later. 'The hippies have gone from the Glebe.'

Father Jerry looked at him, seeking mockery in his smile.

'It can't be true.'

'Prayers *are* sometimes answered. Come here and see for yourself.'

He went to the window and looked down on an empty stretch of flat, sandy ground.

'It's hard to credit. Not one tent left.'

'They went out over the hill, bag and backpack, at seven o'clock this morning. I was in the bathroom at the time, I saw it all.'

'Pity you didn't call me. I'd give anything to have seen it. Now the rabbits will return to the Glebe and everything will be

187

the same again.'

'Everything?'

'Well, perhaps not everything.'

'Certainly not Olga's cottage. Someone broke in last night and smeared the walls with excrement. It's a reeking mess: wardrobes and drawers ransacked, filth everywhere. I rang the police. They didn't seem surprised. They said that they'd already removed all the evidence they needed for the inquest.'

'Who could have done such a thing?'

'McDaid, who else? He was hinting dark things yesterday. He blames me for her death.'

'How absurd.'

'He's convinced that I discovered she was on the game and couldn't face it. A classic case of projection.'

'You overdramatise McDaid. Behind the sinister appearance lies a schoolboy innocence.'

'Then let me tell you a little story. I was fishing in Bolliska two evenings ago, standing on a rock with the cliff behind me. I had just caught a pollack and it was flapping about in the bag between my feet. Then I heard another noise overhead and I saw a big rock rolling down the cliff face. I dived under a ledge, and not a second too soon. The rock landed on the bag and made pulp of the pollack. I lay under the ledge for half an hour, afraid to put out my head. When I climbed up the bank again, I saw the bed where the rock had come from – more than ten feet from the brink. I'm sure you're a good enough Thomist to know that whatever moves is moved by another. Quod movetur ab alio movetur.'

'The mover wasn't necessarily McDaid.'

Hugo was sweating from the exertion of re-enactment. He went to the window and stood with his back to Father Jerry.

'Have you forgotten the cut brake pipes?' he shouted. 'What we've had over the past few months was only a cold war. The stone-rolling is the opening shot in a fresh round of hostilities.'

Father Jerry left him to his ranting and set off down the foot-path to the Glebe. His excitement cooled when he saw the state in which the hippies had left what was once a clean and pleasant strip of ground. He walked across a littered waste land, kicking cardboard cartons, plastic containers and empty cans and bottles out of his way. In the trodden grass were patches of bare earth where the tents had stood, and among them heaps of broken straw with here and there a flesh-coloured condom. Over the whole area hung a heavy burnt smell, heavier than that of a rabbit warren in an airless summer.

The hippies differed from those other travellers, the tinkers, who had an ancient culture of their own with songs, music and an oral literature. The tinkers were country people, skilled in field craft and respectful of country ways. The hippies were dirty, sub-versive and anarchic, contemptuous of organised modes of life, without allegiance to either place or place name. Now, happily, they had gone, and what they had left behind tugged at his innards, opening up a vacuum of despair in his stomach. The Glebe would have to be made fit for rabbits to live in. Tomorrow he would pay two strong men to collect the litter and bury it deep in the sand.

'If I had prayed for them to leave that evening, would I now be a different man?' he asked himself. 'The most contented priests are those who don't take their priesthood seriously. So what is a priest to do who seeks more than bingo and the trivial round can furnish?'

The love of God tested keenly, if only because His face remained unseen. Now and again, as in the recovery of the mountain boy and the departure of the hippies, you might be

189

tempted to think that He had revealed Himself, but you could never be entirely certain. He left you to your own devices. As an Anglican clergyman, with whom he was once friendly, used to say, 'Unlike a wife, God never hides your whisky.'

He walked the length of the Glebe to the shore and stood on the sand dunes looking into the face of the sea. The surface of the water was a thousand broken mirrors flashing and winking in the sun. Waves advanced and retreated, flecking wet sand with quickly vanishing foam. In and out, in and out. No respite. No end. As he watched and listened, he became aware of the first deep stirrings of a grief that was new.

On a warm June morning he had met her returning from the shops with a bulging carrier bag. She was wearing white trousers and a white, crumpled jacket with a light-pink shirt underneath. He felt hot and uncomfortable. She looked cool and aloof as she stood in the road facing the breeze from the sea. They made light conversation for five minutes, a middle-aged priest in heavy black and a young woman in airy white, while a corncrake called from a meadow.

'This morning I watched two men in a field with their hands joined and their heads bent, looking down at the earth between their feet,' she said. 'I stood opposite, concealed by a hedge, wondering what they could be up to. I felt as if I'd made a discovery, that I'd seen all humanity in its abject emptiness and futility. After a while they walked away through the long grass of the field. When they'd gone, I came out from behind the hedge and saw that they'd been looking down at an oblong slab half-buried in moss and ferns.'

'It's St Columcille's Day today, the 9th of June. The stone was once an upright cross. They were praying, "doing the station", as we say.'

'How extraordinary! I had a vision of deluded humanity. Ignorance in my case was a kind of enlightenment. Your explanation has left me naked.'

'You were wrong but at least you were wildly wrong. Never just be wrong. Contrive to be as wrong as Luther, Marx and Nietzsche.'

She flipped back her hair and laughed critically but amicably. She had come to the glen because of a 'remarkable echo in the mountains'. Now he could not help feeling that the remarkable echo had died with her.

He walked back slowly to the parochial house and wrote a postcard to Dr Sharma:

Wherever I look I see motion. Trees in a wind, their branches galloping. A pent-up sea with the back of a wrinkly monster, all the vexation of unavailing thought concealed beneath that writhing, creeping skin. What we long for is perpetual rest. No ebb, no flow, only slack water *in aeternum*. No pain, no pleasure. The burden of thought and feeling shed for ever.

After dinner he took down a book of love poems by Donne. Between poems he would close the book and think of Hugo, McDaid and Olga, because he could not think of one without thinking of the other two. Towards midnight he heard the front door open, then his brother's heavy stomp on the stairs.

'Hugo lives in a hell of his own making,' he said. 'Life is not monstrous enough or lurid enough to satisfy his imagination. He must invest everyone he meets with a history of demonic malignity.'

191

Part III

Dr Sharma

Chapter 16

He was twenty minutes late getting up. He shaved in haste because he disliked keeping the five village women and the middle-aged bachelor who came to Mass on weekdays waiting. As he hurried to his car, he heard a muffled groan from the garden. He peered round the corner of the house and saw Hugo trussed in a net that dangled from the tallest of the sycamores.

With a mixture of anger and impatience he got the ladder from the garage and lowered the net to the ground on a rope. When he'd cut him free, Hugo emitted a litany of curses and touched his ankle where a knot on the rope that bound him had chafed the skin.

'I can't talk to you now, I'm half an hour late for Mass already.'

'Ah, you mustn't keep the faithful waiting but it's permissible to keep your brother hanging from a tree.'

'I didn't leave you hanging. I must go now. We'll talk when I get back.'

The five old women and the middle-aged bachelor looked round when he entered the nave. He told them that he'd been unavoidably delayed and that they would be rewarded at another time and in another place for the loyalty to the Mass that they had shown in waiting so patiently and so prayerfully. He said it to make them feel guilty. He knew perfectly well that they had been seething in their seats for the past half-hour. As a gesture of mollification, he said Mass quickly, struggling earnestly to put the nightmare of Hugo's life from his mind. He returned to the parochial house to find Hugo in bed with a bandaged head.

'How did it happen?' he demanded more with annoyance than sympathy.

'Same as last time. I was coming home after two or three pints at the motel when someone gave me a wallop of a stick on the back of the head. I came round and found myself bound and gagged between earth and heaven. I waited six hours in agony. I thought you'd never get up.'

'You must go to the police at once. This is no longer a practical joke.'

'It's the second shot in a war to the death. I shall be firing the third and last.'

'If you don't go to the police, I shall.'

'It's none of your business. This is a matter between me and McDaid. It's obvious that the net and the tree were Brennan's idea first time round. Poor old Mandamus is so deficient in imagination that he couldn't think of a better trick. I suppose we shall be having a rerun of the brake pipes too – if he gets half a chance.'

Father Jerry went downstairs to get breakfast. There was no talking to Hugo, and there was no living with him, not in a house where love, not enmity, should be the governing emotion. He got up in the afternoon and drove off to Burke's. Father Jerry went to his room to see if he'd been writing up his diary. He found an entry which, to judge by the handwriting, had been written in bed:

September 30th

While Helga lived, I made plans. So many things have come to an end, even small things that should not matter but do. What's to become of the sheep-woman now? Should I give her to Father Jerry for his birthday? She had begun teaching me the rudiments of carving. I was a willing pupil, though my mind ran on matters less artistic. I borrowed two of her chisels and set to work. I wanted to surprise her. Everything she said came true:

'If you want to carve a horse, cut away everything that isn't a horse, or at least everything that doesn't amount to horseness.'

To be honest I didn't know what to carve. Then her breasts appeared out of the wood, aggressively cantilevered, poking and piercing, shouting randiness through the cable-stitch of her pullover. Next came a pair of steatopygous buttocks that weren't hers. I tried to make them callipygous but the grain of the wood ran against me. Finally came the sheep's head and the sporran below. I laid down my chisel and stood back to admire.

'Put money in my purse,' she screamed.

How could I have missed the message of my own clairvoyance? She should have told me. Even money is better than worms. She reminded me so much of Mary Rose, the same quick mind and body. And like McDowd, I wanted to resurrect the Game with her. The game, the game! The thought of it makes me violent. I took her up the hill for a second look at the Termon Stone. I told her everything about the Game, and how Father Johnnie used to play it too. She laughed at that. She must have thought him a right hypocrite, preaching purity and sanctity thirty years on. It's as if Mr Cox had raised his orange pippin at the age of twelve and spent the rest of his days going about

197

preaching that all apples are Dead Sea fruit. As we sat on the Termon Stone, I put my hand on her knee to feel the fabric of her dress.

'It's very elastic,' I said. 'Is it nylon?'

'You're heavy-handed,' she replied. 'Or rather your hand is heavy.'

I wondered if she regarded sex as a bag of sweets that she was saving up till Father Johnnie saw the light – or saw her as his light o' love. Nothing is more blinding than an obsession. I simply failed to see her as she was.

Memories of the Game keep coming back. It was a sacred ritual that never varied, and like all rituals it gripped the imagination of the freemasonry who took part in it. I suppose it was natural that Arty Bradley, McDowd, Father Johnnie, Mary Rose and I should play together after school. First we played simple hide and seek till Brother Johnnie, bless him, gave it a twist that both enriched and impoverished our lives.

As I recall it now, the four of us would sit on the Termon Stone facing north with our hands over our eyes, while Mary Rose hid somewhere on the mountainside behind us. Then she would give a long wail that would echo round the hills and make it impossible to say from which direction it had come. We would all set off to find her, each following his own nose, and then the victor would lead her back to the Termon Stone with one arm round her. She would lie on the Termon Stone with legs splayed while the victor pulled down his trousers. The defeated three would gather round the rock and watch the two of them going through the motions of sexual intercourse as they imagined it. When the business of the Game was done, the lucky protagonists would rise from their bed and the three excited witnesses would give an echoing cheer that would skate round the tops of the hills behind them.

For a man who invented the Game, Brother Johnnie was singularly inept at playing it. So, for that matter, were McDowd and myself. It was always Arty Bradley who found her and enjoyed 'the thrill of the Rub', as he called it. McDowd, Brother Johnnie and I did our best, but it seemed as if she knew in advance where we'd look – or, more to the point, where Arty Bradley would look. Only he had the key to the castle; the rest of us were condemned to remain outside, peeping at the feast through a loophole. We're still peeping, almost by choice, because nothing excites the imagination more than deprivation. Perhaps I'm to blame for never shaking off the voyeurism of the vanquished. In the beds of the sexiest women that New Guinea and the Solomons could offer, I kept seeing Bradley's dimpled buttocks in the sun, while manfully struggling to visualise my own. Throughout my life I've been cursed with double vision. All I wish for is one good eye and the innocence and joy that come with it; to be granted the gift of skating skittishly over life's thin ice without ever looking over my shoulder. Can that be too much to ask, O Lord?

It fell to me to keep the score-book, which regrettably has gone the way of my diaries. I still remember the final reckoning as at June 23rd, 1955, and I'll remember it if I live to a hundred:

On two occasions none of us found her, so Bradley comes out with a success rate of 95.3 per cent, enough to get him a starred first at the most reputable of universities. Undoubtedly, it set him up to win the material success that followed. Sadly, if that's the

Arty Bradley	61
Thomas ('Mandamus') McDowd	0
Hugo McSharry	0
Brother Johnnie	1
	62

word, his luck ran out on Scariff Island within sight of a sea stack that never troubled his dreams. For me, though, a problem remains: how to exorcise those sixty-one humiliations so distant and still so looming.

Helga, Helga, what I miss most is your peculiar way of putting things. On the road to Dublin we stopped for fish and chips in Enniskillen.

'It's expensive for what it is.' I showed her the bill.

'It's gastronomical,' she replied with neither blink nor smile.

Now I shall never know whether it was a witticism or a genuine malapropism. If it was a witticism, it was her last with me. Perhaps it's typical of our relationship that I was too preoccupied at the time to laugh.

Father Jerry put down the diary, regretting the compulsive curiosity that had led him to open it. Hugo's continuing obsession with the Game reminded him of his own no less insistent preoccupation with Mary Rose during his illness in London. Then his memories of their life together in the city had become so oppressive in their vividness that it took Dr Sharma over a year to reclaim him for everyday living.

Hugo was correct in saying that the inventor of the Game was not its most brilliant exponent. At least he'd had the excuse of poor health, which was more than Hugo and McDaid could plead. He was also more ambitious than either of them. Though a poor runner, always last of the field, he could not accept that Brennan should always be king. He, too, wanted to experience the Rub. He dreamt of it nightly. He felt faint whenever Mary Rose touched him at play. One day the schoolmaster read them the story of how Ulysses escaped from the cave of Polyphemus. The next time they played the Game he resolved to win by cunning. Instead of roaming the hillside in search of Mary Rose, he hid in an old sheep pen and waited. As he watched through the holes of the dry-stone wall, it seemed to him that the others had vanished into the ground. Then he heard the thudding of a runner, Mary Rose coming towards him, making straight for the pen. His breathing and heartbeat quickened. She was within six yards of him when suddenly she veered down the hill. He jumped over the wall of the pen and gave chase. There was a shout of anger from his left. He saw Brennan closing in on her, already too late. At last the health-giving Rub was his. He led her back in triumph to the Termon Stone, while Brennan protested and his unpaid lackey McDaid lent boisterous support. Mary Rose was a brick. She lay with her legs wide open and he lay on top of her with his trousers down, but only Hugo raised his fist and shouted at the sky. As he rose, he realised with a gripe of fear that his twin sister Carmel had been looking on.

'Where have you come from?' Hugo asked. 'Don't you know you're not supposed to follow us up the hill.'

'I'm going home to tell Mammy,' she threatened.

'Tell her what?' Brennan laughed.

'What Jerry did to Mary Rose.'

'He didn't do anything,' McDaid swore with a grin.

'He lay on top of her. I saw it all. He pulled her knickers down.'

'Come on, it's bonfire night tonight. We'll all go to the top of the hill and pull a cart-load of heather.' Hugo took Carmel's hand.

They climbed the hillside to the plateau where the heather was deepest, and he prayed to Mary Magdalene that Carmel would forget what she'd seen. It was a rosy summer evening with the fragrance of wild flowers in the air and the bare strand below forming a sweeping sickle half-hidden in grey-green bent-grass.

On the north side of the glen the cornfields and potato patches looked greener than the meadows, the potato tops already obscuring the ridges after being earthed up early. In another two hours every hill and height would be crowned with a bonfire, flames rising hungrily into the twilight, as young men and women made fun and heaped the dry heather higher. It was his favourite time of year, and as he looked down on broken threads of smoke rising from cottage chimneys, he held Carmel's hand and tried to talk to her as if nothing unusual had happened. They came to a sheltered hollow, and she ran on ahead, skipping lightly.

'I'm tired of the Game,' Hugo said. 'I'm not going to play it any more.'

'Neither am I.'

'Was the Rub worth waiting for?'

'There's nothing to it. I got no good out of it at all.'

'Maybe it's time Arty Brennan and Mary Rose played it on their own,' Hugo said.

'Maybe if we don't play it, Mary Rose won't want to play it either.'

'You'd better promise Carmel sweets. If you don't, she's bound to tell.'

He followed her over the rim of the hollow, while Hugo joined Brennan, McDaid and Mary Rose. He tried to take her hand, and she told him that she preferred to skip on her own. Concealing his anxiety, he stooped and pulled a clump of heather. It was long, dry, bushy heather with gnarled roots that tore through the soft peat-moss and suddenly snapped, causing him to fall backwards with his legs in the air. When he got to his feet, he saw Carmel on all fours stealing up on a ewe that was lying on her side chewing the cud. The ewe took off across the breast of the hill. Calling to Carmel to wait, he gave chase as the other sheep scattered before him. He followed the ewe through peat-hags and eroded gullies until she finally jumped a cutting and left him standing.

Puffed, he sat down with his head between his legs and cursed the asthma that had stolen the breath from his lungs. Beside him was a pool with darting tadpoles stirring up brown clouds of mire at the bottom. He began prodding their tails with a stalk of melic grass to make them flit and dive as quick as minnows. He lay for a long time waiting to get his breath back, and observed the busy life of the pool which seemed to resemble the life of a teeming city viewed from high up in the heavens.

'Where's Carmel?' Hugo came up behind him.

'I thought she'd gone back down the hill to you.'

'I haven't seen her. Maybe she's wandered off on her own.'

'She doesn't know this part of the hill. She could get lost.'

'I don't think so,' said Hugo. 'That would solve your problem too neatly.'

He cupped his hands and called her name but he got no answer. He climbed a peat-hag to get a better view and called her name again.

'Don't waste your breath, it's short enough,' Hugo scoffed. 'She's probably home by now helping Mother to make scones and telling her the latest about you and Mary Rose.'

When they came in for tea, their mother asked if they'd seen Carmel. Early the next morning a search party from the townland found her body in the lough not far from where she had been skipping. They carried her home and put her lying on a white sheet on the bed. Her fine, long hair was flattened, her lips closed tight over her teeth. She looked pale and unconcerned. Her bright pink dress was a muddy brown.

'You needn't worry now,' Hugo said. 'I'll never spill the beans.'

'If we had carried on looking for her, we might have found her. She's dead because we gave up too soon.'

Their house was never the same again. Their father talked less and their mother became more bossy and overbearing. They had played the Game with Mary Rose for the last time. On June 23rd, 1955 a phase of his boyhood had ended.

He spent the evening reading a book on Indian philosophy, a parting gift from Dr Sharma. He was not really in a mood for philosophy but he felt that the effort of engaging with an unfamiliar vocabulary would concentrate his mind on the present. He was still reading in bed when Hugo returned from the motel at midnight. He could tell from the way Hugo slammed the front door and the subsequent banging about in the kitchen that he had drunk more than usual and therefore much more than he could hold. He clumped up the stairs and stumbled into Father Jerry's bedroom brandishing half a cooked chicken in his fist.

'I saw the light – if you see what I mean. I knew you were still awake.'

He sat on the edge of the bed, tearing at the chicken and licking his fingers after each untidy mouthful. When Father Jerry suggested that he find himself a chair, preferably in his own room, he replied that since his visit was not a formal one the edge of the bed would serve his purpose. His eyes gleamed wildly as he looked round the room. He knew that he was intruding and he disliked himself for being aware of it.

'You're a man of the cloth, Jerry,' he hiccuped. 'Now you're in pyjamas; the cloth is hanging up in the wardrobe. No soutane, no biretta, no stole, no big, black missal under your arm. Now we can speak as equals without giving either offence or quarter.'

'I think it's time you went to bed.'

'You don't know how funny you look in pyjamas. It's strange to see you look like any normal man.'

He belched deliberately and patted his stomach with the palm of his hand.

'You were always too close to Father, that was half your problem. Father wasn't the hero you imagined. He was never exposed to the unfamiliar, never plagued by uncertainty. He trained to be a country doctor and a country doctor he remained. Now, I've travelled in strange places and thought about him in strange circumstances, and felt his presence in my life as a dead limb that never belonged to me. He's a wooden leg that keeps me standing up but won't bend when I want to sit down. Father Jerry, you and I, we've both got a wooden leg.'

He chucked Father Jerry under the chin and laughed through a mouthful of chicken.

'Never touch me. You must respect the holy ground between us.'

'Think of your bed as a bishopstool and of me as a pope laying hands on you, conferring sacramental graces to strengthen and uphold you in the nightly fight against evil thoughts and impure fantasies. Surely you must recall Olga's bottom in her skin-tight leotard.'

Father Jerry tried to get up but Hugo immediately pinned his arms under the bedclothes.

'I came in to talk to you. We never talk, so now be quiet and listen to your younger brother. I was thinking of Mother last night, a good woman. I won't hear anything said against her. Father was a dreamer but she had her head screwed on. She was an original thinker, not your common or garden, craw-thumping Irish mother. She didn't want you to become a priest, now did she? "There's only one good reason for going in for the priesthood," she said. "And that's to get to be bishop. Jerry, you're not bishop material." She didn't laugh, she meant it, every word. You must wonder now if you should have taken her advice. She gave us more than Father ever did. We've got her restlessness, her sense of misery and dissatisfaction. All we lack is her single-mindedness. If we had that, you'd be archbishop by now and I'd be running my own coffee plantation. It's a fatal combination: Father's unworldliness and her unhappiness. Jerry, me boyo, we're sunk.'

Hugo was leaning over him, holding him down in the bed. He turned his head away and said, 'You're talking a lot of nonsense. You're too drunk to talk anything else.'

'You didn't love Mother, you hated her.'

'Of course I didn't hate her.'

'Do you remember the colour of her eyes.'

'They were grey.'

'I knew it, I knew it,' Hugo crowed. 'They weren't grey, they were a luminous black, just like a woodcock's.'

'They were grey,' Father Jerry quietly insisted. 'Grey with little green specks.'

'Do you remember the colour of Carmel's eyes?'

'Brown like her hair.'

'Brown like her hair! Her hair was black.'

'You're trying to annoy me. I'm not saying another word.'

'Let me tell you why you don't remember. You hated her, just as you hated Mother for loving her. Carmel was your twin sister. She looked like you and you looked like her. Mother kept you in skirts till you were seven, to keep you looking alike. You had curly, black hair then, just like Carmel. You rejected your first pair of trousers, you said they made your legs itch. Father made you wear them. So now it's time to ask yourself why you've taken to the cassock. Did you see it as the only respectable way to get back into skirts? You were jealous of Carmel, you wanted to be a girl like her. Finally, you must ask yourself if you willed her death that day –'

'I told you I'm not talking to you.' Father Jerry almost shouted.

'Mother sensed the truth. She didn't like you. Do you ever wake up in the night and say, "My mother didn't love me"? I'll bet you don't. You've hidden the horror of it from yourself. Your whole life is only an elaborate act of concealment.'

He leant forward as he laughed. Slaver ran down his beard and fell on the sleeve of his pullover. Father Jerry tried to swing his legs out of bed. Hugo put one hand in under the covers and gripped him fiercely above the knee.

'Now, let's see if little Jerry has got any tickles left in him. Poor sister Carmel lost hers a long time ago.'

Father Jerry writhed in the bed, while Hugo kept him down with the full weight of his body.

'You won the Game once. It was your finest hour, and of course you never knew. What was it like? Hot or cold? I'll bet it was cold. It put you off. Confess. It put you off. And for evermore it had to be a life of self-denial, or rather self-delusion, for how can you truly deny yourself something you don't truly desire. That's the secret of your priesthood: not doing. No sex, no cakes, no fun, no ale. Why not go the whole hog and deny yourself milk and biscuits? You have no desires and no appetites. Just consider. There would be rejoicing in heaven if you shook the foundations of this frozen house with a good randy woman and did something that went against the grain of your miserable nature. What is the use of pretending that you've turned your back on the world at great personal cost, if you see the world as a stinking cesspool? Oh, I should have been a priest. It would have been a daily and nightly struggle. That's where the meaning is, in the struggle. All else is only drift and self-indulgence. If I were a priest, I'd work in the sewers, I'd bloat my body with all the filth and stench of humanity.'

'It's bloated enough already.'

'Ah, the priesteen has delivered himself of a cliché ... I'd become an outcast for Christ's sake, a man apart in all his sores and boils, because there's no regeneration without degeneration. Time and example would tell. In my old age I'd become a salt-lick for the faithful, they'd come to me for the minerals of spiritual growth, and as they went away restrengthened, they'd say, "This is one salt-lick that hath not lost his savour." '

'Have you done?'

'Is that your answer? Just another cliché. I'd like you to know that the clichés came later. There is none to be found in the parables of the New Testament. Christ was intelligent. The apostolic succession is a succession of donkeys.'

Father Jerry closed his eyes and pretended to sleep.

'Ah, you're dreaming again, dreaming about Olga. Sing her praises. Hosanna in excelsis. She was worth six of Mary Rose. Remember how she breathed, and how you listened to the breathing above the words. And remember those strong legs and shoulders. She'd lead you into hell and carry you back again without wilting under the burden. In the village they spoke of "Father Jerry's Romance" but you didn't have the courage of your lust, now did you? As you sit in the confessional listening to the lurid ins and outs of the flesh, will you fondly enumerate the sins you failed to commit with her?'

He drove his hand up Father Jerry's leg. Father Jerry jumped a foot off the bed and Hugo fell back with the bedclothes on top of him. His head made a hollow sound as it struck the skirting.

'Out, out, out.' Father Jerry shouted. 'If you don't get back to your room this minute, I'll ring the police.'

'The police won't believe you.' Hugo laughed scornfully as he got to his feet.

'Don't put me to the test.'

'It won't look good, a priest who preaches charity evicting his only brother at two o'clock in the morning.'

'I meant what I said, I'll say no more.'

Hugo crossed the landing and stood on the far side of the stairwell.

'You sold your birthright when you sold the ancestral home,' he shouted. 'Now you're home and homeless. And homesick too. You'll never do any good here, so why don't you follow the hippies over the hill. You're homesick because you're youthsick, because nothing ever happens twice.'

He made a prolonged belching noise and slammed his bedroom door.

Father Jerry locked his own door and put out the light. He lay awake in the dark all night, waiting for the first glimmer of dawn. In the morning, as he left for Mass, he knocked on Hugo's door and told him that he had less than an hour to pack his bags.

Chapter 17

When he came back from church, the Land Rover was no longer in the driveway. He went straight upstairs to Hugo's room to find the sheets and blankets folded neatly on top of the mattress. The wardrobe was empty, the carving of the sheep-woman gone, and the pile of unwashed socks and under-clothes had vanished from the corner. With a sigh of relief he went downstairs and ground a handful of coffee beans in the kitchen. He could hardly believe that Hugo had left so quickly, so quietly, and so early in the morning.

He decided to spend the day about the house and luxuriate in his new-found solitude. He went from room to room and stood by each window in turn looking down on the sea, the Glebe and the village to the east. The parochial house was built on a height; all was under his eyes. A sentence from the *Summa* plopped into his mind: 'That the saints may enjoy their beatitude and the grace of God more abundantly, they are permitted to see the punishment of the damned in hell.'

'Are there any saints, even in heaven?' he asked himself, as he turned away from the window.

He took his copy of the *Divina Commedia* into the garden and

210

sat beneath the trees with his back to the light. The October sun struck sharply through the branches and their leaves cast shadows that ran up and down the yellowing grasses in front of him. *Nel mezzo del cammin di nostra vita* … In the middle of the road of life I found that I had strayed into a wood so dark … As he read in the warmth of the morning, a more joyous life gradually began to wake round him: thrushes, robins, sparrows hopped above his head. Bird song surrounded him. A tiny field mouse crossed the clearing at his feet. The heat of the sun on his neck, the dappling movements of quivering foliage, and the impromptu warblings in the background gave him an intimation of rightness and wholeness after the unspeakable events of the previous night. Gradually he relaxed a little. It was well past noon before he closed the book on his knee.

In the spring what he liked best about the garden was the discordant racket made by visiting rooks. Every year they came to build in the ash trees and rend the air with tuneless cawing. From his window he would watch them swooping in with twigs in their beaks, and sometimes he would smile at the sight of a 'criminal' rook stealing a twig from an unattended nest. With steady concentration he wondered if the tribe had a system of punishment for discouraging such outlaws, but try as he might he could not cleanse himself of the memory of Hugo's drunken ramblings. He tried to imagine the rooks in spring again, then in late autumn when their big black nests disfigured the bare forks of the branches, and finally the return of the birds to the rookery at the beginning of winter … It was no good. With a gesture of impatience he got up and went back to the house.

That evening he went to Hugo's room to remove the sheets for washing. Beneath the folded blankets he found his brother's diary, after which he made a thorough search of the room. The diary was all he had left behind. It contained an entry for the previous day which he read with difficulty because it had been written in a hurry:

October 10th

Yesterday I came across an old sand-eel hook at Burke's that put me in mind of the sand-eel strand of my youth. I decided to give the motel a miss just for once, and as the moon rose I set off for the shore with the hook and an empty sack on my shoulder. The sky was clear and the moon so bright that you could count the furrows in the sand and the silver edges of the waves as they ran. I took off my shoes, rolled up my trousers, and walked out through the shallow water with the sack hanging from my waist. Suddenly I froze. Before me, facing the shore and the moonlight, stood a lanky man whose head and shoulders I could not mistake. My first reaction was to be on my guard. He reached out a hand. Without a smile I returned his uncompromising grasp.

'I'm here to observe an age-old custom,' I said.

'So am I,' said McDowd. 'It's the first year in ages that I haven't had the sand-eel strand to myself.'

'It's big enough for both of us, and that's just as well.'

'If you stand and listen, you can almost hear the laughter and merriment we used to have in the old days here. Arty Bradley, Mary Rose, you and me. Father Johnnie never came, he was not our kind of fisherman.'

We both waded out behind the sand-bank until the water was up to our knees. Then I drew my hook firmly through the sand until the movement of the first sand-eel stopped it. The effect on my wrist had the immediacy of an electric shock. I stooped down, put my free hand in the water, and pulled the wriggling sand-eel into it with the hook. As I dropped the first fish into the mouth of the empty sack, I had a feeling of youth renewed, which was almost as intoxicating as a bottle of whisky drunk quickly for a bet. I was a growing man again. I had never spent a night away from home.

As I fished, I kept thinking about the sand-eels and what they had once meant in the life of Glenkeel. They are small eel-like fish that come into the bay in shoals every autumn, between the end of September and Hallowe'en. Best for fishing and eating are the green sand-eels that live in salt-water rather than estuaries. Some of them grow up to fourteen inches long. They are fished during the low ebb at spring tide, either at the new or full moon, but any fisherman with a glimmer of poetry in his soul would prefer the sand-eel strand at the clear spring. The sand-eels are easier to hook when they lie stiff in the sand at low water. At other times they wriggle and skite, making the fisherman's task pretty well impossible.

McDowd and I fished side by side in silence for over an hour until the weight of the catch had begun to weigh both of us down. We carried our bulging sacks back to the sand dunes, emptied them, and returned to fish once more. I still kept thinking of the old days when the sand-eel strand was part of what Father Johnnie calls the living culture of the glen. It had a serious purpose, of course: it provided sand-eels to be smoked and salted and eaten for supper in the long winter nights. It also provided an occasion of fun for young and old at a time of year when the harvest was saved and relaxation and merriment were possible before the months of cold and rain set in. I dredged up a fund of memories, and now and again I looked at McDowd to see if he were looking at me.

We fished for another two hours, retreating before the filling tide which tugged at our legs and sucked the loose sand from under our feet. When we had each killed another ten score, McDowd said, 'Time to make tracks. Think of the weight of the buggers on the way home.'

We trudged up the foreshore under our sacks to the place where we had dumped the first catch, and then we lit our pipes. We lay on the edge of the bent-grass, looking down on the silvery water and up into the clear night sky. A curlew expressed the loneliness of a long lifetime in one piercing whistle that seemed to retreat from the air like a great wave ebbing from an estuary, leaving bare, black mud-flats behind. Still McDowd said no word. It was a magic hour, a time out of life when two irascible contenders could sit silently side by side as the rest of the world slept soundly.

'It was a good strand,' I said after a while. 'The moon and the tide were right.'

'The sand-eels were a fair size,' he replied after five minutes.

As he smoked, his full pipe glowed and his guts curmurred, probably because like myself he had not eaten since early evening. I thought it a pity that we should spend our lives in enmity, and I wondered if he felt the same. I waited for him to speak, because I had started the last conversation and it was now his turn. We sat for twenty minutes saying nothing, just listening to the rush and hiss of the waves and the whisperings of the breeze in the bent-grass behind us.

'Father Johnnie doesn't care for sand-eels. I'll never get through twenty score on my own.' I knocked out my pipe.

'Why did you come then?'

'To remember the old days and to see if I was still handy with the sand-eel hook.'

'I like sand-eels,' he said. 'I'll give you half a bottle of whiskey for the lot.'

214

'You can have them for nothing.'

'I don't want them for nothing. We'll carry them home now and drink the whiskey before we part. That way our little transaction will be complete – all in one night.'

This was peace with honour and it would have been curmudgeonly not to accept. He was as good as his word. When we got to his cottage, he opened a bottle of Paddy whiskey. Though I felt more in need of food than drink, I drank glass for glass with him till the bottle stood empty between us on the table. Even in our drinking we were contending, and I must have started at least ten conversations only to have them strangled at birth by one of McDowd's quizzical generalisations.

'Now our business is complete,' he pronounced, as I emptied my glass.

'Is it?'

'I mean for tonight.'

'Will you be going to the sand-eel strand again tomorrow night?'

Ignoring my question, he rose abruptly from the table.

'Do you ever wonder why you continue to live?' he asked.

'I know it's because I don't fear death.'

I said good night because it was the only thing to say. Walking home, I felt flushed with excitement. I finally knew that what I had to do must now be done quickly. Father Johnnie won't understand. What a pity we had to fall out – all over a matter of interpretation. Humbly, I shall enter his confessional and ask forgiveness for a certain capital offence that can't be postponed any longer. If one's opponent is Satan incarnate, surely God will overlook a temporary departure from the Queensberry Rules.

He sat on the edge of the bed in the empty room and reread the last sentence of the entry. That night, as he lay awake, he found that he could not pray. Now and again he dreamt of violence in a dark landscape and male and female figures dancing round a boiling pot on the Glebe. Towards morning his dreams became more peaceful. He walked in the shadow of a graveyard wall at midnight. A tired moon, no brighter than a candle flame, hung over him, and then he heard two voices from inside the grave-yard saying, 'Ceann domsa, ceann duitse, One for me, one for you'. God and the Devil counting souls, he thought; God speaking Gaelic (you could tell He was God by His accent) and the Devil speaking English with cut-glass precision. He peered over the coping of the wall and saw Hugo and McDaid dividing a catch of silver sand-eels.

In the morning he went to Burke's, determined to confront Hugo. Burke's was locked and there was no sign of either Hugo or his Land Rover. Next he called at McDaid's cottage and knocked sharply on the door. 'Are you there, Mandamus?' he shouted. When he got no reply, he walked round the house and looked into the barn where a tub of sand-eels stood in the middle of the earthen floor.

Somewhat shaken, he walked back to the parochial house and picked up the telephone in the hallway. He wished to talk to someone, just to hear a normal voice at the other end of the line. He was afraid to ring the police and he was reluctant to involve Canon Hackler. He put down the receiver and stood by the window of the study watching cars passing and women with shopping coming from the village. One of the cars slowed down and crossed over the cattle grid in the gateway. It came up the drive and stopped in the shade of the trees. He could hardly believe his eyes when Dr Sharma opened the door. He almost ran to meet her. He stood before her smiling and grasped both her hands.

'This is a surprise.'

'I was touring Sligo and I thought it would be fun to look you up. Thanks for all your cards. Very cryptic. You haven't changed.'

She was wearing a blue suit with a white shirt and red tie. She looked smaller and thinner now, her nose and chin more pronounced, her face darker with little lines of laughter round the mouth. She was in her mid-forties. Though her straight black hair and brilliant dark eyes hadn't changed, in the two years since they had last met she had gone from what he used to think of as a late girlhood to an early middle age.

'Why aren't you wearing your black-and-gold sari? I barely recognised you in your suit.'

'I thought my sari might attract too much curiosity here. Besides, a suit is warmer. The weather is finally turning cool.'

They drank tea and chatted like old friends. He felt secure and serenely happy. He asked her how long she planned to stay. When she told him that she was staying at the motel for the night and leaving early in the morning, he felt a stab of disappointment and disbelief.

'Why not stay a week? The weather may be cool but it's dry. You'll love it here. There's the sea, and then the mountains full of hidden loughs. You mustn't behave like a day-tripper. You must live with us here for a little while.'

'I must think of my patients. I'm sure they're thinking of me.'

'Then we'll spend the rest of the day sight-seeing. We won't waste a minute,' he promised.

She helped him prepare a packed lunch while he told her about his wayward brother and his feud with McDaid. Finally, he told her about his suspicion that only one of them was now alive.

'You've always had a vivid imagination,' she smiled. 'How can you think such thoughts in such a peaceful place as this?'

'I'll take you down to Scariff Island. All will be revealed.'

He felt excited as he drove her to Smug Rone Pier. He showed her Hugo's boat as if it were tangible proof of all the things he'd been telling her about his brother and McDaid. She sat sideways on the centre thwart, chatting cheerfully about seals and sea birds and the majestic impersonality of the cliff faces that over-looked them from the land.

'Are you happy now?' she asked suddenly.

'At this moment? Oh, yes. In a boat nothing matters except the sea, and that's how it should be,' he replied.

'Is that how it is?'

'Perhaps not. I can't help thinking of the island and what we may find when we get there.'

'I suggest we wait and see.'

He beached the boat on the sloping white shingle and hurried up to the top of the hogsback, leaving her to carry the lunch basket. He wanted to call out Hugo's name; instead he heard distinctly those terrible words he had read again and again since that quiet July evening when he first opened Hugo's diary:

nor is it possible for me to express the horror of my mind at seeing the shore spread with skulls, hands, feet and other bones of human bodies; and particularly, I observed a place where there had been a fire made, and a circle dug in the earth, like a cockpit, where it is supposed the savage wretches had sat down to their inhuman feastings …

'Satisfied?' she asked as she joined him.

'Nothing's changed. It's as if time did not exist.'

'What did you expect?'

'Evidence of recent violence perhaps. To be honest I don't

know.'

'You're lucky to have such a peaceful place to come to.'

'It's a place I can't get out of my mind. I think about it and I dream about it. I can hear the sound of the shingle rolling when I'm talking about something else.'

'It's an Otherworld. I'll bet it has its place in local folklore.'

'There's a story that in the days of sail a merchant ship was wrecked here and kept the mountain people in Indian meal for over a year. That's why it has an alternative name: Oileán na Mine, the island of meal.'

'Now it's an island of sea fowl. I'll sit here and watch them for a little while.'

He ran down the slope and stopped above the shingle. The boat was lying peacefully on her side with a seagull perched on the outboard. It looked lodged and immovable as the rocks on every side. Talking to Dr Sharma above, he had known a moment of panic. Now he was almost surprised to find the boat where he had beached her. He walked round the island, combing every niche and cranny. Then he came back to the shingle and began searching among the stones.

'What are you looking for?' she enquired as she joined him.

'Two beach stones I left behind on my last visit.'

'The things you seek here have no bearing on your brother. The things you seek are irretrievably lost. You must reinterpret your history, confront your experience with a new vocabulary, and remember that there's still life to be lived.'

He smiled ruefully. She had a weakness for summations that he did not always find apt and felicitous.

'My mind is two quernstones grinding,' he told her. 'All my life I've been taking in other people's corn. One day, if only for a day, I'd like to grind my own.'

They had lunch on the high ground above the shingle, and washed it down with coffee from a flask. In his illness he had seen her as a confessor with whom he could share every thought and sensation, every desire and fantasy, no matter how extravagant or personal. She would listen sympathetically with a notepad on her knee as he sought to extricate himself from the obsessions that had risen to replague him in his fortieth year: the Game, the Termon Stone, Arty Brennan and Mary Rose. Exploring with her his early memories was an act of purification in which he sought to recover the serenity he used to feel after confession as a boy, when stealing turnips from a neighbour's field was the most grievous sin he knew.

'I suppose I come to this place to escape from the hippiedrome that the glen has become. Here are only sea fowl and the pure smell of the sea.'

'You have the kind of imagination that will always stoke the inferno. The glen, from what I've seen, is a lovely and peaceful place, unspoilt by the twentieth century. There are no hippies defecating on roadsides. The fishmeal factory doesn't stink all that much and the motel is almost quaint. The twentieth century is in your head. For everyone else it's only a soap opera on television. Have you ever thought of going away and taking the twentieth century with you, leaving behind no eye that isn't innocent?'

Her pupils glinted with secret mirth as she spoke. He could tell that she still saw him as one of her patients, just as a schoolmistress might continue to see a grown man as her pupil. He decided not to give her further cause for summary judgments.

They lingered on the way back to watch seals and cormorants and to inspect narrow inlets and channels between sea stacks. The clarity of the day helped to dissipate his sense of disappointment. He began to take pleasure in her company again and to share her obvious delight in the wildness of every cliff and promontory. When they got back to the parochial house, he gave her Hugo's diary which she read with the help of a magnifying glass from her handbag.

'He's a bit of a showman, your brother,' she said when she'd finished. 'The interesting thing is that he seems to be more obsessed with your life than his own. I think you need not worry, he's well able to look after himself.'

'What did you make of it all?'

'It's difficult to say, it's all distortion and refraction. I'd like to see the Termon Stone, though. It seems to have played a part in more lives than yours.'

They walked up the slope of the Crag of Cats past the sheep pen where he hid the last time the Game was played. He led her to an oblong block of granite, facing east. He laid his hand on the rough surface and with his penknife scratched away a patch of lichen to reveal a black sole underneath the grey.

'It seems so ordinary,' he tried to explain. 'As I look at it, I sometimes sense that a mystery is about to be revealed. Then the moment of intimation passes and I find myself gazing at a nondescript stone. We have all fallen under its spell.'

'Or the spell of your own lives?' she questioned.

'Does the stone speak to you?'

'There's no reason why it should. It has as much to do with my life as the Stone of Scone. Perhaps we should sit on it,' she smiled.

He sat beside her on the edge of the block looking across at the north mountain with its S-shaped road, a calligraphic flourish that had been cut into its heathery flank. Below them the curving strand lay bare.

'It's a beautiful evening,' she said. 'I've been here only a few hours, and already I realise that the magic and the mystery are in the light. A minute ago that hill was blue. Now it's purple. I feel foolish for having missed the transition.'

'Enjoying the view?' A mocking voice came from behind. McDaid stood before them with a creel of turf on his back and a black-and-white sheepdog at heel.

'I was looking for you this morning,' Father Jerry said. 'You weren't at home.'

'I was at Corrloch fair. I've just got back.'

'Was Hugo at the fair?'

'I didn't see him, and I didn't expect to see him.'

'Perhaps I misunderstood him,' Father Jerry replied.

'You're sitting on the Termon Stone,' McDaid smiled at Dr Sharma. 'Don't lie on it whatever you do. Those who lie on the Termon Stone go to the grave not as old men and women but as old children.'

'It's a distinctive stone,' she conceded. 'It's rather warm to the touch. It would make a good penitential bed for a medieval monk who was more than half in love with himself.'

Father Jerry knew that McDaid would give a chew of tobacco to find out who she was. He laughed strangely and looked lingeringly at them both.

'There's no mention of medieval monks in the folklore,' he said. 'But men have lain on it who've become monks. Father Jerry will know who I mean.'

They both watched him pick his way down the slope while his dog sniffed cakes of cow dung.

'That was McDaid.' Father Jerry turned to her.

'I recognised him from your brother's description. He was just as I expected, a harmless, slightly superstitious eccentric.'

'My brother sees him as an evil man of the earth.'

'Your brother is not a scrupulous reporter.'

'Perhaps he's a harmless eccentric who realises how disturbing harmless eccentricity can be.'

'Your preoccupations haven't changed. To grow up you must learn to forget. Say to yourself, "I shall forget something every day."'

'Your advice would make excellent sense if we lived in a world of sense. The worlds we each inhabit are not our own to deconstruct and reconstruct. We may try to read sense into them, which is only an exercise in crossword puzzling. The good thing about them is that they'll die with us. They will never rise to pester other people.'

'So the Termon Stone will revert to being a simple block of granite.'

'There will always be other children and other termon stones.'

She invited him to dinner at the motel, and he suggested that they eat at the parochial house. When he reminded her that he didn't eat meat, she cooked a vegetable curry with carrots, tomatoes, beans, onions, potatoes and chillis. After they had eaten, they went into the study and she sat in the armchair opposite his own. The balm of her conversation drew his mind off Hugo and all the things that had been vexing him. They talked for two hours, and all the while it seemed to him that their conversation could go on till morning. Some time after midnight he made coffee. When he came back from the kitchen, she said rather casually, 'I've got a piece of good news to tell you. I'll allow you to guess what it is.'

'You've been offered a chair at an ancient university?'

'No, it's something more personal. I'm engaged to be married. He's an old colleague and friend whose work I've always admired. After his wife died two years ago, we began spending our

223

evenings together. I left him in Sligo visiting relations whom he thought might bore me.'

'I'm so pleased for you. I've always known you as a single woman. Were there times when you regretted being single?'

'I sometimes regretted my lack of regret. In recent years I'd become aware of a kind of sadness. One evening I came home and said, "Without my patients I wouldn't exist." Surely you must know loneliness too.'

'I've learnt to live with it. Being lonely is now being myself.'

'Are you happy?'

'I have moments of happiness, mainly when I'm alone with a few sheep in the mountains. In my illness I had become aware of a visitor in my life – an alien presence, an invader who was seeking to overcome me. One morning I knew that she had gone and that I was on the way to health again. For a long time I used to wonder if she had deserted me temporarily or for ever. I felt empty, I almost wanted her to come back, and I grieved when I realised that she would not. There was gain and loss, of course. I grieved only for what I had lost. Now I have surrendered to the knowledge that nothing will ever change for me again.'

'Your illness has gone. The "visitor" who has left would have destroyed you. What you are grieving for are the heightened sensations and the excitement of a battle that could easily have gone the other way. Your present life may be an uneasy peace, but any peace is worth having.'

'At any price?'

'Compared with some patients I've known, you got off lightly.'

'I used to write poetry once. It's a great loss to me.'

'If you've stopped writing poetry, you mustn't blame the departed visitor. To use a metaphor you will appreciate, you were possessed by a demon which I helped you exorcise. You told me at the time that you longed to be rid of him.'

'I don't think I said "him".'

'Him or her, it doesn't matter.'

She seemed to have grown impatient. She got up and paced around the room.

'For me it was "her". I must tell you now that there are times when I'd like to have her back. I feel as if I've spent the last two years standing by the door waiting – waiting for just something. I was standing by the window when you came in the gate.'

'You look tired. Why don't you arrange to come to London for a month? I've still got that large, ungainly house in Islington, and there are one or two empty rooms.'

'It's very kind of you.'

'I shan't be seeing you in the morning, I'm making an early start. We must keep in touch. After all you were my favourite patient. I like to think that no one could have cured you but me.'

'I don't think a man could have cured me.'

'I did cure you, didn't I?'

'Yes,' he ventured, as he kissed her proffered cheek.

He watched the tail-lights of her car vanish at the gate, knowing that a relationship he had taken for granted had been severed. He would stop sending her postcards, which were only a sad substitute for the poetry he used to write.

'I faced three tempters,' he said. 'Brennan, Olga and Dr Sharma. The most subtle of these was Dr Sharma.'

When he went upstairs, he looked at Hugo's empty bed and for the first time felt the terror of being truly alone.

Chapter 18

In the morning he went to Burke's again. There was still no sign of Hugo. He returned to the parochial house and found a letter from his brother that had been posted in Dublin three days ago:

Dear Jerry,

As you may have suspected, my diary was a tease, written, as they say, for your eyes only; a mixture of fact and fiction to make you think and possibly act. You say you pursue the Columban ideal of prayer, study, work. Whether you study more than work and work more than pray is something I have been unable to determine. Be that as it may, I thought you might value an opportunity to put the fruits of your studies into practice. I sought to present you with a series of moral choices. I am tempted to conclude that you considered it more politic to offend God than your brother.

Don't get me wrong. I wasn't trying to play God, or, for that matter, Satan. I was simply having a go at playing Novelist. Sadly, the characters got out of hand, which proves at least that they were alive, I suppose. Brennan, McDaid, Olga, you and I – the Game again with its most brilliant exponent *hors de combat*. I mustn't tell you the ending I had envisaged. Regrettably, it's now unachievable. I've lost my omnipotence. My characters have overthrown my tyranny.

It all began when I saw your mugshot in *The Donegal Democrat* after twenty years of exile. It was a face of innocence, unlined and unwritten on. When I looked at my own palimpsest in the mirror, I naturally felt envious. I wanted to write on your cheeks and forehead, then erase what I'd written and write and write again. At first I was at a loss to discover how this might be accomplished. Then I realised that I must shock you into living, and therefore seeing, life in all its naked horror.

Unfortunately, my scheme lost its pristine simplicity. Things got out of hand, or perhaps a greater trickster took a hand and demanded to be outclassed in trickery. If you should turn out to be the loser, please accept my apologies. Comfort yourself with the thought that at least I am not the winner. For all I know, you may now decide to assume my abdicated role of Novelist. It would be a neat and satisfying twist. Please write. I should dearly love to have your thoughts. As for myself, I shall not die entirely. Or to use three words instead of five, *Non omnis moriar*. (You will agree that there is a pleasure in being outclassed by a fellow-classicist.)

You asked me once why I had come back and I gave you an *ad interim* answer. The truth is that in my stomach is a pit of longing that no amount of eating and drinking will satisfy. Perversely perhaps, I concluded that my yearnings could be assuaged simply by proving my primacy. You are my elder brother, my keeper, bishop, pope and abbot all together. Need I say more?

Certain things must be conceded. You proved less predictable than I had expected. I had envisaged a stern and unbending lawgiver. Instead I found a man who never insisted narrowly on his

227

own moral ideology. That impressed me. It demonstrated that you are not just a programmed robot in a cassock, that you're yearning flesh and bone like your younger brother. In fact I could be excused for concluding from your conversation and actions (or inaction) that you are impeccably amoral. Or to put it in more flattering terms, that you are possessed of a godlike objectivity. Perhaps you're a born eclectic. A quick analysis of your *obiter dicta* has revealed trace elements of Sufism, Marxism, Platonism, Thomism, Buddhism, Cartesianism and Cynicism. I am full of admiration.

I claim no godlike aspirations, yet as I consider the last five months I am tempted to see myself as *Deus ex machina* – albeit with a difference. First I created a problem. Then I withdrew to give you time to realise that there was a problem. Finally, I descended to solve the problem, and what do I earn? Ingratitude.

Again I must return to your commendable Olympianism. At several points you could have reproached me face to face; laid down the moral law, as it were. Or you could have invoked the assistance of the police and left judgment to judge and jury. Instead you must have said, 'Punishment is God's prerogative. Let's give Him an opportunity to exercise it.' Or did you say, 'Hugo is a jealous brother, his wrath is greater than Our Father's'? Which was it? You must realise that you owe me a letter.

Now to explain, if only briefly. As Novelist, I was lucky. For starters I had Brennan and McDaid. Since you saw Brennan as your adversary, it was a simple matter to provide him with a cloven hoof and make McDaid his familiar. My first concern was to get the plot going, so, with great difficulty and personal discomfort, I suspended myself from a tree inside an old salmon net purloined from the storehouse on the pier. Next I drove nine black bullocks into your vegetable garden. Need I add that I also cut the brake pipes. Now that was exciting because I was risking my own neck as well as yours. You will agree that I did it rather well.

Then out of the blue came Olga, an unsolicited gift, a kind of *donnée*. She fired my imagination; she looked and smelt like Mary Rose. No sooner had I got the idea of resurrecting the Game than things began to go awry. You refused Arty Brennan Communion. How could I have foreseen an act so wayward and so provocative? As Novelist, I had to get you off the hook, and at first I had no idea how. I needed time to think and I knew that you needed time to pray for guidance. So, as an interim measure, I dropped a sheet over Brennan's head one dark night and removed him to Scariff Island without revealing my identity.

At that stage I had no clear-cut plan. I was relying on the imagination of my characters, yours in particular. Then Brennan's creditors crawled out of the woodwork. You found me sitting on the cliff above the Devil's Pintle wondering who was really writing my novel. Two days later I went out to the island to strike a bargain with Brennan. I searched and searched. All I found was his clothes. The man himself was nowhere to be seen.

You can imagine my sense of disbelief. Had someone rescued him or had he swum ashore? I began to wonder what on earth would happen next. Then his body was found. That solved your problem, though not mine. I was no longer calling the shots. Olga fell in love with you and I fell in love with her. You know the rest. I tried to regain control by getting you to focus on McDaid. I made you a present of Brennan's clothes and told you that they came with the compliments of McDaid. Another moral choice, and again you played Mr Pilate. I suspended myself from the sycamore once more to prepare you for a final burst of action, in which McDaid, like his master, would vanish into thin sea air. I went to the sand-eel strand knowing that he would be there on his own. I accompanied him home and even drank his Paddy whiskey – not my tipple, as you know. At the last moment I held back. I had come to the boundary of devilry beyond which I could not go. Read my account of that evening again. It's one of the few 'true' things in my diary.

So where are you now? Alas, not back where you started. A whole world has been lost. You can't trudge on with head bent and pretend that nothing has happened. You must make an exit. You should leave the glen, as I have done. You will never know peace between those blessed hills. Your great exemplar St Columba went to Iona. You could do worse. His going followed Culdreimhne, a bloody battle. It is fitting that yours should follow a mere skirmish in which no bones were broken. After all, you will grant that you are a lesser man.

Desire and imagination impelled me back to the glen. Now I have left with neither satisfied. I did some good, though. I bought Burke's and saved the glen from that abomination of abominations, the Holiday Village. Now Burke's will be yours. I have instructed my solicitor to see to the details. I hope it will make up for all my truth-telling, which is a privilege I am willing to pay through the nose for. If you don't believe that, just say, 'Hugo's got money. He can afford to indulge himself – and me.'

I am now returning to New Guinea. Life is simpler there; you know when you're about to be eaten and by whom. I travel light. I've shed the past. Nothing remains but a sense of original sin which gives me an intoxicating feeling of irresponsibility. Who knows, I may return again one day. So wherever you are, keep

laying out that extra glass of milk at suppertime. And put a dash
of Scotch in mine.

Yours in You-Know-Who,

Hugo

P.S.

If you suspect that I murdered Olga, you're mistaken. As you
know, I claim to have eaten human flesh but never before someone else had killed, trimmed and cooked it. Seek comfort where
you can. I'm not a murderer. You've been savaged by nothing less
than a moralist. Don't dwell on it. You've been through five
months of spiritual depression, a kind of acedia that manifested
itself in moral impassivity. All that's over. You can now come out
of your cocoon and sing rejoicement in the sun. Spread your
wings and watch them flap. Who knows, some passerby (not
Olga, alas) may think them beautiful.

P.P.S.

A final word of advice. Relax and let your lettuce grow, now that
there are no black bullocks. And once in a while envisage a wild
lettuce growing in the jungle, unobserved by a gardener with
nothing on his mind but green salad.

He slumped into a chair with a stinging sense of bewilder-
ment. Overtly, the letter had been written to explain all. Predict-
ably, it explained nothing. The incomprehensibility of Hugo's
behaviour was only a reflection of a more profound and more
disturbing incomprehensibility. Life itself, it would seem, was
little more than deception. Father Jerry had been schooled not to
trust appearances. Hugo had been at pains to demonstrate that
if you can't trust appearances you can trust nothing.

He took the diary from the bookcase and whipped through

the entries which now seemed as familiar as the Bible itself. They were full of particulars that Hugo could not have invented, and the only purpose of them was deception. Now as he read, the physical presence of the island and the black sea stack merely fostered a suspicion of the natural world and the workings of man within it. All that was real and solid was the heavily bound volume itself – the stiff boards, the cloth and paper – not the words that supposedly gave the book its purpose.

Nothing remained but defilement and desecration. He went to the window to make sure that the north mountain was still purple, but all he could take in was the Glebe, the Glebe, the Glebe below. What only yesterday had been a newly sweetened strip of sandy ground was covered again with brown and green tents, and six more hippies were coming from the village with backpacks high above their shoulders. He hurried down the avenue to confront them.

'You're back?' He did not smile.

'Back from Portnoo,' one of them said, a freckled girl with thin, unrounded breasts that were still pathetically breastlike.

'Was the weather bad?'

'We only went for the rock festival, and we didn't like the place. Too many tourists. It's lovely to be in Glenkeel again, it's so unspoilt.'

'There are more of you this time.'

'Oh, yes,' said the girl. 'We've been spreading the good news.'

'You've been walking through dry places, seeking rest and finding none. Welcome back to the Glebe. It is now empty, sweet and garnished. I hope you'll be comfortable.'

'Thank you,' said the girl. 'It's so kind of you.'

They left the road and took the footpath to the Glebe in single file. He watched their backpacks bobbing and the thin, naked legs of the slender girl. Above them two clouds came together without colliding, forming a great, ungainly bottom, bigger even than Brennan's, with two pale-grey cheeks and a hairy orifice about to rain thin diarrhoea on the hallowed glen – on megaliths and turfstacks, on streams and tarns, on everything in it that was local and holy as opposed to catholic and apostolic. The vision threatened his faith in the life of prayer, study and work. It was a statement from the Opposition – from Brennan and his assigns, from Canon Bingo and Bishop Monopoly ... The scream of a seagull over the fishmeal factory recalled him to the common-place earth under his feet.

He walked back up the avenue, too weary to contemplate lunch. He sat by the fire with the diary on his lap, flicking back and forth, seeking internal evidence and internal contradictions, anything that might lead him to an understanding of his broth-er's motivation. His efforts yielded nothing except a feeling that he had been mercilessly excoriated.

He was immobilised by a sense of failure. In becoming a priest he had failed his parents, and ironically enough he had failed God as well. From the beginning he had known his own weaknesses. He had tried to keep himself unspotted from the world, yet even here the world had found him out. Now it paraded in front of his eyes in a kind of morality play full of stock characters: Evil Thoughts, Fornication, Murder, Adul-tery, Covetousness, Wickedness, Deceit, Licentiousness, Envy, Pride and, last of all in a clown's cap and bells, Foolishness himself.

He heard the voice of his old theology professor, a handsome, commanding man steeped in the scholastic tradition and the belief that the existence of God could be known by natural rea-son. His conviction that reason was not the enemy of religion,

233

and the erudition and intellectual agility he displayed in demonstrating his conviction, gave him a stature that imbued his students with a sense of harmony and wholeness, arming them with certainties that they themselves had not earned.

As a young priest in a world of secular indifference he often felt grateful for the legacy his teacher had bequeathed him. It was not until he had begun discussing morality and religion with Dr Sharma that he realised that the valley of reason was a valley of conflicting echoes. Perhaps he lacked his professor's erudition or even Dr Sharma's oriental subtlety. Whatever the cause, he soon came to realise that the enclosed system of thought in which he had been trained survived in its pristine simplicity only because it was enclosed. It was a hermitage behind high walls with a life that achieved harmony and unity by ignoring the shouting and the rumpus from the Tower of Babel outside.

Dr Sharma seemed well read in eastern and western philosophies. She was not overbearing or disputatious. She listened to what he had to say and now and again asked a question. When he answered, she did not seek to contradict. She merely thought for a moment and then asked another question. He sensed that through him she was searching for a truth that had hitherto eluded her. He felt flattered. He considered it his duty as a priest to communicate his religious experience and the framework of thought in which it existed. After a while she seemed to lose interest, and they talked about more personal and worldly things. Then one evening, as he sat alone in his room, he began to regret having talked to her. He had said too much. He had said so much that all that remained to be said was that he now knew nothing. The Tower of Babel was no longer outside the walls. It was a pandemonium inside his head.

He lay back on the sofa and closed his eyes. It seemed to him that Canon Hackler had entered the room on tiptoe and was standing beside him with his hat pulled down over his jug ears.

'So you've decided to leave us?' he said gravely.

'I'm giving up, I'm no longer able to function as a priest.'

'Ah, cherchez la femme,' the canon smiled omnisciently.

'No.'

'It must be a woman, it always is.'

'Not this time.'

'Was it the German girl who died? Depression and despair after unbearable grief perhaps?'

'No.'

'Then it must be a failure to pray.'

'No, no. Prayer was my pillar of cloud by day as study was my pillar of fire by night.'

'Too much study then. I've always said that theology is to priests what ornithology is to birds.'

'It is simply that I took my priesthood seriously. I wanted to be a priest twenty-four hours a day.'

'Tu es sacerdos in aeternum.'

'Tu es Canon Bingo in aeternum. If I could be a priest, a real priest, just for one day, I'd die a happy man.'

'We could pray together, the two of us. We could go on retreat, give God a chance. You believe in God?'

'Yes, but …'

'But what?'

'His universe is a cold and mechanistic place and life has little to do with love, either earthly or heavenly. The long night of life is loveless.'

'What on earth is the matter with you, Jerry?'

'There's nothing the matter with me. I know what you'll all

say after I leave: "Where did he go wrong? Where did *we* go wrong? Was he fond of a drop? Did he have a hidden weakness for women?" The same old post-mortem, or is it a vivisection? Well, it's simpler and less sensational than you all imagine. It won't make the headlines, it won't even make good sacristy gossip. All I want is to sink back into God's anonymous congregation. I want to kneel at the back of the church and let Canon Bingo, Monsignor Disco and Bishop Monopoly do the incensing. I'm sick, sick, sick, I tell you. Sick of sham.'

'Jerry, you are sick. You need a rest. Why don't you go away for a month? To a monastery or even the seaside. A supply is no problem this time of year. Don't worry about a thing, just leave the arrangements to me.'

He went to the north window again and looked down on the Glebe, a place of many colours and multifarious activity. More tents had sprung up at the far end. Men and women were hurrying here and there. From a grassy knowe a solitary rabbit surveyed the scene. On a squally October day two years ago, just after he had come back from London, he stood at this window gazing at the same patch of ground. The wind was making waves in the aftergrass and wrinkling the surface of the sea. Suddenly it lifted a haycock sky-high. The haycock disintegrated in the air and the wind shook it out over the grey and indifferent water. It was the most startling thing he had ever seen. Hay into hay dust before his very eyes.

'The glen is unpossessable,' he told himself. 'It is as alien and elusive as a dream. Hugo's island and the Termon Stone are dreams. So is my unlived and unrealised life. The dream is not my own. To me it seems like Hugo's and even that is only a reflection of yet another more impenetrable dream.'

He went out to the hallway and rang Canon Hackler who

greeted him with bluff self-confidence.

'Don't say a word. I know why you're ringing. You've decided at last to go for bingo.'

Father Jerry hesitated. 'I'm really ringing about my holiday.'

'I thought you said you weren't having any this year.'

'I've changed my mind. I feel a bit off-colour, I need a break.'

'When were you thinking of going?'

'I'd like to go next week. I'll organise a supply before Sunday.'

'I thought you looked drawn last time I saw you. What you need is three square meals a day. All this vegetarianism can't be doing you any good. You've made your body your sworn enemy. You need to relax. Go to the seaside, it will be quiet now. Put up at a comfortable hotel where the food is good. Eat a solid breakfast and a hearty lunch and, remember, a big juicy steak for dinner. You'll come back like a lion, we won't be able to keep up with you.'

'You're a sensible man, Canon,' he said, ringing off.

The truth was that he needed more than a holiday. He needed to escape from staleness and sameness, from the tedium of knowing in the morning the conformation of the evening. He wished to be shocked into a new order of existence, into a life of fulfilment with the complexity and texture that come from the daily ebb and flow of truly felt relationships. His bishop and parish priest could quote him texts to prove that the union he yearned for was not to be found on earth. They would not know that his need was in his body, a need for spring, new growth and the joy of the never-before-experienced. It was a need that could not be satisfied.

He recalled a summer day in the heart of the country with heat coming up out of the ground. He was walking along a straight lane with a high hedge on each side when out of a

237

gateway came a small curly-headed girl, barely old enough to toddle. Haltingly, she came towards him with a little switch in one hand, small and slightly bow-legged between the hedges. Her light brown hair could have been that of his dead sister Carmel. It was so wonderful to see her alive and smiling in the quiet, dusty lane. He bent over her and took her upraised hand. Her mother, a stocky, frumpish woman, came running out of the gateway.

'Oh, there you are, thank heavens.' She dragged the reluctant girl away.

Neither the bishop nor the canon would understand the profound effect that the incident had had on him, or why he would never forget the straight, grey lane stretching uncompromisingly ahead. Would he find the strength to continue to walk that lane without looking over his shoulder or gazing into the mysterious gateways on either side?

A bell began tolling in the village with a warm vibrancy he had not heard before. In a field between the parochial house and the Glebe a man stopped digging and took off his cap to say the Angelus. Father Jerry hurried to the village where a small group of men and women had gathered in the churchyard. McDaid came out of the belfry, smiling broadly.

'She's a lovely bell, and a pleasure to ring,' he said.

'It's a surprise to mark your second anniversary here,' an old man explained.

'The parish council wanted to give you a present. We collected the money and kept it a secret among ourselves,' McDaid added.

'You bought a new bell against my wishes.'

'We paid good money for it, we collected from every house. The parish council was unanimous. There was a vote, the

238

decision was arrived at democratically.'

Though he was angry, he saw the puzzlement in their faces and the triumph in McDaid's blue eyes.

'I can see you don't think much of democracy, Father,' McDaid said.

'Did Canon Hackler know about this?'

'Canon Hackler keeps his ear to the ground, he knows everything,' one of the women said.

'You should have told me. As a priest I can only forgive you. As a man I am less than happy.'

'Now we'll have the Angelus every noon and evening again. Five hundred people will pray twice a day. A thousand prayers. It can only do good,' McDaid smiled.

Father Jerry hurried away, leaving them to stare at one another in the windswept churchyard. As he walked back to the parochial house, he knew that in showing anger he had done himself less than justice. He felt tired and dispirited, unable to think. For the remainder of the afternoon he sat by the window of the study looking blankly across the fields at the roofs of the village houses.

The dry, brittle days of autumn would pass into winter. Rain and wind would bleach the grass, and the grey boulders on the hillsides would turn into ugly barnacles on the hull of a grounded cargo vessel. Mist would come billowing in from the sea to shroud the mountains before thickening into drizzle and cold rain. The glen would shrink into a hard, ice-bound trough, and night would come down at three o'clock in the afternoon. He was forty-four, still in the mellow September of his life, yet in his heart it was the end of December with the black entrails of the year laid bare.

He recalled an April day in the mountains just before Hugo came back to the glen. He was walking northwards to Glencrow,

239

knee-deep in frost-burnt heather, aware of nothing but the clear sky above and the hard, sharp breeze on his face. Among the roots of the withered heather young grass was peeping, single blades, beautifully green, bright and slender like new corn. He stooped and plucked one blade of 'heather braird', twirling it in his fingers, as he held it up to the breeze. For a moment his whole body glowed with exaltation. The lean sheep would push through the sapless heather and feed on the single blades of new grass underneath. To satisfy their hunger and survive till summer they would search diligently and travel far each day, but they would survive because even in this barren land there was still sustenance for anyone with the desire to find it.

At six the bell rang again and he counted the strokes without moving from his seat by the window. They never varied: three, three, three, followed by nine, making eighteen in all. The bell sounded from an outer world, a voice of health, wholeness and continuity. It was not his bell. He'd had no say in the ordering or making of it. It had been hung and rung against his wishes. As he listened to its rounded tone, he realised how little depended on him. The day-to-day life of the parish went on while he was absent fighting demons from another place and time.

He got up to answer the telephone in the hall, half-expecting to hear Hugo's subversive laughter. It turned out to be the bishop. He spoke softly, almost languidly, like an aristocratic sybarite after a good dinner at his club.

'How are you keeping, my dear Jerry.'

'I've never felt better, I'm pleased to say.'

'You go from strength to strength, I always knew you would. I've got something to tell you. Yet another opportunity has arisen. I've had to make some changes and I thought it wise to remember you. I'm transferring you to Rathmallow next month. Canon

Canty is parish priest there. A live wire. You're certain to work well together.'

'I'm happy here. I don't think I'm ready for a change.'

For a moment the line went taut with silence.

'Rathmallow is a good-sized town,' the bishop continued blithely. 'It will help to keep your mind off country matters.'

'Country matters?'

'I can't help feeling that you care a shade too deeply about the countryside. In Rathmallow you'll have other battles to keep you occupied.'

'I never expected to remain in Glenkeel for ever but I had imagined that when I moved it would be to serve in another country parish.'

'You mustn't be so self-effacing, dear Jerry. The future is to be found in the town. You should look at life as a ladder. For you Rathmallow is the next rung up. You must come to see me soon. There is much to discuss. I'm determined to ensure that you succeed.'

Father Jerry put down the receiver. What the bishop did not understand he could not be made to understand. He was all drive and will; and the will, it willeth every day. He remembered his father and the care he lavished on his patients, even those who were too poor to pay his fee.

'Would you like to be a doctor?' he once asked on one of their walks in the mountains.

'No, a priest,' he'd replied without hesitation.

'Not enough stress,' his father advised. 'You're too sensitive to take on a life behind the lines. Do something that is not in your nature. If you flee far enough from yourself in your youth, you will have some chance of finding yourself in middle age. Now, the priesthood is the right job for Hugo. He's coarse-grained and selfish. It might have a refining effect on him.'

'What should I do then?'

'Do something that no one else has done before.'

He went into his study and ran his eye along the packed shelves of the bookcase. 'Don't neglect your body, it's a machine,' his father had said. 'And don't neglect your mind, it's a system of rivers that will silt up if it isn't dredged regularly. Good books are great dredgers. A man who reads one good book a week will never have a stagnant oxbow lake in his head.' His books had lost their potency. Now all the books in the Bodleian would not dredge the stagnant oxbow lake in his mind.

He went to the cupboard under the stairs and from the single shelf took down a box of cartridges that he'd bought for a clay-pigeon shoot and never opened. To his surprise the seal was broken and two of the cartridges were missing. He picked up his father's shotgun and found it already loaded. Slowly, he turned it over in his hands. The stock was cracked and the foresight scratched from the time his father had dropped it accidentally from a cliff-top. It was strange to find it loaded. He wondered if he had dreamt it all before.

He carried the gun upstairs and stripped to his vest and under-pants. Now the cloth was hanging up in the wardrobe, and, as Hugo had put it, he looked like any normal man. He took a poker from the fireplace and sat on the bed with two pillows to his back. He put the poker through the trigger-guard so that it rested in the curve of the first trigger, and he kept it in place with the toes of both feet. When he bent forward to put the muzzle to his mouth, he found the position too uncomfortable to maintain for long, and he wasn't yet quite ready to push the poker away from him with both feet. He had expected confusion and pertur-bation. His hands were steady and his mind was calm. It seemed to him that he knew absolutely nothing, or alternatively that there was nothing to know. The hallowed practice of a lifetime asserted itself; he began repeating a favourite prayer: *Dominus illuminatio mea, et salus mea, quem timebo … Dominus illuminatio mea, et salus mea, quem timebo … Dominus illuminatio mea, et salus mea, quem timebo … Dominus*

A NOTE ON THE AUTHOR

Patrick McGinley is an Irish novelist, born in 1937 in Glencolumbkille, Ireland. After teaching in Ireland, McGinley moved to England where he pursued a career as a publisher and author. His strongest literary influence is his Irish predecessor, author Flann O'Brien, who McGinley emulates most noticeably in his novel *The Devil's Diary*. McGinley is the author of eight novels including: *Goosefoot* (1983) *Foggage* (1983) *The Trick of the Ga Bolga* (1986) and most recently *The Lost Soldier's Song* (1994).

Made in the USA
Columbia, SC
23 July 2021